To Peggy —

"He will quiet you with His Love, He will rejoice over you with singing." Zeph. 3:17

Thank you for your friendship!

Cris

To my family and friends.
The days would be dull without you.
"... one person sharpens another."
Proverbs 27:17

Chapter 1

There was a time I wasn't in pieces.
I barely remember.
Today, yesterday, tomorrow—
Each day the pieces break a little smaller.
I fear becoming dust.

Lissa Makkinen Maguire, 2003

Every cell in Lissa's middle-aged body howled for rest.

Not a chance. No way was she giving in to that wounded-animal urge. She wasn't bleeding—just dying of a broken heart. Dying for a year and a half, so this summer shouldn't make much difference. She could always dig back into her burrow and lick her grief wounds, after she got her parents moved.

Still, it was unbelievable she'd let her mother talk her into coming home for the entire summer. Not like she had anything else to do, but if she did, she couldn't do it.

She bit the inside of her lower lip to stop the thoughts. Without Sean, absolutely nothing mattered.

Lissa shifted her grip and hauled her suitcase up the stairs. Rather than bang the walls of her parents' house, she let her ankle take the beating. Standing on the landing the rest of the day wasn't going to accomplish a thing.

Stomping on every step would have helped, but the weight of the suitcase made that impossible. Anyway, she was no longer a child storming off to her bedroom; she was a woman raging against the image of her husband ahead of her on the stairs, easily handling the suitcases, his laughter filling the hall. Phantom laughter.

At the top of the stairs Lissa dropped the case on its wheels and flinched, as if dishes crashed. Her heart twinged. She hoped the noise hadn't startled her parents.

She jammed her fingers in her gray-streaked hair and shoved it out of her eyes. Never. She'd never had to carry what felt like a load of pig iron in a suitcase. Sean always…She bit her lip again.

Giving her suitcase a push, she sent it bumping over the threshold. First room on the left—"Melissa's Room," the wood burned plaque on the door announced—her old room. With a grunt, she heaved the case onto the bed where it landed beside its smaller mate.

This homecoming was proving to be harder than Lissa had imagined. Turning her back to her suitcases, she plunked down on the edge of the bed and exhaled. Her body sagged, ready to slip off the mattress and puddle on the floor. Oozing through the floorboards seemed like a good idea.

Lissa closed her eyes, wishing away her life as she now knew it.

She sat—frozen—tried to free her mind of thoughts that stung like nettles. Relaxing didn't come easily anymore.

Tick, tick, tick. The windup clock on the nightstand ticked a heart-calming sixty beats a minute. Deep breath…exhale.

FIFTY DAYS TO SUNRISE

Familiar smells charged her brain as she took in the scents of the old house, a house she'd known for so many years. The sweet smell of Tide drifted off the bed, the tang of wood and varnish, a hint of mustiness. Home.

Lissa let all that was home wrap its arms around her and squeeze.

When she opened her eyes, there was Daisy in black-and-white, gazing at her from the framed photo on the dresser. A sharp breath stabbed the back of her throat, and she stood and picked up the picture frame in both hands. Lissa couldn't hug her old dog around the neck, but could only press Daisy's picture against her chest.

Lissa still missed Daisy. She was the best dog a child could hope for—well, usually. A smile tugged at Lissa. There was a day when Daisy wasn't quite the perfect dog: she was an apron thief—over forty years ago.

Daisy had run around the swing set and the clothes pole so fast, Lissa informed her family that Daisy might have turned into a pool of melted yellow Labrador butter. Everyone laughed, even Mom.

Mom's apron lost the tug-of-war between Lissa and Daisy. Lissa had thumped straight down on her behind when the apron ripped.

The memory of chasing Daisy in the backyard faded and so did Lissa's smile. Setting the photo back on the dresser, Lissa rested her fingertip on Daisy's nose. When Lissa had snapped the picture many years ago, Daisy was in the same pose she had been in after the apron caper—lying in the grass with her paws crossed in front of her, muzzle down on her paws, looking up at Lissa. The old dog's muzzle and a mask across her eyes shone white.

Lissa frowned. The glitter of the afternoon sun coming in the bedroom window caught Daisy's eyes and gave them a disturbing light. Lissa opened the top dresser drawer, laid the photo face down, and slowly closed the drawer.

Her gaze fell on the Bible lying beside where the photo had been; her saliva went sour. She couldn't touch the Bible. Where were You, God? All those years believing in You.

Was God withholding Himself? Invisible? No. It was her—*she* was becoming invisible. Blotted out by grief. Really, the living become the specters, slipping in and around life, unnoticed. And, after a time, uncaring.

Lissa spun back to the bed and her suitcases. Seeing the thirty-five-year-old photo of Daisy in her old age stabbed like a pinprick.

A phone call from her mother had started all this. Lissa replayed the conversation in her head, but it was too late now.

Just six weeks ago, Lissa had been at home trying to write, but mostly she stared at the computer. Five lines of depressing verse. *I fear becoming dust.* Yeah. Blown around. Then gone.

She had wandered outside into the spring air. Past her neglected flower beds. Past the soggy vegetable garden. Until she stood at the end of the dock—watching rain-swollen clouds cast a fractured reflection on the lake.

Her phone vibrated. Lissa had given up not answering calls, since nobody left her alone. It was Mom.

"Lissie, honey, do you think you could come home for the summer? Dad and I could really use your help moving to our apartment."

"What? The summer?"

"I've talked to Ray. He said it would be perfect. The twins could stay at the farm while you're gone."

"Oh?...The twins?...Well, I..."

"And Jack could help out too. He said that would be no problem."

"Sounds like you've got this all planned." Lissa couldn't hold back the sharp edge. Mom had thrown her brother, her nieces, and finally her son at her. Mom had a way of being manipulative, but wasn't usually this obvious.

"Dad and I have talked about this for a little bit, and we

think it would be a good idea. It would be so helpful to have you here."

"Let me think about it, Mom. I don't know what to say. This is out of the blue."

"You know, we've been planning this move for some time. The first of August is our moving date. Remember?"

Remember? No, she didn't. Her nose prickled, and her eyes stung.

"Sure, Mom. Sure. Just let me think about it, okay?"

She had so much to take care of, she couldn't possibly be gone that long. Traveling from Maine to Minnesota seemed like going halfway around the globe when it was an effort just to navigate herself to the next day.

"You could bring your little computer and work on your novel here, couldn't you?"

Oh, that. She hadn't touched her current project for a year and a half. "I could," she said. But she wouldn't.

Lissa changed the subject. Their gardens were something Lissa and her mother could talk about easily. But after a few minutes, silence dangled between them. Before her mother could again bring up the plans she had for her, Lissa said she'd call back in a few days. They exchanged "love you" and hung up.

Six weeks later. How did this happen? Here she was, in her old room at her parents' house. In Gifford for most of the summer. The pity party chafed like a hair shirt, and she shook it off, sick of it. She'd go for a run later. That would help. She groped for normal, familiar. Easy to find in the old family home.

She always looked for changes as soon as she walked in her room, though nothing had changed in over two decades. She had visited home and stayed in her room many times over the years, but this was different. What had changed was that Sean wasn't with her. Again. She drove those thoughts away. Happy times. Those were the thoughts she wanted. Family times.

Little in the room was the same as when she lived here. It had been difficult to leave, and she'd moved out in stages. She hadn't taken much with her going three blocks away to a dorm room up the hill at St. Lucy's, but then moving to New York for graduate school left an empty room for her mother to decorate. Mom had delighted in making the room pretty and pink, somewhat, Mom admitted with a twinkle in her eye, because Sean didn't care for pink, but Lissa loved it. The cushioned window seat was still here, piled with soft pillows and an afghan Mom had knit.

Lissa opened the window and let in the perfume of the shrub roses below. The lace curtains fluffed out.

She stripped off her black summer cardigan and flung it on the bed. It was going to be a long summer.

Lissa had never left the farm in her nieces' care before—not that there was that much to do. One more worry. But the twins were good kids. They had to be, being pastor's kids. And Jack would help out, he always did. Her sweet son.

Thinking about the farm and the girls was pointless: there wasn't anything she could do about it, except go home, which was ridiculous.

She unlatched the biggest suitcase and flung it open—took out piles of T-shirts, capris, shorts, and a plastic bag containing her running shoes. She scooped out the novels grabbed off her bookshelf and tossed them on the bed.

She turned away from the mess, stalked over to the window seat, and sat down hard. A moment later, she sprang up and headed for the kitchen to find her mother.

At the landing on the way down the stairs, Lissa took the left turn down the five steps into the kitchen, rather than to the right, which led to the front entryway. This split stair layout had made running around the house especially fun for three kids.

Mom wasn't in the kitchen. Lissa expected Mom would be starting dinner.

FIFTY DAYS TO SUNRISE

Passing through the kitchen and the dining room, she found Mom and Dad, a tableau of old people sitting in their easy chairs on either side of the fireplace. Dad put his newspaper down; Mom jerked her head up from a doze.

"How about I put the kettle on for tea?" Lissa hitched up her tan slacks, a move she regretted. Mom noticed.

"Oh, that would be lovely. I guess it's near enough to teatime." Mom didn't get up, and Lissa turned back to the kitchen.

Dad called after her. "Missy, I'll have mine with lots of milk please." Dad still called her Missy.

Out of sight, back in the kitchen, Lissa put a hand on the counter to brace herself. Her parents looked so much older, especially Mom. Normally, Mom scurried around, serving people.

She wished Ray and Boots were here. She needed her brother and sister.

Guilt kinked Lissa's stomach; she hadn't come home after Mom's stroke. Couldn't. She just couldn't. But she was here now. And she needed to get a grip and get busy.

She filled the copper teakettle, put it on the stove, and lit the gas burner. Lissa huffed. Mom refused to replace the old Roper stove. Lissa would have to remember the oven temperature ran about ten degrees hot, or she'd have dried out lasagna.

She opened the light-blue painted cupboard to get mugs, but then stopped. Ah, this was an occasion for the good tea set. Start this summer off right.

While the water heated, she crossed back over the pale-yellow linoleum tiles to the dining room and pushed the swinging door against the wall. The golden oak flooring, combined with the rich red and blue of the old Persian rug under the table, gave the room a warm glow in the afternoon sun.

From the bottom drawer of the built-in oak buffet, Lissa

pulled a square blue-and-white checked tablecloth. She spread the cloth on one end of the mahogany table and repositioned the vase of snapdragons.

The Crown Staffordshire tea set was kept in the upper glass-fronted china cabinet. Mom said she enjoyed the view provided by the mirrored back of the cabinet. Lissa gently put the tea set on the table: three cups and saucers, three plates, sugar bowl, creamer, and the teapot.

Lissa had never seen another set like it. The pattern was *Bluebell*: white bone china, with soft, yet vivid blue flowers and green leaves. The teacup handles and the finial of the teapot were a lovely light green. The cups had six deep flutes, just the right size to funnel tea to thirsty lips.

Lissa loved this tea set: so delicate, so English. A wedding present from the family Mom stayed with her junior year in England, the tea set had been a treasured possession ever since, a family heirloom.

Lissa noticed Mom watching her lay out the tea service. Lissa glanced at her mother for approval of her decision to use the Crown Staffordshire. Mother and daughter smiled at each other.

The squealing kettle called Lissa back to the kitchen. Fig Newtons out of the English cottage cookie jar would have to do for biscuits.

During tea, Mom and Dad talked about the plans they had for the next several weeks. They intended to go through the house and get rid of things that wouldn't fit in the new apartment.

Mom and Dad had obviously been discussing this move for a long time, but Lissa only came in on it six weeks ago. The more her parents talked, the more her chest tightened. It didn't help that she had to avoid looking over the mantel where Sean's painting of their children had hung.

"Mom, what are you planning for dinner?" Lissa couldn't sit still any longer.

FIFTY DAYS TO SUNRISE

"Oh, I thought I'd fry some pork chops. Would you like boiled potatoes and vegetables to go with the pork chops?"

"Sure." Lissa's thoughts ground in her brain. She had no interest in food.

"Do I have time to go for a run?" She quickly added, "Leave the tea things here, and I'll wash them when I get back. It should only be thirty or forty minutes." She avoided her mother's eyes.

"I suppose." Lissa caught the edge in Mom's voice. "We won't eat till around six thirty, now that we've had our tea."

"You could go run on campus." Dad took another Fig Newton.

"Sounds good." Lissa usually ran on campus when she visited.

Inside her head she bolted from the table, but on the outside she pushed back her chair and walked at a normal pace through the living room, past the baby grand piano, and up the front steps. Once she rounded the corner on the landing, she flew up the stairs, two at a time, to the relative safety of her room. She needed a run to clear her head. Desperately.

Chapter 2

Lissa escaped out the front door, crossed the screen porch that ran the length of the house, and shot down the front steps. Pausing to stretch, she looked down the street at the familiar neighborhood, then took off down the sidewalk and veered right toward campus.

Years ago, giant elms flanked Manitou Street, but various hardwoods now stood tall in place of the long-dead elms. Lissa barely noticed the trees.

Manitou came to a T intersection with College Drive three blocks from the house. Crossing College, Lissa ran straight up the hill, like her tail was on fire. The cushion of grass brought relief from the punishing sidewalks—familiar grass she had run on since her undergraduate years at St. Lucia College.

She forced herself to think about nothing but her breathing and the thump of her shoes on the grass. Every step took on monumental importance in grasping for nothingness. Breathe...*thump, thump, thump.* She swiped an arm across her sweaty forehead.

She followed her usual route: past the dorms, past the

chapel, the science building, education building, the library. No thought required. Running novocaine.

After twenty minutes, Lissa paused to stretch again. Standing with hands on hips, awareness of her surroundings seeped in. She took a deep breath and let it out. Did it again.

She reached her arms over her head and stretched. She couldn't believe she'd agreed to this project. This was already looking like it was going to be almost two months of looking back and going through a lifetime of the George and Eleanor Makkinen family. She gave herself a mental palm-slap to the forehead. She pulled hard on her elbow crooked behind her head. Two months.

Oh, yes—she was doing this for Mom and Dad. Duh. It was the right thing to do. Of course she'd do this for her parents. Lissa shook her head. She didn't have much confidence she could do this. Ordinarily, she would have jumped in to help, but now everything was a blur: whirling at top speed, or still and indistinct, an out-of-focus photograph.

She loved her family, loved her life here. But she couldn't stand the thought of any more pain right now, maybe ever.

Sprinting as fast and as far as she could, thoughts jostled against each other till they were bounced out of her head.

She was okay again. The stress of the afternoon had subsided. Just to be sure, she ran a lap around the track next to the field house. Two laps.

Jogging down the hill to Manitou, she slowed her pace. Well, she was here. She might as well make the best of it. She *would* make the best of it. Her parents deserved no less.

Back on Manitou, Lissa walked the three blocks home. Now that her head had cleared, she drank in the neighborhood, and it made her relax even more. Gifford, Minnesota. It didn't get any more Midwestern-small-town than this. It was a quaint neighborhood of 1920s houses—many of them Sears Roebuck kit houses—standing shoulder to shoulder, buffers of fences and gardens between them.

FIFTY DAYS TO SUNRISE

A lot of building and remodeling had gone on in the neighborhood since Lissa lived here. A few backyards were reduced in size by additions of expanded kitchens and breakfast rooms, or master bedroom suites, or even two-story additions of both. And of course, new two-car garages.

Dad loved his double garage. The garages were in back along an alley. In a downpour, bags of groceries never made it to the kitchen without getting slightly soggy. That's just the way it was in old neighborhoods.

Lissa stopped in front of her parents' house. She loved this house. What an incubator for love it had been. She took a long look at her childhood home; the wide porch swing still hung from chains where it had always been. Summer evenings, the screen porch was the best room in the house.

A cream stucco Craftsman-style house, but with a large dose of Midwestern modesty, the Makkinen home was different from the other houses on the street because of two large dormers on the second floor. Nothing fancy. Otherwise, not much distinguished the second house in from the corner of Manitou and Seventh Street—not on the outside.

Home. Trite phrases about home and heart came to mind. But trite didn't make it not true. A part of her heart was here, had always been here. Besides, her jaw tightened, there wasn't much back at the farm for her now.

Chapter 3

The Summer of Love, that's what she'd call this summer, since that's why she was here. Lissa stretched in bed: a big get-all-the-kinks-out stretch. Her hand brushed the empty side of the bed. Would she never stop expecting Sean to be there? Or maybe wake up and find it's all been just a bad dream? She slammed the lid on those thoughts and instead, savored being surrounded by the wallpaper garden and pink, and thought about her parents.

The talk with Mom and Dad last night after dinner encouraged her. They were looking forward to this move. Lissa finally remembered looking at the apartment complex with them over three years ago when she and Sean were home for Christmas. Her parents had gotten on a waiting list.

She smiled and yawned. She'd actually gotten to wake up on her own time. Nobody stood on her chest purring, bumping her in the face, demanding breakfast. The brass bedstead gave the room a cozy feel. Cabbage Rose Bed and Breakfast... Makkinen's B&B...Mom's Place. My Place, she decided. She loved this room.

The dormer window seat was unchanged. Dad had built the window seat. So big, it served as extra sleepover space—not just a bench, more of a bed. Mom found a big piece of foam rubber and covered it. Lissa spent hours there as a child: tea parties, reading, studying, writing, and dreaming. Then, dreaming meant looking ahead, now it was looking back.

The wallpaper Mom put up after Lissa left home had been here over twenty-five years, but it still looked cozy. Huge bouquets of flowers covered the cream-colored walls—pink cabbage roses, blue delphiniums, red snapdragons, and yellow black-eyed Susans—tied with pink ribbon. The sensation of lying in a flower bed.

A stick family in purple crayon stood on the wall to the right of the dresser where Shannon drew them when she was three. Mom thought it was cute and left the memento of her granddaughter. At home, when Shannon drew wall art a few weeks later, Lissa pushed the dresser over to cover it and gave Shannon a time out.

Lissa pulled the light quilt up under her chin. The cool June morning breathed on her face. She had left the shade up just to watch the lace curtains dance in the breeze.

She closed her eyes for a few minutes of peace.

Lissa woke twenty minutes later. She dug her toes into the sculpted pile of the rose-colored rug next to the bed. She threw on her robe and, barefoot, made her way down to the kitchen.

Mom sat alone at the large, round table in front of the kitchen window, her hands around a mug of coffee. Eyes closed, she faced the morning sun.

A tear glistened on Mom's lashes. Maybe it was a tear, Lissa wasn't sure.

"Oh, Lissa, I didn't hear you come down."

"Did I startle you?"

"What would you like for breakfast?"

"Co-ffee." Lissa extended her arms, Frankenstein-like, and advanced on her mother.

FIFTY DAYS TO SUNRISE

Mom chuckled and waved a hand in the direction of the pot on the counter. First, Lissa kissed her mother on the cheek. Mom gently pressed her hand to the side of Lissa's face, a cheek-hug, the crazed porcelain of Mom's skin like a soft buffing cloth against her own.

Lissa would have preferred the coffee intravenously, a direct wake-up slam in an artery, but instead she poured it in a mug.

"Let's go outside, Mom."

"That would be nice."

They sat in the old bouncy green metal chairs on the patio. Chilly cement on bare feet—Lissa wiggled her toes. A woman of fifty-three, her feet were rarely cold anymore. She stretched out her legs in the warming sun.

The garden looked good, cleaned up and ready for summer to get under way in earnest. Petunias and geraniums filled the two big pots on either end of the patio. White licorice plants poised to spill over the edge of the pots.

The morning air smelled delicious: hints of damp earth, mown grass, and the intoxicating scent of peonies. Mom's peonies were unsurpassed. Pink, white, red, creamy yellow, frilled, double, single—something bloomed continuously for six weeks. So unlike the scents of woods and water back at the farm. Lissa thought of her mother every time she smelled the fragrance of peonies. Two years ago she had transplanted tubers from the sweetest-scented of Mom's peonies, but it would be a few years before they were this lush, if ever. Mom had the greenest thumb in the family.

"Lissa, do you remember you and Ray chasing Daisy all over back here when she stole my apron?"

Lissa smiled. "I was just thinking of that yesterday." Lissa fixed her mother with an intent look. "You know it was *me* who got your apron back from her, *not* Ray."

"Of course." Mom reached over and gave Lissa's hand a gentle pat. "I saw my apron rip when you and Daisy were playing tug-of-war with it. It happened so fast I couldn't say anything to stop you."

Mom wasn't one to tell jokes, but when she pieced her old apron into the baby quilt she'd made for Jack, they had all laughed.

Mother and daughter smiled. Lissa enjoyed the mirrored aqua-blue she found in her mother's eyes. A taller version of her delicately boned mother, she had her father's thick, wavy hair, several shades darker than Mom's flaxen blond of her youth. Lissa thought her mother was beautiful, but she thought of herself as having big hips.

"Mom?"

"Hmm?"

"Are you and Dad really ready to leave here?"

Mom didn't hesitate. "Yes, we are. We've talked it over for a long time, and we're really ready. It's just way too much work for us. Too hard to live with all the stairs."

Mom took a sip of her coffee. "You know how much we love gardening, but it's too much." She pursed her lips as she gazed at her garden.

"We've lived here forty-eight years….Everywhere I look, everything I touch, reminds me of some part of our life here. And it's been a good life….That isn't to say it won't be very painful to leave."

Lissa nodded, didn't interrupt her mother. For a moment, Mom looked far away, as she did sometimes.

"But pain isn't always a bad thing." Mom stopped, took in a sharp breath, and sighed. She stared into her coffee. "Oh, honey, I'm sorry."

"It's okay." Lissa clamped her jaw and let a few moments of silence hang in the air to prevent the storm rising inside her.

"I just needed that last reassurance that you and Dad are good before we start going through everything. Shall we start today?"

"That would be fine. I've actually got a list started of things that need to be done." Mom smiled, a pink tinge coloring her cheeks. Mom was funny with her lists, a joke among the rest of the family. Apparently Mom enjoyed the joke too.

"Where should I start?"

"How about the attic?"

A dark space full of junk. Just what she needed more of.

Chapter 4

The attic was through a varnished pine door at the end of the hall and up a steep flight of steps. Rough pine boards, nailed horizontally, lined the stairwell.

Lissa flicked on the light switch at the bottom of the stairs. A row of three bare bulbs hanging from the roof peak illuminated the dark space. The only natural light slanted in through the small louvered vents on both ends. No railing guarded the open stairwell.

As Lissa stepped into the hazy light, the floorboards creaked. The age of the house could be seen and smelled in the attic—old wood darkened to velvet brown.

She set down two empty boxes. This wouldn't be so hard. There wasn't that much stuff left. Ray and Boots had already taken any mementos they wanted of their childhoods. What was left behind was left behind. Goodwill or trash. That was about it.

Old toys, games, and puzzles—those went in the Goodwill box. Forty-five-year-old toys passed through her fifty-three-year-old hands for the last time. Old. She smirked. How did they survive childhood with all the sharp edges on toys? Nothing battery-operated and not even that much plastic.

Lissa dragged a couple throw rugs to the Goodwill pile. Then changed her mind and dragged them to the trash pile.

Those old stuffed animals were definitely going to Goodwill.

Sounds of Dad playing the Steinway drifted up to the attic. The music resonated, surrounded by all the wood in the attic. She didn't recall hearing the piano from the attic before.

She ducked down and pulled out a box from the corner under the eaves. "Huh," she said, when she saw her name written on the top of the box in her own handwriting. And *Private* in big black letters.

Goosebumps raised on her arms as she knelt down and opened the box. In this box were all her most personal and private things, put here when she moved to the dorm at St. Lucy's. She had stashed it in the attic out of the way where no one would notice it. Apparently, her plan was quite effective—she'd forgotten it herself.

She carried the box down to her room and set it on the floor by the window seat. She pushed her hair back from her face, grinning at her box of treasures, and wiped her dusty hands on her shorts. She labeled the gnawing in her stomach as hunger. Lunch. Food before memories.

She made her way to the kitchen through the living room. Coming down the steps, she gently swayed to the left, holding the banister in her right hand where the railing gracefully curled away, dramatically trailed her left wrist, floated off the bottom step, and landed elegantly on the floor—her grand entrance into the living room. A widening, even if short, staircase with a sweeping walnut railing was the stuff of a young girl's daydreams. Halfway through this familiar maneuver she thought better of it since she was certainly no longer a skinny little girl and feared for the old banister. But it was too late to stop.

FIFTY DAYS TO SUNRISE

She alighted in front of Dad at the baby grand. He winked at her. Dad playing the piano—such a familiar sound. She put a hand on his shoulder; he didn't miss a note of *Für Elise*.

"Want some lunch?" Lissa ignored her ridiculous entrance.

"You betcha."

She lingered to listen. Dad played the final soft notes, hands poised over the keys, caressing the fading sounds. He lifted his hands only after he took his foot off the sustain pedal, ending the piece. When Dad played at the college, it was then that the audience exhaled in utter bliss before breaking into applause. Dad was that good.

Lissa left Dad to his reverie and pushed through the swinging oak-paneled door into the back hallway and into the kitchen. She made ham and cheese sandwiches while Dad continued with chord progressions and scales that didn't rip quite like they used to.

"Mom, I made some lunch," Lissa called out the back door.

Mom stabbed her trowel in the dirt where she was loosening the soil around the lupines. "Coming."

Lissa noticed her mother struggle to get up. Turning back to the kitchen, that gnawing in her stomach returned.

Chapter 5

After lunch Lissa settled back to her room and sat cross-legged on the window seat, the box of memories in front of her. Was she ready to open Pandora's Box? She closed her eyes and took a deep breath.

Lissa reached in and took out the dry shreds of several pressed corsages. She brushed bits of flowers off the top of a shoe box, lifted it out, and opened the lid.

Lissa unwrapped a miniature china shoe and smiled. The delicate pink shoe with the white porcelain rose was her favorite. She unwrapped each of nine shoes and lined them up on the windowsill—her shoe collection from more than forty years ago. She still thought they were beautiful, and, until today, she had forgotten about them.

Wrapped in tissue paper and packed with the shoes was a small porcelain collie dog a nameless boy gave her when they went to family music camp.

She lined up her George Harrison doll next to the china shoes. And a wooden bug Mom gave her for Valentine's Day in ninth grade. The taped Beatle bangs of her hair hung cockeyed on the bug.

In the box, nine diaries were stacked in chronological order in two piles—her diaries from fourth grade through senior year of high school.

She sat back against the pillows and looked at the diaries. She didn't have to read them now, didn't even have to take them out of the box. But they were magnetized to her hands. Lissa lifted out each stack and set it on the window seat.

She picked up the top volume and held it in both hands—her first diary.

The pink vinyl cover was embossed with a picture of a teenage girl. The blond pony-tailed girl—dressed in pedal pushers, over-sized boyfriend-shirt, and bobby socks—talked on a black 1950s phone. A tiny key to the gold clasp was taped to the back of the diary. The crinkled tape let loose, and the key fell into Lissa's hand.

Such a tiny key, so many memories. A summer of reminiscing. Part of her resisted it—hoped she wouldn't drown in a flood of memories. Her parents' move was going to happen, and nothing could stop the memories that were an inevitable part of it. Thinking about the day her parents moved, or the day the house had be cleaned out, was just a vague abstraction, not something that ever really happened.

Still, it was good to be home with her parents. They shouldn't have to do this by themselves. But memories of all the emotions experienced in this house were overwhelming. *Love encompasses such an array of emotions. Like all the colors in a rainbow.* She frowned at her own sappy poetry. No wonder her muses had abandoned her. Rainbows were nice, but first, the storm.

She opened the diary—and looked through the wrong end of the telescope.

Strange to see her fourth-grade handwriting: scrawls in purple ink, all the *i*'s dotted with circles.

Chapter 6

This Diary belongs to
Melissa Louise Makkinen
216 Manitou Street
Gifford, Minnesota

BOOTS AND RAY KEEP OUT!!!!!

August 14, 1959

Dear Diary,

    Mom bought me this diary today. I love it! You will be my best friend! Not like Sally and Jessica. They are my best best friends. I will tell you everything.
    Today Mom and I went school clothes shopping. We went to downtown Minneapolis. To Dayton's. Mom got me a blue plaid skirt with green and yellow. I love it! Best of all I got a red Lady and the Tramp skirt and a slip to make it stick out. I got some other things too. Mom said

she can let out the hems on some of my last year dresses. I grew some. Not too much she says. We had lunch at The Forum. I had macaroni and cheese. Then pecan pie. Yum!

Mom said I should write my prayers down. She says when she does she sees how God answers prayers. I say this prayer every night.

Dear God,

Now I lay me down to sleep. I pray the Lord my soul to keep. If I should die before I wake, I pray the Lord my soul to take. Thy love guard me through the night, and wake me with the morning light. Amen.

And that was my day.

August 25, 1959

Dear Diary,

Today was really fun. I wrote a short story that I love. It is about the Good Horse and the Bad Horse. Mom really likes it. Daisy does too. I wrote it in my fort in the backyard. I got wet because it rained. Mom says I should be an author. She says that means I should write books. I think I will.

And that was my day.

And this is my story.

The Horse that Ate the Sun
by Melissa Makkinen

FIFTY DAYS TO SUNRISE

The sun was too hot one day. Susie's mother made her come in and lie down...

Lissa remembered the backyard as a place of wonder when she was a child. A white picket fence bounded the yard, making a turn to the back wall of the house instead of going all the way around to the front yard. This was the domain of kids and dog.

Lissa was five when they moved to the house on Manitou Street, so the swing set was one of the first additions to the yard. The swing set quickly became where the Makkinen children ran when they got the command, "Go outside and play."

The other place Lissa ran to was her favorite place in the yard: her fort. Mom cultivated an area to look wild—a thicket, Lissa called it, named after Bambi's thicket. A path to the left of the garage led into an area of overgrown bushes and wildflowers, a magical place to Lissa. It smelled of dirt and sometimes smoke from Dad's burning pile.

In a tangle of bushes, Lissa made a fort. Off limits, unless invited! Lissa tunneled an entrance through the brush, as tall as a big yellow dog. Lissa had to crawl in on her hands and knees. Once in her sanctuary, a clearing opened up—just big enough for a girl and a dog.

She spent hours there: reading, lying on an old rag rug, staring at the clouds, writing about anything that caught her imagination. There she brought her book friends Nancy Drew and Trixie Belden, and devoured pages and pages of their adventures. She wrote about pirates and smugglers hiding in caves on the East Coast shores. She dreamed about being a mother and a wife.

One day, while lying on her back, knees pointing at the sky, studying the clouds with Daisy, a huge white horse galloped

out of nowhere and gobbled up the sun. Inspiration.
Lissa flopped over on her stomach and began writing furiously.

The Horse that Ate the Sun.

Her little almost-fourth-grade mind raced as fast as the wind that sped the giant horse along in the sky. The horse's name was Gabriel.

The sun was too hot one day. Susie's mother made her come in and lie down. It was too hot to play outside. Susie prayed to God that it would not be so hot. So God sent Gabriel to take care of it. Gabriel raced across the sky. He got to the sun. He didn't know what to do. He galloped around. He stopped to think. Then he raced some more. He reared up. When he came back down he had a bright idea. He ate the sun! Then it was not so hot. Susie could go out and play after all.

As she read her story over for about the tenth time, thunder finally got her attention. The white horse disappeared, and masses of dark clouds piled up it its place.
Lissa flipped her notebook shut and scrambled to her feet just as big splashy drops hit the ground. Daisy leaped to her feet at the first growl of thunder. They ducked out of the fort and ran for the back door. Lissa clutched her notebook to her chest and ran as fast as her skinny little-girl legs would go.
"Good girl. You protected me from the storm." Daisy wagged her whole body at Lissa, then shook and sprinkled raindrops all over the back hall.
Seated at the kitchen table, Lissa wrote some more, since she now had more to tell. She chewed on her lower lip and wrote with passion, as fast as the words could fly from her pencil.

FIFTY DAYS TO SUNRISE

The Bad Horse. The black horse came out of nowhere. He started a fight with Gabriel. There was a terrible noise as they fought. They screamed. Their hoofs hit together and sparks shot all over the sky.

From the safety of the kitchen Lissa watched as the rain came down in billowing sheets. She saw the flower heads get beaten down by the rain, then jerked back up by the wind.

Daisy lay at Lissa's feet, her head on her paws. Daisy hated thunderstorms. She looked up at Lissa, as if to say, "Make it stop." And it did. A spigot turned off, leaving no more than a fine mist in the air. The sun peaked out, and a rainbow arced across the sky, a double rainbow.

Gabriel turned and kicked the Bad Horse right in the chest with both hoofs. The Bad Horse flew backwards. He landed somewhere by South America. He was gone.

Gabriel let out a big burp and the sun came back out. Then Gabriel tossed his mane and fluffed up the clouds and put them back to white again. He kicked some soft clouds in front of the sun. It was not so hot anymore.

God saw what Gabriel did. God said, "Thank you, Gabriel." God drew a rainbow in the sky as a present. It looked so nice He drew two rainbows.

Thank you God.
And thank you Gabriel.

Lissa had learned the real story of the rainbow at Sunday School, that when God promised Noah there would never again be a flood upon the earth, He gave the rainbow as a reminder of His covenant. But she didn't think God would mind if she made up a just-for-fun rainbow story.

Chapter 7

September 19, 1959

Dear Diary,

 Boots broke my tea set to pieces! All because of her silly thing about spiders! I am so mad!!!! See if I do anything nice for her again!!!! Mom says she will get me a new one. It will never be the same!!!!
 And THAT was my day!

Mom must have told this story fifty times. Then Lissa took up the telling when it was far enough in the past to be funny. But that had taken a while. And any future tea parties with Boots were held *inside*.

This day was henceforth known in the family lore as the Backyard Tea Party Incident.

One warm fall Saturday afternoon Lissa had the bright

idea to invite Boots to a tea party in her fort. Mom helped Lissa write a proper invitation.

> *You are invited to a tea party.*
> *Time: 2:00*
> *Place: Lissa's fort*
> *Bring a guest.*

Two o'clock was a half hour away, which meant Mom had to keep Boots occupied so Lissa could get tea ready.

Lissa ran up to her room and got her beautiful china tea set out of her closet. Grandma Louise had given her this tea set for her birthday last year: white china, with pink flowers, rimmed in gold. One of the tiny plates already got a chip knocked out when Lissa accidentally hit it against the side of the teapot. She had tried to be so careful passing the cookies to her doll.

This was going to be fun. The cookie jar on the counter was almost full of pecan tassies Mom had made the day before. Being a fourth grader now, Lissa could reach the cookie jar at the back of the counter, but couldn't quite get the lid off without danger of a disaster, so she had to use the stool with the fold-down steps.

She put two cookies for each of them on the little serving platter, poured milk into the creamer, and filled the sugar bowl.

Pretending plain water was tea, she filled the teapot and turned the top to lock it in place like Mom showed her. She put the pink tea cozy that Mom had knit over the teapot to keep the tea warm. Mom said the English served their tea this way. Lissa only pretended the tea was hot.

Mom had gotten out a wooden tray and one of the tablecloths she used when friends came over for tea. Lissa loaded the tray with her treasured tea set and left it for Mom to carry out.

Lissa ran outside to straighten up her fort for the party.

FIFTY DAYS TO SUNRISE

The cardboard floor was still in good shape. She brushed off some leaves and spread the cloth over the cardboard. It wasn't Mom's best tablecloth, but it was Lissa's favorite: pink and brown checks. The tea set would look beautiful on it.

Mom carried the tray out. It was tricky getting the tray into the fort. Mom had to get down on her knees and reach it in to Lissa.

Cups on the saucers, tea ready to be poured—Lissa arranged everything just the way she wanted it.

Mom opened the back door and sent Boots off to the party. At four and a half years old, Boots had almost shredded her yellow blankie. It no longer went everywhere with her, but apparently, taking it to a tea party seemed like a good idea. She clutched what was left of her blankie in one hand, the torn satin binding dragging on the ground, and held Teddy under the armpits in the other arm. Teddy was the guest—*not* Daisy, who trotted beside Boots.

Boots knocked on the pretend door of Lissa's fort. Lissa shooed Daisy away. There wasn't room for a big yellow dog at a tea party.

"Knock, knock," Boots said.

"Why, come in, Boots." They were very polite.

They sat on the tablecloth around the tea tray—Teddy, Boots, and Lissa. Lissa played mother and poured the tea.

"Would you like some milk?" Lissa asked. Boots pursed her lips and nodded sweetly at her big sister. "Sugar?"

Lissa passed the platter of cookies. Teddy got pretend cookies.

They munched their cookies and sipped their tea. They were careful to include Teddy in the conversation. He smiled, as he always did. He was a very friendly bear. Things were going so well.

Without warning, Boots started shrieking—the kind of shrieking little girls do when they can't think of anything else to do. It was surprising the teacups didn't break at the sound of her screaming.

Boots slapped at her legs. The teacup in her hand went flying. She kicked the saucer and platter over near Teddy. Teddy fell forward onto the platter, now empty of cookies. And that was just the start.

Daisy, startled awake from her nap on the patio, came racing to help, and landed smack in the middle of everything. The tray flipped into the air and crashed down, smashing what wasn't already broken. The sound of breaking china made Lissa want to scream.

She yelled, "Stop!" at Boots, and some other not-very-nice words. Daisy was a yellow flash—leaping, wagging, barking—trying to figure out what was wrong so she could help. In between barks she licked Boots's face, which only made Boots shriek some more.

In Boots's scramble to escape, her foot tangled in the tablecloth. When she jerked to free herself, the sugar bowl shot in the air and bounced off the tray. Broken pieces of sugar bowl settled in a pile of sugar. Finally, Boots scooted far enough off the tablecloth that she got to her feet and ran for the back door, pulling her blankie with her until it caught in the bushes.

Boots found a word somewhere in her panic and screamed, "Spiders!" Lissa never saw the terrifying spiders, if there ever were any. Boots yanked her blankie free and fled to the house. Daisy romped after her.

With Boots and Daisy gone, Lissa stared at the scene. She jammed her fingers into her short honey-colored hair, snagging her fingers on bits of twigs snarled in her curls. Lissa didn't know whether to scream, cry, or run.

The tablecloth had been dragged halfway out the door of the fort, and her beautiful tea set was strewn all over, in pieces. Water, sugar, cookie bits, and blood.

Blood!

Then Lissa noticed her knee. Trying to stop Boots and Daisy from wrecking everything, she had cut her knee. It wasn't a very bad cut, so she just sat there and held her knee and cried. Her legs were sticky and wet with milky sugar-water. Lissa pounded the cardboard with her fists and looked around at the mess. She set Teddy back upright. Under Teddy, the cookie platter had survived. She picked Teddy up and gave him a big kiss on his nose for protecting her platter. Hugging the small platter to her chest, she cried some more. How it happened that Daisy didn't knock Teddy off the platter was a mystery.

In the distance, Lissa heard Boots's sobs subside. Mom appeared, as she always did, when Lissa needed her most. Mom blotted Lissa's tears with her apron and took her to the house to clean up her knee. It didn't need stitches, just some mercurochrome and a Band-Aid. Lissa must have knelt on a broken plate or saucer trying to get hold of Daisy's collar to stop her from jumping on the tea set. Daisy had escaped Lissa's grasp and gone after Boots, mercifully ending the incident.

Boots was in her room, still sniffling, when Mom and Lissa headed out the back door to check the damage.

"Oh dear." Mom went back to the house for a paper bag.

They picked up all the broken pieces. Mom said she'd have Dad take a look and see if he could glue any of the pieces back together. But it looked doubtful.

Once all the pieces of any size were in the bag, Mom shook the tablecloth over the garbage can. Lissa stomped back to the house, clutching the platter, determined not to cry any more. Daisy happily ran circles around Lissa as if they were having fun again.

Boots sat at the kitchen table, drawing. She folded the paper she was working on and handed it to her big sister. Lissa put the platter on the counter safely out of any more harm's way and took the paper from her sister.

"Here. I made you a new tea set. I'm sorry I broke it."

Lissa unfolded the paper and saw a teapot and cup that Boots had drawn. Lissa's scowl softened a bit, and she started crying again. She grabbed Boots by the shoulders, and Boots started crying again too.

"Boots, why do you have to be so silly about spiders?" Lissa punched out her words, and Boots wiggled free of her sister's grasp.

"I don't know. I just do!"

Lissa opened her mouth to yell properly at her little sister, but she stopped. It wasn't Boots's fault she broke the tea set, but it was all so upsetting.

Dad pronounced the tea set a total loss, so the next Saturday Lissa got to pick out a new tea set. The only china set the toy store had wasn't nearly as nice as the one Grandma had given her, so she decided on a Melmac set—it was unbreakable. She didn't ever want to go through this heartache again—and besides, it had Lady and the Tramp on it, and it was white, rimmed in red.

Chapter 8

Lissa closed the pink diary and brought it to her nose. It smelled musty. Such old memories. The small china platter was behind a plate rail in the center of her antique Irish farmhouse buffet back in Maine. The gold rim was faded, missing in spots.

Boots still didn't like spiders. Lissa smiled at the thought of her younger sister. At least Boots didn't break things in her wake anymore.

Lissa missed her sister.

When Mom and Dad brought Boots home from the hospital, she and Ray had crowded around their new baby sister, wanting to touch her soft, warm skin, smell her baby smells. Then there were five hearts beating in their house. The rhythm of a family.

Christened Leah Catherine after Dad's mother, Sadie Catherine, Leah earned her nickname "Boots" when she was two and a half years old. The rest of the family was eating lunch around the kitchen table when Leah came clomping down the back hall and into the kitchen wearing Dad's engineer boots. They had all laughed uproariously, and Leah clapped and grinned like she'd just won a prize.

Dad had promptly dubbed her "Boots."

Leah bent at the knees in Dad's boots, bouncing up and down, clapping and giggling, until her dark curls bounced along with her.

Leah, now Boots, had stomped around, minus Dad's boots, the rest of the afternoon saying, "Boots! Boots!" And it stuck.

Boots was always the little sister and Lissa the big sister when they were growing up. With five years between them, they didn't do much the same at the same time. As Lissa got older, the years between them seemed to dwindle, and they grew close.

They got especially close when Boots and her husband, Etienne, were suffering through infertility. Boots would call Lissa and cry. Boots and Etienne came to stay with Sean and Lissa for two weeks. Rest, family love, and work in the vegetable garden helped a little with their grief.

Boots couldn't bring herself to take the route of in vitro fertilization, and Etienne refused to consider adoption, so they threw themselves into their careers. They had met when Boots interned with Amnesty International in Geneva, Switzerland. Partners in a prestigious Chicago law firm, they had the world by the tail.

Boots had a passion to help people subjected to injustice. She still hated spiders, but was a tiger in the courtroom. She and Etienne worked almost nonstop. For years, Lissa had told Boots she needed to slow down.

An idea sprouted, and Lissa went downstairs to find Mom and Dad.

"Oh, Lissa, you startled me again. You've got to start wearing wooden shoes so I can hear you coming." Mom was chopping vegetables in the kitchen.

"Mom, would you mind if I ask Boots to come for a visit?"

"Well, actually, she's coming next Friday. Let me look at

the calendar." Mom opened the cupboard next to the phone and checked the date on the calendar hanging there. "Yes, it's the twenty-seventh. She was going to surprise you."

"Really?" Boots didn't take much time off.

"Yes, when we knew you were coming, I arranged it with her. Oh, maybe a month ago. Dad and I thought it would be nice for you to have her here."

"Great! I can't wait. How long can she stay?"

"Tuesday. I think she has to be back Tuesday."

"I'll go get her room ready for her."

"I already did that, but thanks, honey."

"And, no, I prefer going barefoot, thanks." Lissa noticed her mother had a small furrow between her eyebrows for a moment, but then Mom smiled. Lissa gave her mother a quick peck on the cheek and bounded up the kitchen steps.

She dialed Boots's cell phone. Boots seldom answered, but Lissa left a message. "Hey, Boots, call me."

Alone in the living room after Mom and Dad had gone to bed, Lissa turned off the late news. She didn't want to hear about the war in Iraq.

She caught her phone after the first ring. Boots.

"Hey, Boots."

"Hi, Liss."

Boots had taken to calling her "Liss" some years ago. Apparently "Liss-a" was too many syllables in Boots's busy brain where economy and efficiency reigned.

"How ya doin', big sister?"

"Well, I'm here. And we're actually getting stuff done. But we'll leave some for you to do." The sisters immediately fell into the easy, teasing way they had of talking to each other.

While they talked, Lissa moved from Mom's chair in the living room out to the front porch. "Can't wait to see you,"

Lissa said.

"Yeah, me too. It's been too long." The last time they had seen each other was last Christmas, the Christmas-to-forget, at Mom and Dad's, though they talked on the phone usually once a week.

"Bring an extra suitcase if you want to take any dusty old throw rugs home with you. And that Barbie you made up with war paint."

"Hmm. Probably not. Hey, are you on the porch swing?"

"Yeah, why?"

"I can hear it squeaking." Lissa felt her sister smile through the phone. "Another one of those things Dad was always meaning to fix."

"Yeah," Lissa chuckled. "Do you want me to come pick you up at the airport?"

"Naw, thanks, I'll rent a car and drive up. I'm renting a Mustang convertible, a V8. Won't that be fun?"

"Wow! You bet. What? Are you made of money?"

"Oh, you know I am. High-priced Chicago lawyer and all that, remember?" They often teased about Boots's finances. She never asked, but guessed Boots and Etienne made well over a million a year. Lissa wouldn't do Boots's job for two million—high-priced, high-powered, and high-stressed.

"Well, I get in to Minneapolis around noon, so I should be up there by one thirty or so, if the traffic's not a mess."

"Good. Bring chocolate."

"You know I will. Kiss. Kiss."

"*Ciao, Bella.*" They hung up. Lissa smiled—certain Boots was smiling too.

Talking to Boots revived Lissa like a tonic. Lissa really needed to see her sister.

Back in her room, Lissa glanced at her stack of diaries on

FIFTY DAYS TO SUNRISE

the window seat. She thought again of the Backyard Tea Party Incident, and of Daisy, her yellow shadow.

Daisy wasn't quite a purebred. The truth came out in the brown tips on her fur, her more slender muzzle, and her ears that tried to stand at attention. She probably had some German shepherd in her, but they kept that a secret from her.

Lissa retrieved the photo of Daisy she had hidden in the dresser drawer.

The next thing she knew, a tear landed on the glass over the photo. Lissa sat on the edge of the bed, holding Daisy's photo, staring into Daisy's eyes, crying soundlessly. Teardrops dotted the front of her T-shirt, and her nose started to run. She wiped the glass with her T-shirt.

Losing Daisy was terrible. It happened her freshman year at St. Lucy's. She had known Daisy was sick, but Mom didn't tell her Daisy died until it was all over. Lissa had a final that day, and Mom hadn't wanted to upset her. There was no good way to handle it. Lissa was as upset that Mom didn't tell her as she would have been if she'd known.

Loving was so painful. Pain, an unwelcome companion these days.

Her mind drove her on to memories of Choco. Lissa missed Choco so much. With everything going on the past year and a half, Lissa had tried to put her dog's death out of her mind, but couldn't. The images were still vivid from just three months ago. She wanted it not to be true.

The cancer advanced quickly. Having to make the decision to put Choco to sleep was agonizing. She was furious she had to make the decision, and make it on her own. Jack, her sweet son, was with her. The vet came to the house, and afterward, she and Jack buried Choco in the woods with her favorite ball. But every morning Lissa still expected to find Choco resting her head on the bed, wagging her whole body.

Fighting to shatter the awful images of Choco's death, Lissa tried to focus on the good memories.

"Lord, help me."

She shot up a prayer and squeezed her eyes tight shut, until all she could see was Choco launching herself off the dock into the water after her ball. Shannon threw the ball over and over. Each time, Choco brought the ball back, dropped it at Shannon's feet, and shook herself mightily, sending water and sand flying. Then she'd give Shannon a doggy-grin. "Again!" she barked. True to her Lab blood, Choco never tired of chasing the ball or being in the water—both together sent her into ecstasy.

With a pained twitch of a smile, Lissa remembered her usual request to Boots when they visited each other. She wished Boots could—bring Chocolate.

There must be a thousand chocolate labs named Chocolate, but that's what you get when you let a ten year old name a puppy.

Lissa put the photo of Daisy back on the dresser and sat on the bed. Her shoulders drooped with the weight of grief. She longed for respite from her thoughts.

The memories went on and on. Painful links in chains that wrung her heart. She had been happy talking to Boots, and then, with no warning, she was in tears again.

She fell into her pillow and sobbed until she wore herself out with the effort of trying to let the pain out and trying not to disturb her parents in the next room.

"Lord, get me through another day—please," she breathed.

Chapter 9

After a night wrestling with the bedcovers, Lissa woke early. She had the coffee made and was sitting at the kitchen table, staring at the drizzle, when Mom came downstairs. The sludge-colored sky was about as ugly as a morning could be.

"Good morning, Lissie."

"I suppose." She caught herself sounding Eeyorish, but didn't care enough to fake it.

Mom poured her coffee and sat next to Lissa. Before Mom took a sip, she patted Lissa's hand and said, "Bad night?"

"You could say that."

"Do you want to talk about it?"

"No...no, I don't. Just sit and be with me. Talk about something nice."

"Well,...there's the church picnic this Sunday. That should be nice. Would you like to go?"

"Maybe, I'll see how I feel. I'm not sure I'm up for seeing everyone."

They drank their coffee in silence, except for soft sipping noises. Mom wasn't usually silent in the morning.

"You're not talking about nice things."

Mom set her cup on the table. "Lissa, I have to say something."

Lissa gave her mother a look over the rim of her mug.

"Honey, it looks like you've lost weight since Christmas. Am I right?"

Lissa set her mug down in front of her with a restrained *clunk*.

"I guess. Does it show?" As soon as the question popped out, Lissa wanted to snatch her words back. She couldn't keep her acid tone from seeping out.

"Yes." Mom waited, but Lissa said nothing.

"How much have you lost?"

"Oh, Mom." Lissa let out a huff. It was going to be another one of those conversations. Lissa tried to warn her mother off with a stony look, but it never worked. She didn't want to fight with her mother.

Mom raised an eyebrow, clearly expecting more of an explanation.

"All right," she replied through tight lips. "Probably eight or ten pounds. I haven't weighed myself in a while."

"Are you eating?"

Lissa tried vainly to hold her tongue and fired at her mother. "You saw me eat last night. I eat fine, okay?" She picked up her mug, hoping the skirmish was over.

"How much are you running?"

Busted. Crimson guilt crept up her neck.

Lissa roughly pushed back her chair and went for a refill. She leaned against the counter and counted before she spoke. Eyes closed, she made it to five while her mother waited.

"Well…okay…probably too much." She knew she had gotten a lot leaner in the last few months. Pounding the treadmill made her feel better. She'd never be skinny, carrying two big babies had widened her hips, but her weight loss showed in her face and torso. Her friend Mavis had told her so.

FIFTY DAYS TO SUNRISE

"You know Boots will get after you too."

"Yeah, can't wait." Lissa took a big gulp of hot coffee—and was immediately caught in the dilemma of having put something in her mouth she wished she hadn't. She swallowed and felt searing all the way down to her stomach. Spitting it out might have been a better idea.

Lissa secretly hoped Boots would help her toe the line of coping more constructively. Give her hell is what Boots would do.

"I know, Mom...I know." Lissa saw the pinched look on her mother's face. "I'll try, okay? I won't run so much. That's all I can do." A mouthful of tinfoil would have been easier to swallow.

"That's all I ask, honey."

Lissa poured more coffee for her mother and fixed instant oatmeal for herself. Both women fell silent for a time. Silence was calming.

"Mom, I'm sorry."

"Lissie, you are so precious. I just want the best for you."

Lissa nodded. She didn't know what else to say.

Mother and daughter talked about the flowers in the garden, always a safe topic for them.

After breakfast the drizzle stopped, and the gray morning brightened.

Lissa got up and stretched, reaching for the ceiling. "I'm going for a run, okay?"

Mom threw her daughter a severe look.

Lissa smiled, hands up in surrender. "Kidding."

Mom shook her head with a glance heavenward, her mouth a grim line with a hint of a smile. Then Mom speared the air near Lissa with her index finger and shook it at her. Mom's eyes held enough of a sparkle to let Lissa know her mother accepted the joke, but hadn't forgotten the seriousness of their discussion.

"You are a stinker, Melissa Louise."

Dad appeared, smiling as usual. "What's for breakfast?"

"Humble pie," Lissa said.

Dad looked at his daughter, then back at his wife. Mom didn't explain, and neither did Lissa.

Lissa waltzed out of the room to get ready for the day. In her mind she petulantly stomped out, but it didn't show. She resented being mothered. As soon as she was out of earshot, she bet Mom filled Dad in about their conversation.

Gardening turned out to be good medicine. Both Mom and Dad spent the day with Lissa: pruning, digging, splitting, and replanting. They were muddy, exhausted, and thoroughly happy by teatime.

Later that evening Dad played the piano. Mom knit—she said it helped her arthritis. Lissa lay on the couch, letting the sweet sounds of the Chopin nocturne wash over her, her eyes closed against the world.

The phone rang, and Mom moved slowly to answer it. "I'll get it," Lissa said.

"Hello, Makkinen's."

"Hi, Mel."

The cheerful baritone voice on the other end of the line could only be her brother. Ray called her "Mel" because, when he was eight years old, he declared it was obvious he wasn't going to get a brother, so he was going to call Lissa "Mel" and pretend she was his brother.

"Hi yourself, little brother." Lissa took the cordless phone into the kitchen and let the door swing shut behind her.

"How are things at the homestead?"

"Pretty good. We're getting things done."

"How are Mom and Dad doing with this move?"

"Pretty good to that too. They've given this a lot of thought."

FIFTY DAYS TO SUNRISE

"Yeah. They told me they were ready to make the move." Ray paused. "Mel, you okay?"

"I guess. It's weird though." Lissa left it at that.

"Hey, Amy and I were thinking of coming up there in July. That gives me plenty of time before I go back to pick the up twins at your place in August."

"Your flock won't miss their shepherd, huh?"

Ray chuckled, "No, I'll leave them in Dan's capable hands for a few days."

Ray was senior pastor of a Missouri Synod Lutheran church in Toledo. Lissa and Sean had visited Ray's church several times. With compassion and depth of teaching, Ray served his congregation as only a man who genuinely loved his church could.

It didn't hurt that he was just about the most gorgeous pastor ever, in Lissa's unbiased, proud, older-sister opinion. He was a sandy-haired version of Dad: tall, muscular, with dark blue eyes to melt little old ladies' hearts. His wife, Amy, was his perfect complement. The 1971 Gifford Homecoming King and Queen.

"Boots is coming next weekend," Lissa said.

"Yeah, I know. Mom told me. You two should have fun." Lissa fought a frown. How was it that everyone but her knew what was going on these days?

"Well, I'm looking forward to seeing you and Amy. Anything special you want to do when you're here?" Ray didn't sit still at Mom and Dad's.

"We'll be loading up some things to take back with us, so that should keep me busy."

"Oh?" Out of the family loop again.

"Yeah. Mom wants us to take the dining table and chairs. You good with that, Mel?"

"Absolutely. Really"

"Hey, why don't you let me talk to Mom and I'll firm this up with her."

"Sure. Love you."

"Love you back." Lissa took the phone to Mom, and Mom disappeared into the kitchen while Dad continued playing. Lissa heard the kitchen cupboard click open as Mom checked the calendar.

Lissa went to the buffet in the dining room and poured herself a sherry in a cobalt-blue etched cordial glass. An accompaniment to reading her diaries.

She passed Dad at the piano on her way to her room.

"Don't stop," she told him, kissing him on the cheek.

He smiled and continued playing the dreamy Chopin that was tonight's recital. As she climbed the stairs, Lissa peeked at her father. His eyes were closed, and his head moved rapturously to the melody. She turned upstairs and heard Dad seamlessly switch to the familiar tune to which her brain automatically supplied the lyrics, "Lullaby, and good night,..." When they were little, he often sent his children up to bed to the strains of Brahms's lullaby. Not everyone was lucky enough to have a dad like hers.

Carrying the sherry carefully, she watched the liquid slosh lazily in the glass, and her stomach dropped a step or two. The honey-colored alcohol crooked a withered finger at her.

Chapter 10

Three days already. It seemed like a week. The contentment Lissa had a moment ago blew away, fragile as a stray thread of a spider's web. But no regrets. Not about being here for the summer. What good would that do?

She set the blue glass on the windowsill and nestled into the pillows on the window seat. Light from the streetlight shown through the sherry glass, setting the liquid and the etched lines dancing.

The stack of diaries beckoned, and she snapped on the wall light in her alcove. Taking a sip of sherry, she reached back to fourth grade when life was good.

November 3, 1959

Dear Diary,

Steven Reese kicked me! I think he likes me!! Jessica

thinks so too.

We were lined up to go home from school. Steven made a face at me. Then he kicked me. I have a crush on Steven. He looks so cute in his crossing guard belt.

Mom could not come to my school program tonight. We sang songs from other countries. Mom gave me a doll dressed like a German girl. I wish she could have come. She had to teach cello. Mrs. Christiansen was there. She waved at me.

Dear God,

Thank you for all your blessings. Thank you the program went great tonight. Thank you Mom gave me a doll. Thank you for my friends, for Dad, for Boots and Ray, for Scamper and Daisy, for our house. And most of all, thank you that Steven Reese likes me. Amen.

And that was my day.

A kick in the shins as a sign of true love. How silly. Steven Reese moved to California at the end of the school year and that was the end of him. A love story that wasn't.

Her parents—now there was a love story.

Lissa could recite the details from all the times she had asked Mom or Dad to tell her the stories.

Mom and Dad had both taught at St. Lucia College. Mom taught private cello students in the Music Department, but mostly she stayed home with her children. Dad was a professor of piano and music theory. He served as Chairman of the Music Department for eighteen years before he retired, making his tenure at St. Lucy's thirty-five years.

They met at Northwestern University. Back from the war, Dad studied music on the GI Bill. That was 1946, when they were both sophomores, though Dad was three years older. Mom told the story of how they made beautiful music together. Dad accompanied Mom for her senior recital. They were engaged by then, and the story goes that their passion raised a few eyebrows. Mom and Dad laughed about it.

Lissa had always imagined Dad pouncing on the keys and casting a look at Mom. Then, with a toss of her head, Mom bent into her cello and drew the bow firmly and with great flourish across the strings.

They were beautiful together. Dad had movie-star looks: tall, with his dark thatch of wavy hair, and cobalt eyes. In spite of his efforts to tame his hair with Brylcreem, a lock always worked loose and flopped onto his forehead to bounce along in time as Dad attacked the piano keys. At faculty recitals, Lissa and Ray waited to see how long it would take the lock to escape, and then had to stifle giggles when it did.

Mom was dramatic in her own, more quiet way—so the story goes. She looked like a china doll: silken blond hair in a fashionable bob, delicate features, and flashing dark, aqua-blue eyes. A head shorter than Dad, Mom was the bride every daughter dreamed of being.

As a child, Lissa loved to gaze at her parents' 1949 wedding photo on the dining room buffet. They looked so happy. Post-war love with the promise for a better future. George and Eleanor—quite a love story could be written about them. Maybe Lissa would write it.

Dad still had his movie-star looks, only now his hair was thick silver, curling around his ears and over his collar—a kind of wild, retired-professor look.

Though he didn't perform anymore, Dad still played a stirring *Polonaise*—just not as fast. He used to rip through it, lock of hair jumping.

Mom no longer played the cello; she gave it up over ten years ago when the arthritis in her hands got bad. It was a surprise when she sold her cello. "Let someone else enjoy it,"

she had said.
 Mom was beautiful—young, old—her age didn't matter. She was simply a beautiful woman.
 Tipping back the last of the sherry, Lissa closed the diary on fourth grade.

Chapter 11

Comfy memories. Lissa didn't want to stop. She'd make the first run to Goodwill tomorrow afternoon—no rush to get to bed.

It was difficult to get around the house silently at night, but she needed a refill. The stairs popped, as did certain spots on the first floor. After years of experimentation and practice, Lissa had developed a pattern of treading on the stairs that was nearly foolproof for silence—going down, take the first four steps on the left, then cross to the right the rest of the way down.

Certainly Mom couldn't hear her, and probably Dad wouldn't either. Dad snored. But, not only did Dad have perfect pitch, he had hearing like a bat. Without thinking, she stepped into her familiar pattern and padded back downstairs for a refill of sherry.

Two. That would be two glasses. But who's counting?

Safely back on the window seat without waking her parents, Lissa set the very full glass on the window ledge. Laying 1959 aside, she picked up 1960, another fun year, and continued her reverie.

July 2, 1960

Dear Diary,

Today we drove to the cabin. We stopped at McGregor as usual. I bought a really pretty necklace with my own money. It was $2.50. It's a gold cross. It has rhinestones all around it. I thought they were diamonds. Mom said they were rhinestones. It's just as pretty to me. I'm wearing it right now. I'll take it off before I go to bed.
The cabin is the same as always. Gram and Gramps are already here. I love the lake. Tomorrow morning Gramps is taking Ray and me fishing. Gramps says Boots is too little. We have to get up early. That's when he says the fish are biting.

Dear God,

Thank you for our safe trip to the cabin. And please let the fish be biting tomorrow. Ray would really like to catch a big fish. Me too. Amen.
And that was my day. Tomorrow should be a good day too.

At least once every summer, the Makkinen family made the pilgrimage to Lissa's grandparents' cabin. A small community of cabins dotted the shore of a lake a few miles outside one of the small, no-longer-prosperous towns on the

FIFTY DAYS TO SUNRISE

Iron Range. When iron ore mining was booming in Northern Minnesota, so were the towns—but then the ore dwindled to taconite, and taconite gave way to a museum about mining. Now, more money came into the area from tourism than from mining. The fishing was still good.

Lissa's great-grandparents on her father's side were Finnish immigrants. Her great-grandfather worked in a deep-shaft mine in Soudan. They bought the cabin in the late 1920s when they could finally afford a little piece of land that reminded them of Finland—a cabin on a lake, with a log sauna on the shore.

Lissa loved being at the lake. With the last name of Makkinen, it was like waving a Finnish flag. Back home, no one but her own family rallied to the flag, and she was often asked, "What kind of name is *that*?" Probably no Finns were allowed south of Brainerd. She never met any in Gifford. At the lake they were surrounded by Finns: Ahonen, Oja, Lamppi, Hakala.

In the old days her father's entire extended family spent the summer at the lake. Gramps's brother built a cabin next door. The men worked in town during the week and drove out to the lake Friday evenings.

During the week the cabin was an enclave of women. Judging from the stories told, they cooked, laughed, and swam. Dad, being the only boy, ran errands. The cabin had running water—meaning Dad ran down the path to fill pails with cold spring water.

Mrs. Johnson, a widow who lived in the farmhouse down the road, let Dad practice on her piano most days. In exchange, Dad brought in wood and collected eggs from wherever the hens dropped them. A small price to pay for the escape—so Dad said. No wonder Dad learned to play the piano proficiently.

Family pictures showed the generations growing up and growing old at the lake. Lissa had a picture of Gramps with a forty-two-inch northern pike he caught in 1952. Her great-uncle had to shoot the fish to get it in the canoe. It seemed strange to take a pistol fishing, but it was a good thing, since the canoe would have capsized with a fish that size thrashing alongside. That was the Big Fish Story throughout the years. Dad said it was true.

Lissa let her mind drift to the lake: clear, sun-sparkling water the color of strong tea.

Or the color of sherry.

Folded up, tucked into the diary, Lissa found the story she wrote about seining minnows that summer. If, when she got to fifth grade, the class was given the assignment of writing *How I Spent My Summer Vacation*, her homework was done. But the teacher didn't assign the story.

Lissa unfolded the yellowed pages and began reading and remembering.

Here is my fish story. I helped Gramps seine for minnows. I liked doing that. The seine was a cotton net on poles. The wooden poles were made by my great-grandpa. They were straight branches with the bark peeled off. The poles were worn smooth.

Gramps unrolled the net on the shore and we each picked up a pole. We waded out into the lake until the water was just above my waist. We held the net flat over the water and stretched it out. Then we lowered the net into the water with the poles straight up.

Now to catch the minnows. The trick was to keep the net close to the bottom so the minnows would not get away. I could barely keep my mouth out of the water. I had to bend at the waist.

We slowly walked to the shore. We dragged the net with us. The net was not easy to drag. It took all my

> *strength. I wanted to do a good job. It got easier when we got closer to shore.*
>
> *Now the tricky part. When we got close to shore we had to tip the net back. Not so far back that the minnows got out over the top. We had to scoop the minnows out of the lake in the net. We made a quick scoop and put the net flat on the sand to see what we caught.*
>
> *The minnows flopped around in the net. They were all sparkly because of their silver bellies. We had to quick pick them out of the net and put them in the minnow bucket of lake water. We had the bait for fishing tomorrow.*
>
> *Gramps and I took the net back out in the lake and flipped it over. We shook it over the water and got out any minnows and seaweed we missed. We walked the net over next to the sauna and put it out to dry on the long tufts of grass. I felt very grown up.*

Lissa absently sucked in her lower lip, lost in her memories of time spent with her family at the cabin. Happy times that shaped her way beyond her awareness.

Probably partly because of the cabin, she had been so thoroughly happy at their little seventeen-acre farm on Lake Wabanaki. When she and Sean drove down the lane for the first time, in spite of the fact they could see the house needed work, she knew it was home. Lissa had taken Sean by the hand and strolled to the water's edge, skipped a rock on the lake, and only then, turned to survey the house and outbuildings.

Fishing beat a part in the rhythm of Maguire family life. Often, after a day of painting in his studio, Sean relaxed casting off the dock. Lissa watched him from the kitchen window.

A vision of her husband's muscles rippling across his broad shoulders as he worked the fishing line floated across her mind.

"No!" Startled by her own voice in the nighttime silence,

she bit her lip and took a deep breath. Two.

Lissa refolded the seining story and put it back where it had been for the last forty-three years. She settled in the pillows and held the blue glass to the light. Closing one eye, she noticed how the cut lines of the pattern in the glass shifted.

Lissa thought of her little brother and their friendly childhood rivalry. The fishing trip the next day settled the contest for a while—her fish was *much* bigger.

In the morning dark, Dad rousted Ray and Lissa out of bed. A loon laughed. Apparently, the loon thought it was funny the fishermen had to get up so early.

For breakfast, Gram set big bowls of oatmeal in front of them—Lissa's favorite. She poured on the cream and stirred in puddles of melted butter and brown sugar. Gramps had already loaded up the Alumacraft with the fishing gear.

Ready to go. Mom sent them out the door with a quick kiss just as Boots called from the back bedroom.

Bundled in their life jackets, Ray and Lissa plopped down on the middle seat together. The reek of gas and oil faded as Gramps cruised away from the shore.

The sky showed a faint promise of dawn. The damp air smelled of water and pine. Across the lake, a thin trail of smoke rose from a sauna.

They went around the point and into the bay. A great blue heron hunted for his breakfast along the misty shoreline. The elegant bird lifted into the air, his legs dangling, until his huge wings grabbed enough air to gain speed, and he disappeared over the treetops.

Gramps killed the motor, and Dad pitched the anchor over the side.

Dad had the minnow bucket, so he baited all the hooks.

FIFTY DAYS TO SUNRISE

Lissa could have baited her own hook, but she preferred not to. She had done it once.

Gramps and Lissa fished on one side of the boat and Dad and Ray on the other. Fishing was hard work—hard work sitting still and not talking much.

It took a ten-minute eternity until Gramps got the first fish, a crappie. Not a big one, but a keeper. Onto the stringer it went and back over the side.

Then Ray got a bite. Gramps told him how to jerk the line and reel it in. Ray landed his fish, another nice crappie. All together they hooked six crappies at that spot. Lissa's was the smallest, barely legal.

Dad hauled up the anchor, and they moved on to try another spot. Gramps steered them across the lake and into a bay clogged with lily pads. Gramps said this might be a good spot for northerns: pickerel, he called them. He cut the motor down to trolling speed and putted around the bay, just along the edge of the lily pads. Nothing.

They were almost out of the bay when a hard strike hit Lissa's line. She jerked the line, the weight of the fish heavy on the hook. She yanked the pole up and reeled the line. Gramps and Dad coached her, and Ray whooped in excitement. Lissa strained to hang on. Dad reached over and grabbed the pole to help. If he hadn't, she would have lost the fish, pole and all.

Lissa got her first look at the huge fish when she pulled it alongside the boat. The fish thrashed its tail, splashing Lissa in the face, and she grimaced as the water slid over her lips.

Gramps got the net and scooped the fish into the boat. A quick *whack* with a wooden pin, and the fish lay still. Ray and Lissa were stunned that Gramps killed the fish, but then the thrill of the catch took over. The fish wasn't quite as big as it looked when Lissa saw it in the water, but it was still a big fish, a northern pike. Gramps measured it—twenty-three inches long, its teeth vicious-looking needles.

With all the hooting and hollering when Lissa landed her

fish, any other fish had no doubt run for cover. Gramps revved up the Evinrude and headed back.

As soon as they touched the shore, Ray and Lissa launched themselves out of the boat. With a splash, they landed in the shallow water. Yelling and kicking up sand in their wake, they pelted toward the cabin. Gram opened the door and stood on the porch wiping her hands on her apron. Ray and Lissa tugged their grandmother toward the boat with Mom and Boots close behind.

Mom and Gram admired the catch, especially Lissa's. Ray and Lissa recounted every detail of the battle to bring in the big fish, both of them talking at once. Boots hung back. She thought fish were "icky."

Gram wanted a picture of Ray and Lissa together, each holding their fish. Ray pouted, but he smiled again when Gramps told him there would be another fishing trip tomorrow, just the two of them.

For dinner Gram made fried fish fillets, boiled potatoes with butter sauce, and peas. Lissa puffed with pride to have caught a meal for her family. There was even enough for two meals.

The next morning Gram simmered the big head of Lissa's fish in a pot of milky water to make *kalamojakka*, fish stew. Lissa lifted the lid and peeked at what was left of her fish. She wished she hadn't.

It was late. Lissa drained her glass, set it on the window ledge, and nestled back in the pillows. She had told her own Big Fish Story countless times. Life was so simple then.

Her shoulder-length hair fluffed around her head in unruly honey-brown waves. She pushed aside the hair that fell over one eye.

FIFTY DAYS TO SUNRISE

The corners of her mouth twitched at the memories of family and fun at the cabin. She closed her eyes, resting her hands on her fifth grade diary. Just for a minute.
Lissa started awake. She heard herself make a small noise —something less than a cry, but not exactly a moan. Nightmares. Again.
She shook the unwanted images from her head. How much longer could she take this?
Lissa got up and made her way down to the sherry bottle— one more time. This time she took less care to avoid the creaky spots on the stairs.
Refill in hand, she stood in the living room. She bit her lip hard and tried not to look where Sean's painting had been.
Sean had painted Jack and Shannon, their faces alight with childhood wonder, peering into a tide pool along the seashore near their home. It was one of his best paintings. Dad had taken it down before Lissa came home last Christmas, thinking it would upset her too much to see it. In its place, Dad hung a cheap print of an English garden.
Lissa took a large gulp of sherry and turned back to grab the bottle. She marched silently upstairs, determined to get lost in 1960.

Chapter 12

September 6, 1960

Dear Diary,

Today was the first day of school. I like my teacher. Her name is Mrs. Fenstad. Sally is in my class, but not Jessica. Our room is really fun. We have a white rat! Every weekend one of us gets to take the rat home for the weekend. I hope Mom lets me. Boots will freak. I can't wait.

Dear God,

Thank you for this beautiful day. And for all the kids in my class. Keep us safe every day on the way to school. I pray that poor people have enough to eat. And that sick people would get better. And I'm sorry I like to tease Boots sometimes. Amen.
And that was my day. I hope tomorrow is a good day.

Fifth grade was fun for Lissa—though it would have been more fun if Jessica had been in her class too. But, Lissa admitted, they probably would have gotten in even more trouble. Sally and Lissa were manageable for the teacher, but when the three of them were together, they were like naughty kittens in a basket.

The first day of school started well, but the week ended in trouble. Sally and Lissa cooked up quite a caper, just the two of them.

"Pssst," Sally hissed across the aisle separating their desks.

"What?" Lissa barely let out a sound.

Sally propped her math book open on her desk and leaned down to hide behind it. She must have thought it would look like she was studying the math they were supposed to be working on. Mrs. Fenstad was teaching the new modern math and was talking about sets and intersections, or something.

"Want to have some fun?" Sally said.

Lissa put a finger to her lips, silently saying, "Shhh."

Sally raised her desk top just enough to slip her hand in and draw out a small piece of paper. She wrote on it, hidden behind her book, and quickly passed the note across the aisle.

When we feed the rat this afternoon, let's hide it and pretend it's lost. Susan will be standing on her desk, screaming!

Susan Anderson was really prissy—nice, but irritating—way too clean. Most of the girls played kickball pretty hard right along with the boys, but Susan spent most of the game trying to avoid the ball. Nobody wanted her on their team. Susan inspired the phrase "runs like a girl."

The plot was hatched. Lissa smiled at Sally and nodded.

They had to wait until math ended. It was Friday, and Sally was the first to get to take Snowball, the rat, home for the

FIFTY DAYS TO SUNRISE

weekend. Her mom was picking her up after school and taking Snowball, cage and all, home with them. Sally got to feed Snowball today to make sure she knew what to do to take care of him. This was perfect for their plot to scare the pants off Susan.

Lissa had some time to think until math was over.

She wore her favorite gray wool blazer with the red and gold crest on the breast pocket. It had two pockets in front just like grown-ups' blazers. Pockets and a rat seemed made for each other.

Waving a discreet finger at Sally to get her attention, Lissa pointed to her pocket. She pulled the top of the pocket open to show Sally there was plenty of room for a rat.

Sally put a hand over her mouth to stifle a giggle and nodded.

Math was finally over. Time to feed Snowball.

Mrs. Fenstad got the supplies out, and they gathered around for the taking-care-of-Snowball ritual. This was the first week of class, and Snowball was skittish. Sally had to chase him around the cage with her hand before she caught him.

So helpful, Lissa stepped in to hold Snowball while Sally cleaned his cage. Other kids wanted to pet him. Lissa passed Snowball to Tom Grossman, knowing that wouldn't go very well. Snowball crawled up over Tom's shoulder and onto the back of his neck. Lissa rescued the rat before he fell to the floor.

"I'd better let Snowball calm down," she said.

Lissa moved to the side, hoping to attract less attention. Sally drew Mrs. Fenstad off, asking questions about how much to feed Snowball, and whether or not he ate vegetables.

Tom wouldn't go away. Finally, Lissa just had to make her move.

She slipped Snowball into her pocket and pooched out her lips, a silent "shh" to Tom. He smiled a conspiratorial grin.

Lissa mingled back into the crowd around the cage.

"Where's Snowball?" She tried to sound innocent.

"I thought you had him," Sally said, looking only a little concerned.

"No. I gave him to Tom."

"*I* don't have him. I thought *you* had him." Tom looked offended, happily playing along.

"*I* don't have him!" Now Lissa put some alarm in her voice.

"What? Where could he be?" Sally really played it up.

Lissa carefully kept her hand over the top of her pocket so Snowball wouldn't give away the game.

"He must have gotten loose!" Lissa barely contained the mock hysterics in her voice.

Classmates started scurrying around, looking under desks and on bookshelves. As predicted, Susan ran for her desk. She sat on the top of it and clutched her skirt tight to her legs. Susan looked worried. Her face turned light red and she bite her lip, trying not to make any scared silly-girl noises.

Lissa couldn't help herself, she tapped the lid of Susan's desk and said, "Maybe the rat's *in your desk*!"

That did it. Susan let out a scream and bolted for Mrs. Fenstad.

At that moment, a warm, wet sensation spread in the vicinity of Lissa's left pocket.

Snowball had piddled in her pocket.

"Oh, no!" Lissa let out a long, drawn out wail that nobody missed. All eyes were on her.

Game over. She slowly drew Snowball out of her pocket.

Mrs. Fenstad did *not* think it was funny.

That was the one and only time Lissa got sent to the principal's office. Her punishment also included that she wasn't allowed to take Snowball home until after Christmas.

The principal and Mrs. Fenstad talked sternly to Lissa. She didn't rat on Sally—she just couldn't.

Released into her mother's custody, Lissa rode home in

FIFTY DAYS TO SUNRISE

terrified silence. She'd never gotten in trouble this bad.
She was immediately sentenced to her room.

The prisoner was allowed to eat, but after dinner, Mom and Dad sat her down for a talk. In a flood of tears, Lissa told them the whole story. Lissa wasn't allowed to talk to Sally all weekend. That was torture.

Mom called Sally's mom and filled her in. Sally got in trouble too.

Monday morning, Sally and Lissa found their desks at opposite sides of the room.

Lissa quietly chuckled. She twirled the stem of her cordial glass, watching the little bit of sherry in the bottom glide around like a silk ribbon. Snowball piddling in her pocket was just about the funniest thing ever. At a slumber party at Jessica's, out of earshot of either Sally's or Lissa's parents, they had laughed until their sides hurt. But Sally and Lissa decided that was enough trouble for one lifetime.

Lissa missed Sally. Forty-seven years they'd been bosom buddies. Bosom. Hah. That was a fact. One of the things Lissa used to envy about Sally. That and her blond braids down her back. Being around Sally was like soaking up sunshine on a Caribbean beach. Sally bubbled with stories about her kids and the funny things Marv said about his patients. Apparently drilling teeth was a source of comedy.

This would no doubt be one of the countless times they'd picked up right where they left off, as if no time had elapsed. She hoped. Lissa had avoided Sally last Christmas. Not an unforgivable sin. But really—inexcusable. She'd call Sally tomorrow.

Finishing the bottle suddenly seemed like a very good bad idea.

Chapter 13

November 14, 1960

Dear Diary,

Today is my lucky day! Hurray for me!! I won! I won! The Young Writers Short Story Contest picked my story in all of Minneapolis. For all fifth graders. I'm so excited! I got a $100.00 US Savings Bond. Mom and Dad said I can put it away for college. They said it will be worth a lot of money by then.
 I got to go to Ole's Soda Shoppe to celebrate. Mom said I could get whatever I wanted. I got the biggest hot fudge sundae.
 I can't wait to tell Mrs. Fenstad tomorrow. She really liked my story.
 I think when I grow up I'll be a famous author. I'll have lots of cats in my house. They'll sit on the desk with me and I'll write books. Books and books and books. So many books. I'll be so rich. I'll buy Dad a new car. He likes

new cars. I'll buy Mom a mink coat. For me I'll buy a big house where all my friends can come visit me. They can stay as long as they want.
   Oh, Diary, I love my life!

   Dear God,

      Thank you. Thank you. Thank you!!!!!!! For letting me win this contest. You make me so happy. I'll love you forever. Bless me to be a writer. Please God. Please let me be an author. Amen.
      And that's my day.

   Lissa smiled. So many years ago, so many words. Even as a child, Lissa loved words. She wrote short stories, poems, and of course, her beloved diary.
   This particular day, November 14, 1960, was a defining moment in Lissa's life. Without such encouragement in the direction of creative writing, it might not have become a career for her. The *Minneapolis Tribune*, the contest sponsor, launched her into the stratosphere of writing. She completed a Master of Fine Arts at Columbia University and then landed at *Country Journal* magazine.
   The magazine was an exceptionally good job, one which she was able to continue from the farm when she and Sean fled New York City for country bliss in coastal Maine. Renovating an eighteenth-century farmhouse and outbuildings was ideal fodder for her monthly feature, "Life in the Country, Heaven on Earth," although sometimes causing a sardonic twist to her musings.
   A monthly feature was nice, but Lissa and Sean were both getting their careers started, and they needed more income, so Lissa freelanced. When she wasn't wielding a crowbar, slashing

FIFTY DAYS TO SUNRISE

at undergrowth, or stripping woodwork, she was writing.

Lissa's freelancing resulted in a book of short stories, *Lavender Stories*. It was a book for women, about women, and it was a pretty book.

Lissa knew there was a copy on her mother's bedside table, and that her mother had given a copy to just about everyone she knew.

Lissa was a writer—an answer to a childhood prayer. Commuting to New York on occasion, she enjoyed working at *Country Journal* for three years. Lissa then passed the job on to the next aspiring writer, so she could be a writer *and* Jack's mother.

Between feedings, diaper changes, and cleaning up spit up, Lissa started writing the *Ben Stories*, a series of children's books based on the life of her cat. It amazed her that she could even think straight, let alone write anything comprehensible. Baby fluids were shocking and took some getting used to. And sleep was a joke. Just a concept.

Her first book, *God Takes Care of Ben*, was published in 1977. It sold well, so she was given an advance on the next book. It wasn't much money, but it helped. Renovating an old farmhouse took more time and money than expected.

The next book, *Ben Does Flips*, sold even better. Lissa soared on the wings of a real writing career. The back flap of the book jacket had a picture of Ben and her next to the barn. Standing on top of the fieldstone fence that ran up to the barn, Ben stretched to touch Lissa's nose, his tail an exclamation point. The camera caught Ben just as he squinted his eyes shut in the rapture of their nosekiss. A luminous cream tabby, Ben was the star of the books, but as far as Ben was concerned, the sun rose and set in Lissa.

Ben and Jenny, *Nanny Ben*, and *Good Old Ben* completed the series. Sometimes Lissa wanted to pinch herself: see if this life they were living was real. She was a published author, actually making decent money, and Sean was becoming a well-known artist on the East Coast. And they were parents of the two most beautiful children in the world.

She dug in the box she'd brought down from the attic and found her winning short story, way at the bottom to keep it flat. *That's Silly*, it was titled, by Lissa Makkinen.

Lissa had spent a long time trying out different versions of her name and imagining how her name would look on the cover of a book. She even made a brown paper bag mock-up of a book cover to see how her name would really look.

Mom called her Lissa, though at the time, most people called her Missy. Lissa Makkinen—very Finnish—she liked it. From thence forward she informed everyone that her name was Lissa.

She continued to write as Lissa Makkinen even after marrying Sean. Waving the Irish flag under the name Maguire took some getting used to.

That's Silly was about Cora, a six-year-old girl, who was tired of everyone telling her, "That's silly." The story followed Cora through a week in her life when she had all kinds of adventures: ate weird foods, read books not on the first grade recommended reading list, imagined what it would be like to be a doctor in Borneo, and learned to play the drums. The story ended with Cora asserting, "That's *not* silly! That's *me*!"

What a confidence-builder winning the contest had been.

Lissa poured the last of the sherry and leaned back in the pillows, savoring the night air wafting in the window.

Publishing her first adult novel in 1995 had been a big boost, but now she was stuck—stuck up to the hubs of the wagon wheels. Stuck in mud so deep she couldn't see her way out. She gulped down the sherry. Her second novel was hopelessly mired. It had sat for a year and a half. Sat—rhymes with splat. If she'd looked up and seen a seagull passing overhead, doing what seagulls do, it would have fit. *Splat.* Nothing was right.

Closing her eyes was a mistake. The darkness behind her eyes lurched. Who was this person? She hardly recognized herself anymore. Confidence? Who was she kidding? She snapped her eyes open and tried to focus on a spot on the ceiling.

Lissa reached to put her empty glass on the windowsill, and missed. She let go, and the glass plopped onto the cushion. She crumpled against the pillows and fought the threat of the room being set in motion not of her making. Drunk again.

Great. Time for another pity party. Couldn't she just have a little peace? Her anger rose, but she didn't have the energy.

"To sleep: perchance to dream." Out loud, Lissa quoted the melancholy Dane. Hamlet wasn't talking about a good night's sleep. Maybe the big sleep wouldn't be so bad.

Lissa mentally slapped herself. Thoughts of death leered at her, as they had on occasion during the last eighteen months. She tasted bile. She didn't want to die, for heaven's sake. She pushed her hair out of her eyes and left her hand resting on her forehead, as if that might forestall the brewing headache. She just wanted this pain to stop. She could never do anything to hurt Jack and Shannon.

Profanity roiled in her mind. There wasn't much she could do about being in this state now. She was furious with herself for letting this happen again. Unlike at the farm, Lissa had to be quiet so she didn't wake her parents; she couldn't scream; she couldn't stomp around the house; she just went to bed.

Rising unsteadily from the window seat, Lissa tipped over the empty bottle. Her diaries thudded to the wood floor. A vague thought that her parents might have heard the noise crawled through her brain, but she couldn't grasp the thought.

Lissa staggered across the room. A trail of clothes followed her, ending in her bra left dangling from the lampshade on the dresser.

Chapter 14

The shower pounded on Lissa's head—punishment. Twenty minutes later, Lissa descended the kitchen stairs. Her wet hair hung to her shoulders, dripping onto her oversized, purple-and-yellow tie-dyed T-shirt. Barefoot, as usual, Lissa wore sky-blue sweatpants, not her size: too long, and a little snug across the hips, with Columbia Lions in white letters down one leg.

A quick glance at Mom, then Lissa said nothing. Instead, she made straight for the coffee pot, poured herself a mugful, and sat down at the kitchen table with her back to her mother.

The silence between them was painful, but not as painful as Lissa's head. Cutting off her head and setting it on the counter had an appeal. Mom continued to pit cherries.

Lissa rested her elbows on the table, hands clasped around her mug. She brought the coffee to her lips and sipped, breathing in the rising steam, hoping for a miraculous hangover cure.

Neither woman said anything for a few minutes. Lissa seethed.

She heard her mother pouring coffee. Mom sat down next to Lissa at the round table.

Lissa stared out into the backyard, her empty mug on the table in front of her. A movement in the garage caught her eye—Dad. Elbows still on the table, she supported her head with both fists under her chin.

"Lissie?" Mom stopped to sip her coffee. She waited. "How do you feel?"

A groan bubbled out of her, and Lissa raked her fingers into her hair. It hurt to the roots. She leaned her head into her hands. This morning her neck couldn't support the weight of her head. Not surprising, since she had bricks for brains.

"You were in my room this morning, weren't you?" Lissa again fixed her gaze somewhere in the backyard.

"Yes," Mom hesitated. "Why?"

Lissa rubbed her temples. "Did you have to *tidy up*? Was it to let me know you'd been in my room, seeing me like that?" She clipped her words through tight lips. Still refused to look at her mother.

Mom set her cup down. Lissa could feel her mother's eyes searching her face.

"I didn't mean to upset you. I was worried. You never sleep so late." Mom fluttered her hands helplessly. "I didn't know what else to do."

"I'm fine!" Lissa fired out the words, then bit off her breath to stop herself from saying anything more she might regret.

"Lissa, I'm concerned that you've been drinking too much lately."

"I suppose Jack told you." She riveted her mother's eyes.

Mom seemed startled. "Yes...yes he did." Mom looked away. Lissa had her mother's eyes, but not today.

"Mo-ther!" Lissa spat out the word like an unpleasant taste. "It's none of your business!"

Mom blinked, sat up straight, and locked on her daughter's glare. "Well, yes...yes indeed it *is* my business."

FIFTY DAYS TO SUNRISE

Groaning again and kneading the back of her neck with one hand, Lissa opened her mouth, but didn't say anything. She closed her eyes and sighed.

"Melissa Louise, you have to deal with—"

"I'll deal with it when I'm good and ready! I told you that! Now leave me alone!" Lissa's whole body tensed for a fight. She cut her mother off, hacking with an expletive that cut more viciously than a knife.

"And don't call me Melissa Louise! I'm not a child!" Her face twisted with the irony, but she ignored it.

"Lissa, I've never had to confront any of my children about their drinking. Forgive me if I don't know how to do it." Mom's voice sounded pinched and tired.

Lissa covered her face with her hands, wishing everything and everyone would go away. Squeezing her eyes shut, she thought of how this was a reprise of the Christmas mess.

Her head throbbed, and she fought rising nausea.

Just then, Dad appeared in the kitchen. "What's going on?"

Getting no response, he held up a roll of packing tape. "I found what I was looking for."

Lissa shot her father a metal-melting look. She pushed her chair back, got up, and ran up the kitchen steps—and almost tripped over the corner of the rag rug in front of the sink.

She barely made it to the bathroom before she vomited.

Lissa brushed her teeth, took three ibuprofen, and went back to bed. This day was going to be a write-off. The best she could do was sleep it off and try again. She didn't call Sally.

Late in the afternoon Lissa woke. The aroma drifting up from the kitchen smelled delicious. She lay in bed awhile to make sure she wasn't going to dash for the bathroom again. Her eyes too big for their sockets, the headache at the base of her skull was downgraded from a hammering throb to a dull ache.

Slowly, Lissa tested her reentry into reality. She pushed back the sheet. Still wearing her sweatpants and T-shirt, she tentatively sat up on the edge of the bed. She combed her fingers through her hair, straightening the tangled mess—massaged her scalp. Physical sensations, but little brain activity yet.

Lissa tried again to descend to the kitchen and start the day over. She took the long way around, through the living room, past the Steinway, avoiding the steep steps.

Mom was at the stove stirring a big pot of something. Lissa crossed the kitchen before Mom turned around. She came up behind her mother, put her arms around Mom's waist, and hugged her. Her mother stiffened initially at Lissa's touch, but then relaxed.

"Mom, I'm so sorry. I don't know what got into me."

Mom patted Lissa's arm with her free hand. "It's all right. I'm sorry too. I should have been more patient."

Mother and daughter stood briefly in this embrace, like nothing hurtful had been said.

Lissa released her mother. "Can I make some tea?"

"Your dad and I already had ours, but you go ahead."

"That smells wonderful," said Lissa, peering into the pot. "Mmm, chicken noodle soup." An offering of love and care from her mother. "Thanks, Mom." Lissa gave her mother a peck on the cheek. Mom smiled. She quietly stirred the soup while Lissa made tea for herself.

Once again seated at the table with a mug in front of her, Lissa faced her mother. "Mom, I know I've been really awful lately. And I know it's hard on everyone around me. But I just…can't deal with it yet. I will. I know I have to…okay?" Lissa absently ran her thumb up and down the handle of her mug.

Mom turned to Lissa. "We just want to help." She took a deep breath. "Sean—"

FIFTY DAYS TO SUNRISE

"Mom, *please*," Lissa pleaded, almost too softly for her mother to hear. She looked down at her tea, trying to hide tears that threatened.

Mom sighed a small sigh. "All right, honey." She set the spoon on the pineapple-shaped spoon rest and wiped her hands down the front of her apron. "Do you think you'd like to go to church tomorrow, and then to the picnic? I made a cherry pie."

"No, I'll pass. But I will—soon—I promise. Just not tomorrow. I feel like my head's spinning, like I just got here." Lissa hastened to add, "Really, I'll be fine here on my own. Scout's honor." She held up three fingers in promise. "I'd actually like a little time alone."

Her mother said no more about church or the picnic.

A clatter of soft thuds against the hallway walls announced Dad's entrance. He dropped his load of empty boxes at the kitchen door, causing louder thuds. Lissa winced.

"Everything all right?" Dad waited before he said anything more.

Lissa noticed her father glance between her mother and herself. She rose and walked into her father's outstretched arms.

"I'm sorry, Dad. I promise never to do anything like that again. The drinking, or the screaming. I feel so *stupid*."

Dad patted his daughter's back with one hand and with the other hand gently pressed her head onto his shoulder.

"It's all right, Missy. We understand." Lissa disengaged herself. Eyes fixed on the floor, she turned aside to retrieve her tea.

"I'll be outside if you need me to do anything for dinner." She picked her way through the boxes on the floor and padded silently on bare feet toward the back door.

Lissa heard the sounds of a gentle kiss. "All right, my love?" her father said.

Chapter 15

The evening air revitalized Lissa. She had promised Mom she wouldn't run, but she had to get out of the house. In truth, she couldn't have run if she wanted to. The chicken noodle soup had been medicine, but the headache wasn't quite gone. A walk was just what she needed. It was only a few blocks to downtown—Saturday night in Gifford. The tang of charcoal smoke and grilled meat scented the air. A breeze fluffed her loose hair.

Four blocks to River Street. The Dakota River cut a wide gully through town. On the riverbank, at the intersection of Manitou and River, stood the old mill: a three-story building built on a shelf of rock next to the river, just out of reach of the spring flood. One level extended down from ground level, clinging to the short cliff.

The great waterwheel took huge gulps of the river from the spillway channeled to the side. The wheel had churned for a hundred years, turning the local farmers' grain into flour. When her family moved to Gifford, the mill had still operated as a co-operative for a year or two until the farmers gave up and shipped their grain south to the huge mills in Minneapolis. Abandoned in the 1950s, the mill was bought in the '80s by a group of local entrepreneurs, including Sally's husband, and converted into retail space creatively named The Old Mill. The restored mighty waterwheel again turned the huge millstones, producing specialty flour from local grain. During the day the old iron shaft creaked as the river slapped at the wheel. Tonight the spillway was shut, the wheel silent. The flour shop was closed.

Further upriver to the north was Mom and Dad's apartment complex, their home-to-be. Booth Park was next on River Street, and across the river, the grand old houses of Gifford lined the bluff.

Lissa turned south for one block, toward downtown. The Bridge Street bridge was the largest of three bridges crossing the Dakota River in Gifford. Lissa took the pedestrian walk over the bridge. Stopping midway, she leaned against the railing and gazed back toward the mill. If she took a postcard picture of Gifford, it would be from right here.

The river flowing below the bridge fascinated Lissa. The water was constant, yet continuously changing—one of those great paradoxes.

The streetlights winked on. She stood next to one of the glossy black nineteenth-century-style light poles and looked down at the shadow of the bridge cast onto the water. She could barely make out her own shadow next to the rail.

The reflection mirrored her: a barely discernible shadow projected onto a space that wouldn't stand still, hardly distinguishable from her surroundings. She kicked a pebble over the side and waited for the *plop* and the ripples. Nothing. Too noisy and too dark.

Traffic behind her rattled the iron bridge structure beneath her. A carload of teens yelled something in her direction, but she didn't catch it, or care.

Gazing over the rail into the black water, Lissa resolved

that this was going to end: this living between spaces, between trauma and recovery. She had effectively wrestled herself into denial. But now, she was so entrenched in it, denial had a chokehold on her.

Way too much pain. Seeing the pain on her mother's face when she once again screamed at her—that was simply not going to happen again. And she was *not* going to yell at her son for squealing on her about her drinking. Jack had his own grief to deal with, not to mention the stress of running his restaurant. Shame convicted her, and she repented of all the attention she had unwittingly demanded.

Nearly dark. She turned toward home. She was done worrying Mom and Dad. The soft lights in the closed shops of The Old Mill looked cozy. She decided again to call Sally, soon, and meet her at their favorite coffee shop in the mill.

Mom and Dad had gone to bed, but left the front porch light on for her and the door unlocked. The light was still on in their bedroom, so Lissa knocked softly.

Dad called, "Missy, that you?" Lissa poked her head in. Her parents were both propped up in bed, reading.

"It's the boogie monster. I'm back."

Dad grinned, "Yes, it appears you are."

"I had a nice walk."

"Good, honey," Mom said. "See you in the morning. Oh, do you still want to stay home from church tomorrow?"

"Yes. I've got some things I want to take care of."

They exchanged good nights. Lissa stopped in her room to take off her shoes before going downstairs to make herself a cup of chamomile tea.

She settled on the porch swing and listened to the night sounds. The scent of the pink roses along the front of the house wafted up on the rising heat from the soil around them.

Her parents had lived here so long, almost her whole lifetime. If they had the courage to adjust to this enormous change, she could learn to adjust too.

Tomorrow, while her parents were gone, she would spend the day with Pip.

Chapter 16

Sunday morning and the house was quiet. Lissa again settled in the window seat with her diaries. She knew exactly where to look: 1963, that was the year she met Pip. She pulled her eighth grade diary out of the stack, took a deep breath, slowly let it out, and resolutely turned to the first week of school.

September 5, 1963

Dear Diary,

There's a new girl at school. I met her today. She's in my grade. Her name is Pip. It's really Philippa, but she's called Pip for short. I think that's an odd name. I guess it's because her dad's from England. Pip says it's not an unusual name in England.
She just moved here a month ago. Her dad's teaching

history at St. Lucy's. It turns out she only lives a couple blocks from me. I think I'll like her okay. Sally and Jessica like her, so I guess she'll be a friend. At least I hope so. I'd be really upset if anything happened to my friendship with Sally and Jessica. It'll be okay. I'll just be nice to her. Maybe I'll have all three of them sleep over next weekend, and we can get to know her. She's so pretty. I've never seen anything like her hair. She has masses of long, curly red hair. And lots of freckles.

Philippa Lucille Farnsworth—a big name for a little girl. Pip had corkscrew-curly red hair just past her shoulders and loads of freckles. Her Irish-setter-red hair sparkled in the sun like fire, especially when she shook her head and her curls bounced, sending flashes of gold and red all around her head—a human sparkler.

Pip was much shorter than Lissa. By eighth grade Lissa was five feet eight inches tall and towered over Pip. At five feet one, Pip looked like a porcelain doll. Everything about Pip was cute and tiny, which Lissa certainly was not. The boys made fools of themselves over Pip. Bill Penrod couldn't take his eyes off Pip and bumped into an open locker door.

Lissa had that slumber party the weekend after meeting Pip. It seemed Pip had been with the three of them forever—and now they were four.

Pip was not only cute, she was funny. She and Sally told jokes and stories that had all of them rolling on the floor squealing with laughter. They listened to rock 'n' roll and set each other's hair on pink sponge rollers.

Pip was also nice. Sally's grandma died just before Christmas that year. Pip made a batch of chocolate-chip-gumdrop cookies and took them over to Sally's family.

Pip helped Lissa with math when Lissa got so frustrated

FIFTY DAYS TO SUNRISE

she wanted to throw the book. Pip would sit her down, look her in the eyes, and say, "Now Lissa, being frustrated isn't going to help you learn this stuff—is it?" She'd skewer Lissa with a serious look, but then Pip's green eyes sparkled with mischief, and Lissa dissolved in laughter. So frequently did Pip use this line, eventually she could shorten it up to, "Now Lissa...," accompanied by *the look,* and Lissa was helpless with laughter and love for her friend—and ready to tackle her math.

Pip and Lissa got really close. Sometimes she and Pip got together, just the two of them. The final bonding between them happened on February 9, 1964, when all four of the friends were lying on their stomachs, chins propped on their hands, as close to the TV as Pip's parents would allow—waiting.

Ed Sullivan announced, "Ladies and gentlemen...The Beatles."

As one, all four friends leapt to their feet, screaming. Sally screamed, "John!" Jessica screamed, "Paul!" And Pip and Lissa in unison screamed, "George!" Pip and Lissa were sealed as friends forever. They screamed some more, jumped up and down, hugged each other, and screamed, "George!" It turned out George didn't marry Pip or Lissa, but not for lack of either of them willing it to be so.

Beatlemaniacs to the core, they all trooped together to the Beatles concert in Minneapolis on August 21, 1965. They paid four dollars and fifty cents for third-baseline seats at Metropolitan Stadium and screamed their little hearts out.

Pip's dad being from England was a real bonus. Lissa told him he was part of the British Invasion. He laughed and coached Lissa on a British accent, which she tried out on her Anglophile mother.

"Mummy. Oh, Mummy," Lissa said, as she dramatically swept into the kitchen, Pip and her curls bouncing in behind. "Could we have a spot of tea please?"

"But, of course, dahlings," said Mom without skipping a beat. "Would you like one lump or two?" She busied herself with putting the kettle on and then got out the Crown Staffordshire tea set. The girls giggled and so did Mom. They all sat down to proper English tea and nattered away in their best British accents.

Lissa and Pip had such fun together. There wasn't anything they didn't talk about. They knew each other's secrets, and they planned their futures. Because their dads were professors at St. Lucy's, they knew they were going to college there, and they planned to be roommates.

They dreamed of moving to Denver after graduation. Lissa would be an author, and Pip would be a high school history teacher. They'd fall in love with the most wonderful boys, have a double wedding, and ski happily ever after. They'd be godparents to each other's children.

Pip was one of those once-in-a-lifetime friends.

Lissa closed the 1963 diary and contemplated her next move. She knew what she was doing now. She had to face the past before she could live with the present that was suffocating her. She wrapped her arms around herself. She didn't want to go on like this, but it had gotten all too familiar, this escape by one means or another.

She turned to the exact date—August 6, 1966—and tensed, braced for what was there. She hadn't read this entry since she wrote it thirty-seven years ago.

Chapter 17

August 6, 1966

Oh God!! God, how could you do this!!! Pip's dead!!! I can't believe it. I'll never forgive you for letting this happen. Her poor parents!
This is the worst day of my life. Nothing could be any worse than to have your best friend killed in a car accident! I just don't know what else to say. God, I'm so mad at you!!!!!

As she read these words, Lissa's tears dripped onto the already tear-stained page. She reached for a Kleenex from the box she had set beside her in preparation for this ordeal. Oh, God. She pressed a fist to her mouth. It had seemed unthinkable that anything could be worse than Pip's death.
But then, Sean...
Her heart's blood drained. Sunrise extinguished.

She hugged herself for fear she'd come apart. Pleading with God hadn't helped so far, but she kept trying—hoping God would unstop His ears. Living with this grief was impossible. She'd thrashed in it for too long. Something—she had to do something. Maybe by making herself face the pain of Pip's death—and then letting the agony of losing Sean rise from where she'd tamped it down and chained a lid on it—she could manage. Maybe.

She was terrified she wouldn't be able to control her emotions—that she'd shatter into a million fragments—that she'd never again be any recognizable form of what had been Melissa Louise Makkinen Maguire. But thinking of herself was sickening. It was Sean and Pip who had died. This shouldn't be about her. But sometimes she was sure missing Sean was going to kill her.

She tried to contain the wracking sobs surging in her throat. Strangled sounds escaped. Then a low howl, and Lissa crumbled. A wounded animal gone to ground, she gave up and let the pain in—to let it out.

Collapsing onto her side, bent over her arms clutched against her abdomen—as if that would help—she sobbed.

No one should have to cry like that alone.

No comforting hand stopped her tears. Lissa cried until she was done—for now.

She flopped onto her back and stared at the ceiling. Slowly her breathing settled to normal.

Caught in a web of memories.

It must have been a fool who said tears were cleansing. She reached for another Kleenex. Stuffed up and a headache behind her eyes, she rolled off the window seat and went to the bathroom for ibuprofen.

Like a soldier standing on the edge of the battle, she leaned against the doorframe of her room and wished deeply, so deeply, that she didn't have to do this. But amputation was inevitable, and the bone saw was poised. Couldn't she keep

FIFTY DAYS TO SUNRISE

going by denial? Stupid question. She knew the answer. With a sigh, she returned to the window seat.

Memories of Pip's death had never gotten as dim as she wished they would. She saw the scene clearly in her mind as she had many times in her dreams and in her waking nightmares. A resurgence of terror had flooded in when her own children learned to drive, and she had to reluctantly turn them over to God every time they got in a car. It was especially hard when they rode with friends. That was what happened to Pip.

Pip and Lissa were sixteen the summer after their sophomore year of high school. Their parents had conspired and set the age when they could date at sixteen. Before that, they could only be with boys in a group. Lissa hadn't turned sixteen until just after school was out, so Pip, with a January birthday, had gotten a head start. The first boy to ask her out was a senior, Brad Zimmer, the captain and quarterback of the football team. Brad was one of the most good-looking boys in the school, his grades were good, and he and his family attended the same church as Pip's family. Pip's parents didn't think they had grounds for saying no, but they weren't pleased Pip was dating an upperclassman.

Brad had a football scholarship to the University of California, Berkeley, and he had to be at school early for training. These were the last few days Pip and Brad had together before being separated by half the country. Pip told Lissa she really loved Brad and was going to miss him desperately.

August 6 was a Saturday morning. Lissa heard the phone ring unusually early. It didn't bring her fully awake; it only rang twice. She wasn't conditioned yet by life's tragedies to have that immediate dread that's more felt than thought when the phone rings at odd times.

"Lissa, honey. Wake up."

"Mmm."

Mom gently touched her daughter's shoulder, urging her awake.

"Why? It's too early," Lissa protested. She really liked to sleep in on Saturday. Her summer waitress job was hard work on the weekend, and she'd gotten home at ten thirty the night before. Her feet and the rest of her needed the sleep.

"Come downstairs, honey. Your dad and I need to talk to you."

Lissa was awake now. This wasn't normal. Mom looked like she might have been crying. Lissa lay there for a moment, her mind racing to all the things that could be wrong. Her grandparents were the most logical concern, but they weren't that old. Gramps had only just retired last year. She slipped into her pink fuzzy slippers, threw on her robe, and followed Mom downstairs.

In the kitchen, Mom turned to face Lissa. Now Lissa could see that Mom definitely was crying. Dad looked pretty grim too. He was standing with his hands in his robe pockets.

Mom took Lissa by the shoulders and looked her in the eyes. "Honey,…" Tears streamed down Mom's face. The agony in Mom's eyes terrified Lissa. "Pip was killed in a car accident last night."

The sunlight streaming in the window flared in brilliance, and every object in the room flattened to one-dimensional.

"It happened late last night, a little before midnight."

Lissa stared dumbly at her mother. Maybe her ears were ringing—she couldn't tell.

"Brad's in the hospital, in a coma. He's in bad shape." Dad stroked his daughter's hair.

Her father's touch sent a jolt through her. Lissa looked at him and blinked, trying to resist comprehension. She let out an animal wail.

FIFTY DAYS TO SUNRISE

Her mother held her, but no amount of sobbing was getting out the swelling pain deep in her gut.

The rest of the day was a blurred nightmare. This massive grief was all too reminiscent of when President Kennedy was assassinated. No one knew what to do then, but cry and pray. It was the same now, only worse.

Sally and Jessica came over, and the friends cried together in Lissa's room. It was hard to be together because they were so painfully aware of Pip's absence, but it was reassuring to be near each other.

They tried to pray, but they were so distracted by their grief, it was more tears than prayers. They prayed for Brad. He needed a miracle. Trapped behind the wheel of the car, Brad had been mangled along with the front end of the car. His head had hit the windshield, the steering wheel broke multiple ribs and fractured his pelvis, and both legs were broken under the crumpled dashboard. And now Brad was clinging to life.

The phone rang many times that day. Everyone, parents and kids, seemed to need to keep in touch with each other.

Lissa knew, or at least suspected, what had happened. Pip had told her Brad liked to drive fast. The week before, Pip told Lissa Brad had gotten up to ninety miles an hour on the road by Newsome's farm. Pip had been scared, but she also thought it was fun.

News coverage throughout the day confirmed Lissa's fears. A Minneapolis TV station picked up the story and made the most of teen reckless driving and the consequences. Mercifully, there was no picture of the smashed car.

Skid marks indicated Brad had probably braked and swerved to avoid a deer. Apparently he was successful at avoiding the deer, but he lost control of his car. The GTO rolled in the ditch and hit a tree. Brad was going over eighty miles an hour. The only thing that saved Brad was that the car slowed down when it rolled. The news showed Brad's and Pip's pictures. Lissa shouldn't have watched.

Pip was thrown from the car. She died instantly, her neck broken. "Died instantly"—Lissa guessed that was supposed to convey some small comfort, knowing the person didn't suffer. It was no comfort at all.

Mr. Newsome had been awakened by the crash and, having heard the sound before, immediately called the ambulance. This was a stretch of road that was notorious for accidents. It had claimed the lives of three teens when Lissa was in grade school. Kids called it Roller Coaster Road because it was hilly and fun. She thought of how she had driven the road earlier in the summer, shortly after getting her license, and had showed off a little for her friends.

Sally and Jessica stayed for dinner that night, but none of them could do anything but pick at their food. At Mom's encouragement they finally managed to eat a bit. Mom suggested that after dinner they go over to the hospital and pray for Brad.

As the girls left, Mom gave Lissa a hug. Mom didn't say, "Drive carefully," but Lissa knew she was thinking it. Mom looked intently at her daughter's face, as if memorizing her features, and Dad kissed Lissa on the forehead.

Clutching the car keys, determined not to cry while she was driving, Lissa wiped away tears and marched to the car. She didn't know how her parents could let them go; she had only had her driver's license for two months. Lissa didn't look back, but she was sure Mom and Dad were hugging each other.

They arrived at St. Luke's Hospital. They stood in the entryway—not knowing what to do, where to go, or even why they were there. The receptionist came around from behind the counter and put her hand on the back of Lissa's arm.

"Are you here for Brad Zimmer?" she asked.

"Yes," Lissa said, distracted, still trying to figure out what to do. They certainly didn't want to bother Brad's family. They already knew Brad was in Intensive Care after hours of surgery.

FIFTY DAYS TO SUNRISE

"Come with me." The receptionist guided them to the chapel.

It was like being caught in dense smoke: hard to breathe. The announcements over the loudspeaker could have been in a foreign language for all Lissa knew. The light seemed an odd color, and the smells were awful. She had no idea if the receptionist told them to follow the yellow or the green line to get back to the entrance.

"Brad's friends have gathered here in the chapel. Maybe you'd like to join them. Brad certainly needs your prayers." She turned and went back the way she had brought them.

Thirty or forty kids and parents were there, including Brad and Pip's youth pastor. *Amazing Grace* usually sounded sweet, but tonight the guitar accompaniment jangled Lissa's nerves. The three girls sat on the floor next to Bob Gowan, a friend of Brad's. When the hymn ended, the pastor started praying. Other people prayed out loud in turn. They prayed a long time for Brad's healing and for Brad's and Pip's families.

Lissa couldn't imagine what their families were going through, especially Pip's parents. The unspeakable agony of losing a child—the anguish of not knowing if your child would live—all because of a stupid decision gone so terribly and irretrievably wrong in an instant.

Bob prayed the Lord's Prayer. Clearly, Bob had been crying. It was unnerving to see some of the boys crying.

"Thy will be done, on earth as it is in heaven."

Those words really bothered Lissa tonight. How was this tragedy God's will? Did He really want Pip to die and Brad to be near death? How could that be? What had they done to deserve this? Questions were a torment.

The pastor read the Twenty-third Psalm. "Thou art with me..." But how could God have been with them if something so bad happened? Was it a punishment? For what? Pip had told Lissa they were trying really hard to behave like God wanted them to and not go too far sexually. Lissa agonized, unable to make any sense of it. The more questions she thought of, the more angry she got at God.

"Let's go!" Lissa hissed to Jessica. Lissa jumped to her feet, ready to flee.

Jessica shook her head without even opening her eyes.

Sally's eyes implored her friend not to leave just yet, but Lissa let Sally see the dark anger brewing in her own eyes.

"Bob, would you please take us home later?" Sally asked quietly. He nodded.

Sally got up and hugged Lissa. She didn't exactly shake off Sally's hug, but Lissa didn't hug back.

She turned on her heels and somehow found her way to the entrance.

Sitting in her father's car, the door slamming made her jump. Utterly alone, her heart ached, and her head pounded. She grabbed the steering wheel, pressed her forehead into her hard knuckles—and sobbed—sobs that rolled up from her belly. She clung to the steering wheel as if her own life depended on it. Time disconnected from her.

Tapping noises on the window got Lissa's attention. Jessica called her name. Lissa had never been so glad to see Jessica and Sally. At that moment, they were a life raft. Sally said she'd drive and told Lissa to scoot over, while Jessica got in the other side. Pressed between her friends, Lissa wasn't alone anymore.

Back home, she dropped the keys on the kitchen table. Mom and Dad were watching the late news. They looked pale and strained. Lissa told them there was no change in Brad's condition.

"Good night." Was that it? Good night. The best she could come up with to say to her parents? Lissa was exhausted and couldn't wait to go to bed—and she dreaded going to bed. She tried to say more, but no words came out.

"Good night, honey. Remember, Pip is with Jesus praising His name, and Brad is in God's hands." Mom's words would have been reassuring before tonight.

There was an awkward moment. Lissa didn't know whether to hug her parents or cry. She was empty.

She quickly escaped for fear she might see something on the news about the accident.

In her room she wrote in her diary—the entry that haunted her for a long time. She was uneasy about having written that she'd never forgive God. But there it was in permanent ink. Would God punish her too?

It didn't feel right totally ignoring God as she pulled the summer quilt up under her chin. All she could pray was her old childhood prayer.

Now I lay me down to sleep. I pray the Lord my soul to keep. If I should die before I wake, I pray the Lord my soul to take. Thy love guard me through the night, and wake me with the morning light. Amen.

Lissa prayed so fast in her head, she didn't hear the words until the prayer was ended. She buried her face in her pillow and sobbed some more. Pip was dead.

Sleep came eventually, but gave her no rest.

Chapter 18

How could today be such a beautiful day? It should be gloomy, maybe threatening a hurricane. The day after her best friend was killed, Lissa woke up mad. Her eyes hurt, like sand ground in her eyeballs.

The sheet was twisted around her and pulled out from the foot of the bed. She untangled herself, throwing off the sheet. Lissa splashed cold water on her face and went downstairs. She hoped her parents were up.

The house was quiet. Daisy raised her head from her pillow on the kitchen floor and thumped her tail in greeting. She struggled to her feet. At ten years old, Daisy was aging and had arthritis. Lissa could hardly bear the thought of losing Daisy too. Lissa sat on the floor and put her arms around Daisy and hugged her.

Scamper came in from her chair in the living room to see what was going on and rubbed white cat hair on Lissa's robe. "Purrt," Scamper kept repeating, which meant, "Where's my breakfast?"

Daisy squirmed out of Lissa's hug and moved to the back

door, wagging expectantly. As Lissa turned back from letting Daisy out, Dad appeared. She rushed into his arms.

"My precious Missy." Dad gave her a firm hug.

"Oh, Dad. I just don't understand why God took Pip."

Dad held his daughter by the shoulders and set her at arm's length. "Missy, honey, God didn't take Pip. We just don't understand God's ways. But we have to trust His promises of who He is and how much He loves us."

"But if He loves us so much, how can He allow such suffering?"

"I know."

Dad kissed her on the forehead and let her go. He started the coffee. Normal activities seemed strange, but Lissa poured her orange juice and sat down at the kitchen table. Dad put the cereal and bowls on the table, along with the milk bottle, and sat down, waiting for the coffee to perk.

"Remember Romans 8:28?" Dad started his answer to Lissa's question. "'And we know that all things work together for good to them that love God, to them who are called according to his purpose.'"

"I guess." Lissa shrugged as if trying to get something uncomfortable off her shoulders.

"It seems impossible right now that anything good could come of this tragedy and suffering, but God says it will."

"What? Well, then God's mean." She refused to believe it.

"Think of how our suffering helps us identify with the suffering Jesus experienced on the cross."

Lissa went sullen, she just wanted to be left alone with her misery. She wasn't getting the answers she wanted to her questions.

"But why?" She was frustrated and whiney.

"Anything that brings us closer to Him is good in His eyes. Because He just wants to love us and have us love Him back. So if this tragedy brings anyone closer to God, that's working for good."

FIFTY DAYS TO SUNRISE

Lissa didn't understand how her best friend breaking her neck and dying in a car accident could have anything to do with God's love. In a huff, she pushed back her chair, took her cereal bowl, and exited out the back door to have breakfast by herself. Flopping down in a bouncy chair, she almost slopped milk on her robe. Daisy dropped down next to her on the patio. When Lissa finished her cereal, she set the bowl next to Daisy and let her lick out the last bit of milk.

Sitting with her arms folded across her chest, bouncing absently, deep in dark thoughts, Lissa flinched in surprise when Mom came out and sat down in the chair next to her. There was a small metal table between them; Lissa was glad of the distance.

"How did you sleep?"

"Lousy," Lissa said.

"I'm not surprised." Sometimes Mom's habit of stating the obvious was irritating, but this morning it was reassuring. Lissa could feel her scowl ease a bit.

"Do you want to go to church this morning?"

Mom's question caught her off guard. Lissa could never remember her parents giving them a choice whether they wanted to go to church or not. She looked at her mother, not knowing what she wanted to do, and at a loss for words to articulate anything. Lissa was still trying not to think about what Dad had said.

"I think we should," said Mom.

"But Mom, I'm so mad at God."

"I know, Lissa, but God has big shoulders. He can take it. Look what he listened to from David in the Psalms."

"But what if God's mad at me too?"

"What could God be mad at *you* for?"

Then Lissa's tears flowed again. She brought her feet up onto the chair, propped her chin on her knees, and tried to hold herself together with her arms around her legs. She confessed how shamefully she had behaved at the chapel last night, wanting to leave.

"It'll be all right," Mom said, patting Lissa's back. "I'm sure Pastor Eckberg will have some words of comfort for us this morning. I think we should all go and be together. Pray together."

Mom sipped her coffee, this time letting Lissa's lack of response go unanswered. Lissa sat in a tight ball listening to the birds chattering in the early morning. The backyard smelled sweet—of flowers and grass. It was a peaceful place. She shook her head, not in disagreement with Mom's suggestion, but in total confusion.

"Okay." Lissa couldn't argue with her mother, so she agreed.

She couldn't tell Mom the real reason she feared God might be mad at her: that she had written damnation on herself in her diary last night.

Church was full. Tragedy had a way of bringing people together and turning them back to God—if only to plead for the survivors and to try and make sense of the deaths.

Pastor Eckberg used the Twenty-third Psalm as his sermon text.

Lissa tried to listen to the sermon, but her mind wandered to the crash scene. "The valley of the shadow of death." She thought about Brad, still in a coma, and about Pip's visitation and funeral tomorrow.

The only funeral Lissa had been to was Grandpa Henry's when she was six. The casket was open during the visitation, and she remembered Grandpa didn't look right. She was horrified to think there might be an open casket: that she might have to see Pip dead.

"In the name of the Father, and of the Son, and of the Holy Ghost. Amen."

FIFTY DAYS TO SUNRISE

Pastor Eckberg made the sign of the cross in the air. The service was over. The organ postlude was quiet and somber as people filed out, not the usual joyful send-off to the rest of the Sabbath. No one was in a hurry to leave. Lissa could only imagine what it was like at Brad and Pip's church this morning.

Sunday dinner at home was quiet too.

"How about we all go to Sjostrand Woods this afternoon and hike to the falls?"

Dad was a genius. Hiking in Sjostrand Woods was a favorite family activity. That would take their minds off of sorrow—for a moment—if anything could.

In no time, the table was whisked clean—dishes washed, dried, and put away.

Boots and Ray ran out of the kitchen like untethered puppies.

Chapter 19

Lissa couldn't get the fear of seeing Pip dead out of her mind. Pip's visitation was Monday afternoon followed by a funeral service at Pip's church.
    Another disgustingly beautiful day. She had to watch herself so she didn't say hurtful things to her family. She wasn't mad at them, it was just that they were there, and Pip wasn't.
    At the funeral home, Jessica and Sally waited outside. Tears started as soon as the friends saw each other. They clung to each other like there might not be a tomorrow.
    The line to pay respects to Pip and her family spilled out of the main room and wound back and forth a couple of times in the vestibule. Another room on the side was set up with chairs set in conversation groups. Harp music played softly over the loudspeaker. Surreal.
    Jessica peeked into the main room and came back with the report Lissa dreaded—Pip's casket was open. Lissa's knees turned to jello, and the room momentarily blurred. She clutched Sally's arm for support, and the feeling went away.
    Bravely, the girls got in line. Their parents were ahead of

them. Mostly people didn't say much, and if they did, it was in hushed tones, like they'd wake somebody up. People talked about the accident and how Brad was doing. There was a low drone of crying.

When they got to the main visitation room, Lissa watched Mr. and Mrs. Farnsworth greet people. Pip's parents stood at the head of Pip's casket, next to their dead daughter. They looked like they had been crying for forever, especially Mrs. Farnsworth, but they smiled and thanked people for coming. There was no sign of Pip's ten year old brother.

Lissa was afraid to look at Pip, but the closer they got, she couldn't avoid it. Jessica went first, then Sally. Mrs. Farnsworth tightly hugged each of them. They were Pip's very best friends. Then Lissa found herself released, standing right in front of Pip, looking down at her.

A casket on a white-draped bier held her friend. The copper-colored casket matched Pip's hair, and the ivory satin lining matched her skin. She was dressed in her favorite white cotton dress. The froth of narrow lace around the high neckline was repeated in vertical rows on the pin tucked bodice and ended in a pink satin ribbon tied under her small bosom. Her hands rested, relaxed and natural looking, below the pink bow, the wide lace on the gathered sleeve half covered her hands.

Her luscious red hair lay on the pillow like she had just flopped down for a nap—fluffy curls framed her face. On her head was a circlet of fresh flowers: pink, purple, and yellow. She was a fairy princess—or a child bride.

But her face. Lissa couldn't take her eyes off Pip's face. She was so perfectly beautiful. Lissa tried to memorize every feature.

Clapping a hand to her mouth, Lissa stifled a gasp. Something was terribly wrong; something was missing.

"Her freckles are gone!" Lissa blurted out.

Sally put a comforting arm around her friend. "Shh."

Next to her, Lissa heard Mrs. Farnsworth make a small

FIFTY DAYS TO SUNRISE

sound. Pip's mother cleared her throat and said, "It's the makeup, dear."

"I'm so sorry." Lissa was mortified she had intensified Mrs. Farnsworth's pain.

"It's all right, Lissa." Mrs. Farnsworth's faint smile looked so exhausted.

Grief, humiliation, and guilt collided in her, and she clenched her fists at her side. Idiot. She couldn't stomp off and end the situation, so she stayed with her friends. This would all be over soon.

When they got to the other room where more of their classmates were, it hit Lissa—she'd never see Pip again.

Lissa spun around. "I have to go back and see her one more time."

"Do you want us to go with you?" Jessica asked.

"No. I need to do this by myself."

She got in line again. It was much shorter now. Lissa found her mother in the crowd. Mother and daughter exchanged I-love-you looks, and Mom turned back to talking with Sally's parents.

"Mrs. Farnsworth, I just have to say goodbye to Pip one more time. Do you mind?"

"Not at all, dear." Mrs. Farnsworth put her arm around Lissa's shoulder. Lissa put her arm around Mrs. Farnsworth's waist. Shared comfort.

"Pip...I know you're in heaven. And I know you're looking down on us." Lissa's words quavered. "Don't be sad for us. We'll all be together in heaven someday." Tears streamed down Lissa's cheeks, and she could hardly get the words out. "I'm so glad you moved here and we got to be best friends. I'll never forget you.

"Can I touch her?" Lissa wiped the tears off her cheeks with a hankie and looked at Mrs. Farnsworth. Her stomach flipped—Mrs. Farnsworth was crying—but she wanted to touch her friend.

"Of course you may, but remember, Pip won't feel the way she used to."

Lissa reached out, slipped her hand under the lace, and laid her hand over Pip's. Abruptly, Lissa drew back. Pip's skin felt strange and cold—but then Lissa let her hand rest again on Pip's and gently patted her friend's hand—one last time.

Sitting in church, singing, "For all the saints, who from their labors rest," Lissa was overcome by the immensity of being sixteen years old and attending her best friend's funeral. She stopped singing. No tears. No nothing. She was done trying to make sense of it.

She stared at the empty cross high on the wall behind the altar. She had no idea what Pastor Smith said. Whatever it was, it wouldn't have made her feel any better, nor would it bring Pip back.

Six pallbearers, members of the football team, carried Pip's casket out to the waiting hearse. Pip's parents and her brother followed.

Pip was buried, all by herself in the cemetery. Her body was committed to the earth—dust to dust, ashes to ashes. And Lissa committed to giving God the silent treatment.

Sean...Her arms ached—empty of Sean.

Lissa reached for another Kleenex and mopped her face. She had never wanted to cry again. She was torturing herself, but looking back at Pip's death seemed to be a key to unlocking her prison of grief. The walls were closing in lately. She was no longer sure of much of anything, except that the sun kept coming up every miserable morning.

Last Christmas she had come home to her parents'. It

FIFTY DAYS TO SUNRISE

would have been better if she'd spent Christmas by herself on an ice floe. She had just pulled a repeat performance of what she did at Christmas: drank too much and screamed at her family. She could puke. She honked into the Kleenex and continued reading and remembering. She couldn't feel any worse.

Chapter 20

August 30, 1966

Dear Diary,

   I can hardly stand the thought of going back to school. I miss Pip so much.
   Oh, I can hardly write, I feel so bad. Like there's a big, huge hole in my heart. My brain hurts from trying to not think about it. Sally and Jessica and I get together and just hurt because Pip's missing from us. We try to keep busy and do stuff, like tonight we went to see the Sound of Music. But it's not the same. Everything's gray, boring, blah, dragging myself through the days. I'm so tired I can't sleep very well.
   Yesterday I wasn't thinking and poured a customer's coffee right over the top of the cup. I couldn't believe it. I almost burned his hand. At least he was nice about it.
   Sometimes I think about Brad. He's awake now, but does he know that Pip's dead? I guess they don't know

how much brain damage he suffered. Sally's mom talked to Brad's mom yesterday. She said it's still day to day. Why did Brad have to drive so fast?! This isn't the way it's supposed to be! I wish I could turn back time, that I'd said something, anything, when Pip told me how fast Brad liked to drive. But Pip thought it was kind of fun. I should have told her to make him stop, to get out of the car! I should have told Brad to stop it before he killed my friend!! I can't stand it!!!!

And, God, I'm still not talking to you! You could have stopped it!!!!!

The days droned on toward the start of school—Lissa's junior year of high school. Life should have been easy.

Brad came out of his coma after two weeks. He was moved to Fairview Hospital in Minneapolis to continue his recovery. Brad would live, but the doctors didn't know what kind of a life he would have.

Lissa and her friends visited Brad once in the hospital, but they didn't know what to say. They were shocked to see him, his legs in traction. He really couldn't talk to them. He kind of waved and mouthed, "Hi."

The girls babbled on about what was going on at school. Nothing was said about Pip or the accident.

When they left, Brad struggled to say something, but it was unintelligible. A tear slid down his temple. Lissa tried to smile at him, but it was a pitiful smile.

The ride back from Minneapolis with Sally's mom was a quiet one.

Over the next few months, Brad's bones healed, but his brain was damaged. He learned to walk again, with two canes. Relearning to talk took longer. He came home just before Christmas.

FIFTY DAYS TO SUNRISE

In time, Brad was able to get out of the house. Once, Lissa saw him at the grocery store with his parents. His dad pushed him in a wheelchair. Brad the muscular football player was gone.

Brad's life was changed beyond comprehension. He wasn't at UC, Berkeley playing football. He wasn't still going with Philippa Farnsworth. They weren't going to be married after college. And they weren't going to raise a family and grow old together—ever.

Finally, Easter seemed to spark something in the dullness that consumed Lissa. Easter Sunday was always a special day in the Makkinen family, and she was looking forward to church. Dad got corsages for each of his girls, and company usually came for dinner after church. Sometimes it was two or three students from St. Lucy's who weren't able to get home for Easter.

Sitting in church that morning, Lissa turned her head to breathe in the delicious spicy fragrance of the carnation in her corsage. The small red spots in the center of the white flower startled her. Drops of blood. She didn't want to think about blood today, but there it was. She was getting pretty good at pushing thoughts she didn't want out of her head, but on Easter it was difficult to push out blood and dying.

And this had started out such a good day. It was ruining fast.

Lissa was overwhelmed by the Easter Story. The contrast between God's love and her raging emotions that she'd had to bottle up was too much.

Jesus sacrificed Himself on the cross, shedding His blood, so believers could have forgiveness of sins and spend eternal life with Him. Lissa stared at the vacant cross on the altar. What must it have cost God to send His only Son to die for sinners? She couldn't understand the depth of such love. And she didn't understand why Jesus had to die. Unfair.

Death, resurrection, repentance, redemption, forgiveness—these words whirled in her head like a tornado—gathering debris, threatening destruction if they touched down. Did she have to forgive Brad?

Fear slashed at her heart when Pastor Eckberg read a passage in Matthew: "For if ye forgive men their trespasses, your heavenly Father will also forgive you: But if ye forgive not men their trespasses, neither will your Father forgive your trespasses."

Did that mean if she didn't forgive Brad she'd go to hell? Her brain crashed against the question.

For the first time in a long time, tears welled up and trickled down her cheeks. Lissa blew her nose. Her mother reached over and patted her knee.

Later that evening, after company left and the leftovers of the Easter ham were put away, Lissa approached her father to ask him about forgiveness. Dad was the one she took her really big spiritual questions to.

"Dad?" He dropped the Sunday paper to his lap and faced her. "I have a question. A big one."

"Sure, Missy. Shoot." Dad moved his feet aside to make room for her on the ottoman.

"Today in church I got to thinking about what Pastor Eckberg said about forgiveness and what Jesus did for us by dying on the cross." She bit her lip and thought a moment before proceeding. "I don't get it." She had to work up to the would-I-go-to-hell question.

"Well, what don't you get about it?" Dad believed in not answering a question that wasn't asked.

"First of all, why did Jesus have to *die* for our sins for us to be forgiven? That seems pretty extreme and cruel."

"I know. But God had a plan all along to bring all people to Him. By Jesus dying on the cross and taking all sin for all time on Himself, He defeated Satan and death. Jesus was the last sacrificial lamb that God required." Dad lit up talking about Jesus.

Lissa nodded. She knew this from years of Sunday school classes.

"But, Dad, why did He have to *die*?" She couldn't believe she was asking "why?" after all these years. What was really astonishing to her, was that she had never asked the question before. Today she really needed to know the answer.

"Why did He have to suffer? Couldn't He have just died of old age?"

"Jesus's death by suffering was part of God's plan to let us know how much He knows our pain. And the way Jesus suffered was part of what shows us His perfection, that He was a man *and* fully God. None of us could have suffered like that. Most of us would have fought back." Dad paused, but not the kind of pause that invited Lissa to blurt out another question.

"But here's the most important part of Jesus's suffering." Dad leaned forward, crumpling his newspaper. "God can't look at sin. That's why Jesus's worst agony on the cross wasn't the physical pain He suffered, but the moment when the sin of the whole world was on Him, and it seemed His Father turned His face away from Him. Jesus suffered that separation, so we wouldn't have to."

Lissa pictured the scene—imagining if her father had ignored her and kept reading his newspaper when she came to talk to him. Her dad never turned his face from his children.

Dad reached for his Bible on the end table. Dad always turned to the Bible for answers.

"Matthew 27:46 says, 'About the ninth hour Jesus cried with a loud voice, saying, "Eli, Eli, lama sabachthani?" that is to say, "My God, my God, why hast thou forsaken me?"' Missy, why do you think Jesus said that?"

"I guess because He felt deserted by His Father."

"Yes. But deserted by His Father because He was bearing

our sins at that moment, and that was the first and only time Jesus was ever separated from His Father.

"And, Missy, did you know that Jesus was really quoting Psalm 22?" She looked at him dumbly, not understanding. "He was probably so weak that those were the only words of the psalm He could get out—a psalm that was written a thousand years before He was even born on earth as a man. It tells how Jesus would suffer and die for our sins, and be raised from the dead for our salvation. It's prophetic, and Jesus fulfilled that prophecy. He knew people would recognize Psalm 22. I'm telling you, Missy, it's amazing."

Lissa was stunned. She'd heard that Bible verse in Matthew many times, but never grasped its meaning of sacrifice and completion of God's plan. And she certainly had no idea Jesus was quoting the Bible while He hung on the cross. Why couldn't God just make things clearer? But she kept that question to herself.

"But there's more." Lissa wasn't sure she could take in much more, but Dad continued. "Jesus asked God to make us, you and me, one with Him as He was one with God. So when Jesus defeated sin, God sent the Holy Spirit. Now when we accept Jesus as our Savior, the Holy Spirit dwells in us. And it's the Holy Spirit that God sees in us, not our sin, when He looks at us."

She sat silent for a moment—then her secret gushed out in a flood of tears.

"Oh, Daddy, I've been so mad at God since Pip died. I've hardly even prayed. I've even told God I'd never forgive Him. I'm afraid I might go to hell." Shuddering sobs poured out of her.

Dad laid his Bible back on the table, and he patted his lap. It had been years since Lissa had crawled into her father's lap, but she didn't hesitate. Dad put his arms around his daughter, and she sobbed on his shoulder.

"Honey, we just have to keep coming back to God. He

forgives us and wipes our slate clean every time we ask His forgiveness."

Lissa's fears tumbled out. "But what about forgiving other people? Pastor Eckberg said if we don't forgive others, God won't forgive us. What does *that* mean? I never heard that before. That scares me." She sniffled, embarrassed to have to wipe her nose on the back of her hand.

"God is serious about love. He wants us to become more like Jesus every day, and that means loving God and loving others like Jesus did."

Dad reached around her for his Bible again and pulled out a folded yellow piece of paper.

"I heard a great sermon on forgiveness years ago. It was so good, I wrote down the main points. Here, read what it says about forgiveness."

Lissa settled back on the ottoman and unfolded the paper. She read about forgiving people, over and over again if we have to, whether they deserve our forgiveness or not. She read about grace, God's unmerited favor, that we extend to others in gratitude for His gift of forgiveness to us. And finally, she read about accepting that other people make mistakes just like we do. "Forgive us our trespasses, as we forgive those who trespass against us." She'd prayed that a million times, but never thought about it as the words passed her lips.

Carefully, she refolded the paper and placed her hands over it in her lap. She thought for a minute—and then it became very clear. She sat up straight.

"God will *help* us forgive others." Lissa now had an understanding deeper than she'd ever experienced before. "We really can't do *anything* without Him. He just wants to bless us with His love and have us bless others. He'll *help* me forgive Brad. Because it's too big for me to do on my own."

Dad beamed at her. "That's right, Missy."

Relief flooded her heart, and she hugged her father around the neck. "Oh, thanks, Dad! You're the best!"

With much lighter steps, she went into the kitchen to help her mother with the dishes.

Before bed, Lissa sat on her window seat and looked out at the moon. Knees hugged to her chest—she poured out her heart to God. She emptied herself of the bitterness that had built up over the months since Pip's death.

That night she slept peacefully for the first time since the accident—snuggled in her heavenly Daddy's lap.

Chapter 21

Lissa didn't want to lose her momentum on this forgiveness thing.
Brad answered the door. He took longer than expected since he had to struggle with two canes. He invited Lissa into the kitchen and motioned her to the kitchen table.
"Wan' a...pop?" It took him a second to get out the word "pop"—it sounded like "poff."
Lissa guessed what he meant, since he had his hand on the refrigerator door. "Sure. Whatever you're having."
Brad propped one cane against the counter and managed to balance himself. He took two bottles out, one at a time, and set them on the counter. It was all Lissa could do to keep from jumping up and taking a bottle from his hand. He rummaged in a drawer and found the bottle opener. He had to let the other cane rest against the counter with its mate while he used both hands to open the bottles, then he lurched toward the table and handed her a Coke.
"Here ya go, Mak," he said. Brad gave her a broad, twisted smile. She knew part of his smile was at himself for his

accomplishment. Less than a year and a half ago, Brad grinned at friends and family in the stands after he threaded the football through a crowd of defenders for the game-winning touchdown. Now he was proud of himself for getting a pop bottle opened and offering it to a friend. Lissa was also sure he was smiling because he called her Mak. He liked to tease her about her name and had called her Mak since they were in grade school. Lissa almost started crying right then.

Turning back to get his canes, he knocked them both to the floor. The clatter sounded like gunshots. Lissa leapt to her feet, but Brad put up a hand to stop her. "I'll get 'em."

Brad sat down at the table across from her. He'd forgotten his pop. Lissa quickly retrieved it before he could protest.

"Thanks, Mak." Again he smiled crookedly, and a slight flush crept into his cheeks. He tipped the bottle in toast and took a swig. "So, how ya been?"

"Okay, I guess." How stupid. She was not okay at all, and neither was Brad, and they both knew it. "No, sorry, not so good really. You?"

"It's really hard." He spoke slowly and deliberately, carefully forming every word.

"I'll bet. You're walking pretty well," Lissa lied.

"No. I mean, it's hard without Pip."

There it was—her name—the memory of her. They both dropped their eye contact. Lissa studied the black-and-pink squiggles on the gray Formica and tried not to cry. When she looked up, Brad had his eyes covered with one hand, his elbow on the table.

Gently, Lissa said, "That's what I meant too, really."

Brad wiped a tear toward the bridge of his nose and looked at her, placing both hands, palms down, on the table in front of him, as if bracing himself.

"Lissa," he said earnestly, "I'm *so* sorry for what I did." And then he broke into sobs. "Please forgive me."

Seeing Brad's suffering, Lissa was ashamed of herself for

not having had this conversation months ago. She reached over and put her hands on his. She didn't think she had any more tears to cry, but there they were again.

"I think about her every day." Brad pulled his hands back. He didn't look at Lissa. "I can't sleep much 'cause I keep seein' her face. She was so beautiful. I can't get outa my mind what she musta looked like after what I did to her. I'm such a monster!"

It dawned on Lissa that maybe Brad didn't know how Pip actually died. "Oh, Brad, didn't anyone tell you? There wasn't a scratch on her. Pip's neck broke when she was thrown from the car. She didn't even have time to be scared or feel any pain. She died instantly."

Lissa immediately wished she could take back her words. She remembered—that's no comfort at all. Yet she wanted to tell Brad that Pip was still beautiful—lying in her casket—but she couldn't.

Brad shook his head. He stared, looking somewhere over Lissa's shoulder—a blank, pained gaze—fixed on a future, Lissa guessed, that he could no longer see.

"Brad, I do forgive you."

He blinked and looked at her; he seemed surprised to find her sitting at the table.

"I forgive you," she said.

His eyes widened a bit, and he started to say something. His lips moved, but no sound came out.

"I realized God wants us to forgive each other. I thought forgiving you was because God says I'm supposed to so He'll forgive *me*. Now I understand it's for you too. You need my forgiveness to help *you* heal. And, Brad, I'm so glad to give it to you."

Brad let out a breath through tight lips.

"Brad, I know Pip would forgive you too. She was like that."

Brad closed his eyes and sighed deeply. Tears slid down his

cheeks. Several seconds passed. "I'd like to believe that. Maybe I will someday, but thanks for sayin' it."

Something inside Lissa broke free and fell into place. "Forgive me for not being a better friend."

They both sat there crying, smiling through their tears, like they had just exchanged precious gifts.

They were rescued from the awkward moment of what to say next when Brad's mom came in the back door with an armload of groceries.

"Hi, Lissa. So nice to see you." She set the groceries on the counter. "Oh, I see you've been talking about Pip. I didn't mean to interrupt."

"It's okay, Mrs. Zimmer. It's been a good talk."

"Hi, Mom." Mrs. Zimmer bent over Brad and kissed the top of his head. Brad wiped his face with both hands.

Lissa had been so consumed with her own grief in recent months, she hadn't given more than a passing thought to the grief Brad's family was going through—not just the grief over Pip's death—but the grief of their hopes and dreams crushed. Now she understood.

She left Brad's house that day—changed.

It was hard, but Lissa and Brad became friends again. And when he called her Mak, it no longer mildly annoyed her; she remembered the sweetness of forgiving each other.

But the tragedy refused to end. Brad died of complications from a prolonged seizure two years later.

And Lissa attended another friend's funeral.

Chapter 22

Jerked out of the past by her ringing cell phone, Lissa rubbed a hand over her face. It was Shannon's ring, a peppy Irish jig.

"Hi, honey."

"Hi, Mom. How are things in Gifford?"

A little snort laugh escaped before Lissa could catch it. How are things indeed? She could hardly get her bearings. She had a headache, and she was feeling decidedly wary, since the last phone conversation with Shannon ended less than pleasantly.

A month ago Shannon had tersely responded to Lissa's question as to whether she might be coming home *this* Christmas, since she had missed the last two. Lissa didn't even know why she had brought it up in May, but she was hurt. In Lissa's fogged mind, she forgot Shannon had been home for her father's memorial service.

Shannon hadn't exactly hung up on Lissa, but she'd quickly said, "Gotta go, Mom," and hung up before Lissa could get another word out. It felt like Shannon slammed the phone down, so Lissa had slammed the phone into the charger on her end.

"Mom? You there?"

"Huh? Oh,...I'm sorry. Pardon?"

"I said, how are things at Grandma and Grandpa's?"

"Pretty good. We're going through fifty years of family stuff. Do you want an old hamster cage?"

"How's Grandma?"

"She seems good." Lissa didn't have the energy to elaborate on how her mother was slowing down.

"Oh, that's good."

"How are *you*? I haven't heard from you in a long while."

"Mom, I've been busy." Lissa caught Shannon's warning tone and backed off. It was sometimes a struggle for mother and daughter to find the right words that didn't irritate each other.

"What have you been up to?" Lissa tried to sound brighter.

"Well," Shannon paused, "I got a...promotion!"

"Wow, that's great! Congratulations! Promoted to what?"

"I'll be on the auditing team for one of our biggest accounts."

"That's great."

"And I get a raise! I'll get $10,000 more a year. I'm so excited! I probably can't spend *all* that on skiing, so I might have to get a new car. What do you think? A red Rav4?"

Lissa laughed. Shannon's excitement was infectious. "Sounds like fun. Don't forget the ski rack."

Shannon often made Lissa laugh. And Shannon had the Maguire determined streak. Immediately after graduate school, Shannon moved to Denver to take a job with a large accounting firm. She hadn't looked at jobs in any other location, since her job was for the purpose of funding her obsession with skiing. Lissa understood that—the entire Maguire family was fairly obsessed with skiing. But the accounting—how did they get an accountant in the family?

FIFTY DAYS TO SUNRISE

How could a writer and an artist have produced an accountant?

"Matt's gonna take me car shopping. Just looking for now."

Lissa stiffened at Matt's name; her grip tightened on the phone. "Oh? How's Matt?"

"He's good. Great, in fact."

Lissa didn't take the bait. The boyfriend of a year, whom she had never met, got under her skin. Lissa hadn't asked, but she assumed they were living together. She pictured Matt as a snowboarder, pants hanging way below decency, freeloading off her daughter.

"Your Aunt Boots is coming up next weekend."

"Oh yeah? That'll be fun for you."

Fun? Not unless she gained some weight by next weekend.

"She's renting some hot convertible and we're going bombing around the countryside."

Shannon was silent for a minute. "Mom, there's something else," she said, sounding strained. "I just have to say something to you. I can't keep it in anymore."

She knew it. The admission they're living together. Lissa braced herself.

"I really miss Daddy." Shannon's tear-choked voice was so soft, it hardly sounded like her. "I'm sorry, but I just had to say it."

"Hmm," Lissa started crying too, trying not to let Shannon hear. She pinched her running nose rather than sniff into the phone.

Finally, Lissa choked out, "I know, honey, me too." It was hard to say those words that had needed to be said for almost a year and a half. Lissa was surprised Shannon had brought it up, and relieved.

"You do? You never said."

With a sigh, sapped of the energy it took to maintain her denial, Lissa said, "I know. I haven't been very good at..." She struggled. "I haven't helped *you* grieve."

Shannon had probably known her mother to be more angry than sad since her father died. No wonder Shannon didn't want to come home. "I'm...so sorry." Lissa clutched the phone, willing her daughter to accept her apology.

Shannon let out a strangled little, "Yeah."

The silence over the long-distance connection warmed: a gentle touch between mother and daughter.

Something inside Lissa dislodged, fell back into place, and started working again.

"Shannon, I've been thinking about your dad this morning."

"Really?" Her voice had a ring to it.

"Yes, honey,...I can't tell you how much I loved him." Both of them were quiet, trying to stifle sniffs.

"I know, Mom, I just needed to hear it." Shannon took a shuddering breath.

That seemed to reassure her, and she said no more about her father. Shannon slowly resumed her chatter, catching her mother up on the changes slated for the next ski season at Breckenridge.

She fed her mother a little more information about Matt. He was a skier, not a snowboarder—a ski instructor at Breckenridge, which was where Shannon met him. Lissa smiled.

"Send me a picture of him."

"Yeah, one of these days." No edge in her voice this time, but Shannon wasn't one to be pushed.

"I'm so glad you called, honey."

"Thanks, Mom. I enjoyed our little talk."

Lissa caught the humor restored in her daughter and gladly responded. "You *are* a stinker, you know."

"I know, that's why you love me."

"One of the thousand reasons. And, hey, congratulations on that promotion."

"Thanks. Love you."

FIFTY DAYS TO SUNRISE

"Love you. Bye, honey."

Lissa pushed the End button and let out an exhausted sigh. She loved her daughter so, even if at times Shannon seemed like an alien two-headed monster that couldn't possibly have issued from her womb. Lissa thanked God for her daughter's courage and her honesty.

Now what?

Sitting on the window seat in a state of utter exhaustion, Lissa had no idea what to do next. The conversation with her daughter had thrown Lissa on her face in the present. But once prodded, the past wouldn't go away—she thought again about how much she missed Pip—would always miss Pip. But Lissa had survived.

She cautiously thought about Sean. Shannon had been brave to bring up her father. Others had tried to talk to Lissa about Sean, thinking that might help her. But she had rejected those efforts, sometimes rudely. She'd always known she'd survive—she had to—but she hadn't been ready to try.

Shannon unwittingly, out of her own need, had reached in and grabbed something that got Lissa's attention. Listening to Shannon reminded Lissa that she wasn't in this grief by herself. Much as she wanted to, she couldn't sit down and draw her life over herself, a shroud for the living, keeping everything at bay and on her terms.

Tears slipped silently down Lissa's cheeks. Tears for Shannon. For Jack. Her children grieved for their father as much as she grieved for her husband. Didn't they? But Jack had Meagan, and Shannon had Matt, sort of. She had no one. Or did she? She had her children. But children don't fill the same place that a husband does, they don't fill that place in bed, spooned together—Sean nuzzling into her hair, kissing the back of her neck. The images threatened to unhinge her.

Grief was so terribly lonely. Despair lurked around the next dark corner of her heart. She realized she didn't know how her children felt, missing their dad—not really. And she was certain no one could possibly know how she felt.

Lissa got up abruptly and changed into her running gear. She fiercely tied the laces on her shoes, snapping the bows into double knots.

Mom and Dad—gone running—won't be long.

She left the note on the kitchen table where her parents would see it and headed out the back door. She stretched briefly on the patio, then let herself out the white picket gate, clicking it shut behind her. At first, Lissa pounded the cement beneath her feet, stomping out all the warring feelings within her. Aware she was doing this, a faint smile tugged at the corner of Lissa's mouth. She heard her mother's voice, "Melissa Louise! You quit that stomping!"

Instinctively, Lissa turned toward St. Lucy's. Something about all of the solid old brick and stone buildings always calmed her. It was a place of good memories from when Dad taught there. St. Lucy's was also the scene of her happy days as an undergraduate, when home was three blocks away.

Her pace slowed, and the pounding subsided into a more gentle rhythm, until Lissa was trotting easily as she rounded the corner of the chapel. She glanced up and noticed the door of the chapel stood open, but nobody was around. The Sunday morning service was over.

Lissa stopped and breathed deeply, hands on her hips. She propped her right heel up on the top of the railing next to the steps and stretched. Then the left leg. Still no one around. She had been in this chapel countless times, but yet, she was cautious as she mounted the steps. She had never been in the chapel sweaty before and hoped she wouldn't have to explain why she was there, since she didn't know.

It was silly, creeping in, but each step took her closer to the front. She sat on the end of the second pew. The cool, familiar surroundings settled over her, and she leaned back against the pew, hands folded in her lap.

The beauty of the stained glass behind the altar was entrancing. There were four scenes of Jesus's miracles topped by a large panel showing Jesus's Ascension. The colors shone in brilliant reds, blues, and yellows. Lissa had studied these pictures in glass since she was five years old and still found them captivating. Jesus changing water into wine, feeding the five thousand, walking on the Sea of Galilee, raising Lazarus from the dead—miracles. Unfair. The word grated across her mind, and she pushed it away.

Her gaze moved from the precious jewel tones of the glass images to the large brass cross on the altar. Polished by loving hands over the decades, the four-foot-high cross stood in testament to the simplicity of the faith, unadorned and empty —Jesus was risen. The brass pedestal on which the cross stood was graduated in steps leading to the base of the cross. As a child, Lissa had often pictured herself as a tiny fairy mounting those steps to the foot of the cross. She was sure that if she had touched the cross, it would feel warm to her fingers.

The Bible readings and the hymn numbers for the service were still posted on the wooden board on the wall next to the pulpit. She reached to take the Bible from the rack in front of her and turned to the psalm—Psalm 146.

"Praise the Lord. Praise the Lord, my soul. I will praise the Lord all my life; I will sing praise to my God as long as I live...."

Verse nine stopped her.

"The Lord watches over the foreigner and sustains the fatherless and the widow,..."

Lissa read the verse over a second, and a third time. She had never, in a year and a half, thought of herself as a widow, nor had anyone referred to her as a widow. But she was.

She closed the Bible and rested it on her bare legs, then laid her hands flat on it. Lips parted in astonishment, she stared unseeing in the direction of the stained glass windows. She closed her eyes.

Someone put a comforting arm around her shoulder. She jerked her head to see who was there, but there was no one. Maybe she imagined it. Strange. As she closed her eyes again to hold on to the feeling, a wave of exquisite relief washed over her.

"Thank you, Lord. Thank you, Lord," was all she could whisper. Tears of sad joy slipped down her cheeks. She would mourn, but now she was certain she would not have to mourn alone.

Unsure how long she had sat there, Lissa left the chapel and stepped out into the white June sunlight. It was undoubtedly past the time when her parents would be home from the church picnic. She didn't want to worry them and started back at an easy pace. She hadn't run as far as planned, but she wanted to get home. She sprinted the last block.

Dad's Crown Victoria was in the garage, and she braced herself for Mom's disapproval. Shutting the gate behind her, Lissa leaned on her knees, breathing heavily. She straightened and met Mom's gaze. Mom and Dad were sitting on the patio reading the Sunday paper. It could have been a head-on collision of the two women's wills, but Lissa disarmed her mother with a big smile.

"Hi ya, parents." She marched up to them, hands on her hips, talking in big gulps of air.

Dad looked up from the paper and smiled back. "Did you have a good run?"

"I had an excellent run. I didn't go very far." Dad apparently perceived nothing incongruous in this statement, nodded, and went back to reading his paper.

"Mom, I'm sorry I'm late. I totally lost track of time. I meant to be home before you were."

"I saw your note and thought you'd be home shortly. We've been home over half an hour. I thought you weren't going to run as much." Mom never wasted time getting to the point.

Lissa resisted bristling, and instead, put both hands up in surrender. "Mom, I *didn't*. Honest. I didn't go very far. Believe it or not, I spent most of the time I was gone in St. Lucy's chapel."

"Oh?" Mom's look requested further explanation.

"The door was open and no one was around, so I just sat there." Lissa didn't know how to explain to her mother what she had experienced. "It was great." More than great, it was—sustaining.

Lissa gave her mother a peck on the cheek, then did the same to her father, and started for the back door.

"Lissa," Mom called to Lissa's retreating back, "I brought a plate of food home for you. And a piece of my cherry pie."

Lissa turned back toward her mother. "Oh, good. Thanks, Mom, I'm starving." She saw her father reach over and give her mother's hand a squeeze.

The final notes of the Bach prelude Dad had been playing faded into the evening.

"Dad?" Lissa looked up from her book.

"Missy?"

"Can we talk?"

"Sure." Dad sat beside her.

Lissa lowered her voice. "How's Mom?" She was reasonably sure Mom couldn't hear her—Mom had gone to bed early to read, and anyway, she was hard of hearing.

Dad shifted into the corner of the couch and faced his daughter. "She seems to be doing well. The doctor said she could even drive again, if she wanted to."

"Really? That's great."

"The only thing I notice is that once in a while she struggles with names. And she gets tired more easily. Today was a big day for her."

"Yeah, I noticed she rests more."

"The doctor said the stroke was just a ministroke. There's a chance she'll have more of them. But, you already know that."

"Dad, I'm sorry I didn't get here when it happened. It was so selfish of me, but I was just a basket case after Choco died." Tears welled up unbidden, and she swiped them from her cheeks. Her face hot crimson. "Not that a *dog* is more important than my *mother*."

She shook her head and frowned, floundering, trying to find words that didn't sound stupid. "It's just that...it was more than I could take." Lissa hated the whiney tone she heard in her voice and stared at her hands in her lap. "I...I miss Sean so much."

Dad reached over and took both her hands in his.

"I know, Missy. Your mother and I know how hard this has been for you. We've been so worried about you."

Lissa nodded. "I'm so sorry. For that too. I'm done being such a selfish baby." Lissa gently twisted her hands out of Dad's grasp. "It kills me that worrying about me might have contributed to Mom having a stroke." Lissa avoided her father's eyes.

"Please, honey, don't do that to yourself. Your mother's family has a history of strokes. Remember, Grandpa Henry died of a stroke. You know she's been on medication for high blood pressure for years."

Lissa nodded, unconvinced.

"She really does a pretty good job of taking care of herself. She relaxes gardening. And she's always baking a pie for someone. In the last couple weeks she started knitting again." Dad smiled and shook his head. "Your mom's a tough old bird. It's the German part of her, I guess."

She gave Dad a weak smile. He patted her hands. "Don't forget, Mom and I pray for you every night. It's a big comfort to us, knowing that you're in God's hands."

More than he knew.

"Dad? That reminds me. I had a weird experience when I stopped in the chapel today." Dad was Lissa's God expert. "I was sitting in the pew, and it felt like someone put their arm around me. I swear it felt like it was real, but the chapel was totally empty. What do you make of that? Pretty weird, huh?"

Dad sat back and rubbed his chin with his hand while he thought, his eyes twinkling. "Hmm, sounds like someone I know got some comfort from the Lord."

"Really? Do you think it really was God?"

"I don't see why not. What do *you* think?"

She considered for a moment. "I think it was." More certain the more she thought about it, she nodded an emphatic nod. "Thanks, Dad, I needed to hear that."

"Well, there you are then. That God, He's just full of surprises." Dad chuckled and wrapped his arms around her. His hug went deep and patted the walls of Lissa's insides.

Dad kissed the top of her head. "Sleep well, Missy." He held her face between his hands, looked her straight in the eyes, and said, "The Lord will sustain you." He gave her face a gentle squeeze and went up to bed.

After Dad left, she finally blinked and closed her mouth.

She hadn't told Dad about Psalm 146 in the chapel.

Chapter 23

Pip's grave was on top of the hill, nestled under an enormous maple tree. Her parents had planted the tree shortly after Pip was buried. In the fall the leaves were the color of Pip's hair.

It had bothered Lissa that Pip's parents moved back to England and left Pip's grave. An irrational thought, but it didn't seem right.

The pink granite headstone sparkled in the sun. Lissa hadn't been here in many years.

Careful not to step where Pip was buried, she stood looking down at Pip's name and the dates of her life. Sounds were far away, and she had little sense of her own body. A mower in the distance sounded like no more than a buzzing bee. Emotional novocaine blunted reality, but it didn't feel good.

Finally, Lissa sat down with her back against Pip's headstone. It was hard and warm. She rested her head against the rock. She knew her friend wasn't really here, that she was in heaven, that this was just a memorial to her—but it was comforting, in a way.

But why was she here? What did the Lord want?

Tired, Lissa had trouble forming thoughts. A thought started, and it would vanish like a wisp of smoke, barely leaving a trail. Then the next thought rose to tease her. Her mind wandered off in ten different directions.

"Our Father, who art in Heaven,..." She tried to pray.

"Hallowed be Thy name,..." She stopped. "Hallowed...be Thy name. Hallowed..." The words flowed, thick and rich, from her lips. A strong breeze whooshed the leaves of the maple tree overhead, and was gone, leaving a soft rustling in its wake. Lissa gazed up. Was the Lord in the wind? Maybe.

She closed her eyes, the sun warm on her face—and turned her palms up to the Lord. She remembered Psalm 146, God's gift to her in the chapel. "I will praise the Lord all my life."

"I praise your holy name. I worship you...."

Praise and thanks poured from Lissa's lips. An hour could have passed, or ten minutes. She only hoped her offering of worship was a sweet aroma to God.

Her body felt without definition. Where there had been bone and skin, there was the presence of the Lord. Where there was grief, the hope of peace grew as a seedling.

"Amen."

Slowly, as reluctantly waking from a sweet dream, she opened her eyes. She had been singing.

She rested her cheek against the headstone, pressed her hands flat on Pip's name, and thanked God for her friend.

When Lissa got up, her legs were stiff, she had been sitting cross-legged so long.

She plucked a leaf from the maple tree and turned to go. Jogging down the hill and back to Dad's car—she smiled—and wondered how many people smile in a cemetery.

Chapter 24

The Old Mill Coffee Shop smelled of coffee and cinnamon. Lissa followed her nose down the hall, past the teddy bear shop and the knitting shop, to the double doors with the etched glass panels. In the center of the acid-etched tracery, the words "Coffee Shop" stood out clearly, just in case the aroma of coffee wasn't alluring enough.

Sally had called to say she'd be a few minutes late; something had come up at the food pantry that she had to take care of, giving Lissa time to walk to The Old Mill. As soon as Lissa opened the door to the coffee shop, she knew Sally wasn't there. Normally, Lissa's entrance was met with a squeal and a rush of spangles and perfume, as Sally enfolded Lissa in the warm embrace of friends happy to see each other.

Lissa headed for her favorite table in the corner between two windows. One window overlooked the millrace and the waterwheel, and the other provided a view downriver to the Bridge Street bridge. Lissa sat at the round, butternut table and ran her fingers over the marks of a hundred years. A sprig of yellow freesias in a pink pottery vase marked the center of the table.

    Lissa fidgeted. She hadn't seen Sally since she'd flown out for Sean's memorial. They'd never gone that long without seeing each other. Lissa had been home twice during that time, but hadn't called Sally either time, also unheard of in their forty-seven year friendship. Last Christmas was such an embarrassment to Lissa she couldn't even talk about it. Sally and Lissa had continued to write, as always. Writing was safe—eyes dulled by grief can't be seen on the page. Lissa decided not to mention visiting Pip's grave.

    The double doors both opened, and Sally made her grand entrance. Waving her arms, rattling her bangle bracelets like tinkling bells, Sally spotted Lissa and squealed her friend's name. A large flying squirrel swooped down on Lissa as the bat-wing sleeves of Sally's purple top unfurled when she spread her arms, ready for the hug.

    Lissa glanced around the coffee shop to see to whom she had been unexpectedly introduced before she was wrapped in all that was Sally.

    Sally was shorter than Lissa and considerably rounder. Four kids, a fondness for food, and her idea of exercise being shopping, left Sally forever plump. And cracking jokes about her weight.

    Sally was big and round everywhere: in front, behind, even her head. Her stiffly coifed short hair was a helmet of sculpted waves, dyed a little too blond. Dressed in red capris and three-inch-heeled red canvas espadrilles with red laces fluttering around her ankles, Sally radiated flamboyance: a modern-day fairy godmother. The two-carat diamond wedding ring and the ruby and diamond cocktail ring sealed the impression. Only the magic wand was missing.

    Apprehension fell away as Lissa waited for Sally to reach her. The two friends embraced, melting away the months between them. Sally pushed back and held Lissa at arm's length.

"Oh, it's good to see you." She gave Lissa a gentle shake.

"You too. I've missed you."

Sally gave Lissa a slightly reproving look, but didn't say anything. The missed opportunities to see each other were past, and Lissa didn't say anything either. They sat at the table and pulled their chairs close to each other.

"I heard you were in town to get your parents moved to the old folks home."

Lissa gave her friend a you're-naughty look. "They're moving to the Dakota River Apartments, piano and all. But I'm sure you know that." Sally's and Lissa's mothers were friends, and what the girls didn't hear from each other, they heard from their mothers.

"Of course I did. Just teasing."

"I really can't believe I agreed to this, but I know it's a good thing. Mom and Dad have a lot to do. They're home right now getting ready for a rummage sale. They weren't going to do one, but they changed their minds."

Sally folded her arms under her substantial bosom and gave her friend an appraising look. "You've lost weight."

In response to Sally's stark comment, Lissa tightened a corner of her mouth and cocked her head to the side. She gave Sally an exasperated look, hoping Sally would get the hint and leave her alone about her weight.

But Sally didn't. "Okay, okay. *My* mom told me *your* mom was worried about you. I don't think you look so bad, how could you, you look too much like your mother. I, of course, haven't lost an ounce, and I want to....But seriously, Lissa, you *are* too thin."

Deciding not to make it a battle, Lissa chose honesty as the best defense. "Yeah, I know. I was running too much, but it made me feel better."

"Feel better?" Sally squinched up her face into a yeah-right look.

The young server appeared at their table. Sally waved at

Lissa to order first.

"I'll have a medium iced caramel macchiato, whole milk, please."

"Whipped cream and sprinkles?"

"Sure. Why not. Thanks." Sally smirked. Lissa rolled her eyes.

"And I'll have a large skinny latte, extra hot, please. Thanks, Mandy."

"Well, nothing like starting off with a bang." Sally sat back and relaxed. "This is a little weird, you've got to admit."

With a worn out smile, Lissa lifted both hands off the table in a gesture of surrender before laying them back flat on the table. "Don't I know it. I'm sorry. I've been working hard at being Queen of Denial. But, honestly, Sally, I just *had* to." Lissa pleaded for Sally to understand. Maybe this meeting wasn't such a good idea.

Sally leaned forward and put her hands over Lissa's, the bracelets clanking as they hit the table. "I know. We don't have to talk about it."

"Thanks. Maybe later." Lissa changed the subject and tried to sound brighter. "Tell me about the kids." Lissa knew this topic was always good to get Sally wound up and usually good for a laugh.

Sally dug in her gold leather duffle purse and produced a small photo book. She clutched the album to her bosom.

"The first grandchildren! Twin girls! They were born only three weeks ago." Lissa gasped in shared glee. "I didn't write to you because I knew you were coming, and I wanted to surprise you."

"Oh, how wonderful! What did they name them?"

"Violet and Verbena."

"What?" Lissa couldn't help herself. She couldn't keep her eyes from widening, and she burst out laughing.

Sally jiggled with laughter. "I know. You should have seen Marv's face when Jimmy told him the twins' names. I thought he was going to explode. His face turned red, and his mouth twisted up like he couldn't decide if he'd laugh or puke." Lissa was laughing so hard she had to take a deep breath to refuel her laughter. "How he ever managed to keep himself together, I'll never know. I had to put my hand over my mouth. You know me, it's *so* hard to keep a straight face. Finally Marv said, in this little squeaky voice, 'That's nice.' I thought I'd bust a gut!" Laughter rolled up and down Sally's body. Her belly and her more-than-ample breasts bounced along.

Lissa wiped tears from her eyes. "What were they thinking?"

"I don't know. I guess they like flowers, though you'd never know it to look at their yard. They said they wanted something different." She shook her head.

"I guess we could call little Verbena 'Verbie' or 'Bena'.... Maybe I'll just call her 'Petunia'." Sally held her side. She let out a sigh as her laughter subsided and looked at Lissa. "Kids. Whatcha gonna do?"

Lissa sighed too, her laughter trickling to a stop—the kind of sigh that wants to be a word, but isn't recovered enough to articulate anything.

She didn't think about a little girl growing up with a silly name, but just enjoyed laughing with her friend. It was a good thing Jimmy and Gwen lived in Cincinnati, or the gossip grapevine would have informed them that Grandma Sally thought their children's names were really funny.

The drinks arrived. "You guys sure are having a good time."

Sally let out a simultaneous laugh and sigh again and reached for her latte. "Thanks, Mandy." She blew the fancy swirl into a new design. Fortified with a sip, she pushed the photo album across to Lissa.

The first picture was of the proud parents—each holding a pink-wrapped bundle, topped with little round heads in pink stocking caps over apple-red faces. Both babies' faces were scrunched up: screaming that soft, newborn scream, the harbinger of sleepless nights to come.

"Lissa!" Lissa startled at her name being called in a loud, male voice. She jerked her head up.

"Humpy!"

Lissa jumped to her feet and stood riveted to the spot.

Humpy Humphrey was advancing toward them.

"Hi, Sally. Hey, Lissa, it's good to see you." By this time Humpy had reached Lissa and Sally. "Sally told me you two would be here."

Lissa shot Sally a narrow-eyed look. Sally shrugged and smiled, revealing guilt, but no remorse.

Humpy took hold of Lissa's upper arms and gave her a peck on the cheek before she knew what was happening. He drew back and looked at Lissa, still holding on to her. Humpy was only a couple of inches taller than Lissa and their eyes met easily.

The shock of seeing Humpy quickly changed to discomfort at being held by a man. Lissa tensed and broke their eye contact. Humpy let go of her. They hadn't seen each other in ten years, not since the twenty-fifth class reunion in 1993.

Recovering herself only slightly, Lissa blurted out, "Oh, Humpy...Dwight, I mean," Lissa blushed hot pink. It didn't seem right to offer condolences using his nickname from junior high. "I'm so sorry about your wife." She got even redder. What a stupid thing to say. How about "Hello" for starters.

"Thanks, Lissa."

Still rattled, Lissa waved at the chair next to Sally. "Sit down. Please. We were just looking at the pictures of Sally and Marv's first grandkids. Twins. Violet and Verbena." She stifled a giggle.

"You're kidding." He started to apologize, but was let off the hook by Sally's renewed chuckles.

Humpy pulled a chair over close to Lissa and sat down. He dutifully admired all the photos of the newborns.

FIFTY DAYS TO SUNRISE

"Lissa, you got any grandkids?"

"No, not yet. Jack and Meagan have been married two years, but no sign of grandkids yet. They live close by in Seaton. It would be such fun to be a grandma. Are you a grandpa?"

"Nope. Neither of my girls are married, so I guess it's a good thing I'm not yet."

The photo album was stowed in Sally's cavernous purse, and they all sat back. Since this meeting was Sally's idea, Lissa wished Sally would jump in and help out with the conversation.

"Wow, it's been ten years since I've seen you." Lissa broke the awkward silence.

"Yeah, a lot's happened." Humpy leaned toward Lissa. "I was so sorry to hear about Sean. Was it a heart attack?"

She stabbed her straw at the whipped cream on her drink.

"Oh, sorry, Lissa. I didn't mean to pry."

Lissa blanched, answered, even if she didn't want to.

"No, not really. It was something with a long name. You'll never remember it—idiopathic hypertrophic subaortic stenosis. We had no idea there was anything wrong with him. He was a runner, you know."

Lissa ran out of words to go on with the explanation of what happened to Sean. The words were in her head, but she was too tired to get them out. Sally was uncharacteristically quiet, intent on her latte. The Judas.

Lissa sighed and reluctantly added, "I guess it looked like a heart attack." And it probably felt like one. Lissa stirred the whipped cream into her macchiato.

Humpy nodded. He said no more about Sean. "You back for a visit?"

"Yeah, I'm helping Mom and Dad move into an apartment."

"That's nice. That's a big job. I moved back here a couple years ago to help my mother move. You knew my pa passed away five years ago?"

"I didn't. I'm sorry."

"It was one of those cases where it was a blessing. He was really suffering with cancer."

Death. It seemed hard to avoid.

"I retired from the Navy. Thirty years...And after Becky..." He cleared his throat and leaned forward, resting his arms on the table, hands clasped in front of him. "Well, I thought, why not move back to Gifford and help Mother. My girls live all over the place, so I might as well live here for a while. I do some consulting, but I can live anywhere and do that. Just so I can get to an airport."

"That sounds great. Where are you living?"

"I rented one of those old houses up the river."

Lissa knew the area: beautiful Victorian houses overlooking the river.

"It's way too big for me, but I like the view."

Humpy waved Mandy back to the counter. "Listen, I don't have much time right now, but I wanted to catch you. How'd you like to get together for dinner or something?"

Lissa didn't know what to say. Humpy had been a buddy since junior high, but the year after Pip died, Humpy was an anchor for her. He had done his best to make sure Lissa was all right. He'd taken her to Homecoming and Prom, just as friends, and they studied together.

But dinner? She'd hardly talked to him since he graduated a year ahead of her. He'd gone off to Purdue University. And that seemed to be the end of their friendship, except for brief chats at class reunions.

Lissa noticed the anchor tattooed on Humpy's forearm and smiled to herself. She wasn't sure she was up to dinner with Humpy, but she was done hurting family and friends.

Sally patted her hair and shook her bangles a little too loudly.

"Sure. I'd like that," Lissa said.

"Great. I'll call you."

"Oh, yeah. Not this weekend. Boots is coming for a visit."

Humpy shot her an "okay" with his forefinger and winked, including Sally in the gesture.

He got up and strode out of the coffee shop.

He'd changed a lot over the years. Humpy had been the school nerd. Large black glasses constantly falling down his nose, and a plastic pocket protector crammed with pens, pencils, and slide rule marked him with a bull's-eye for teasing. But he now had a confident look and a swagger that he certainly didn't have as a teen.

Apparently the Navy had made a man of Humpy, a very fit one—a man with a brilliant career in nuclear engineering. His brown hair was no longer slicked back with Brylcreem. What hair he had left was a light brown fuzz dusted around the sides of his head, and he no longer wore glasses. Studying his receding back, Lissa wasn't sure she knew this man anymore, but it was done, she'd at least have dinner with him.

The doors closed behind Humpy, and Lissa turned to Sally, who was engrossed in sipping her very hot latte. Sally looked innocently at Lissa over the rim of the large cup.

"So what kind of plot is this?" Lissa let the edge in her voice clearly cut through.

"Plot? What evah do you mean, dahling?" Sally put on her best Southern sticky-sweet-cream accent, and then dropped it with a *splat*. "He wanted to see you. Don't be mad. It's Humpy."

Lissa took a big pull of cold, milky coffee through the straw and let her stiffened hackles settle. "True. But you could have said *something*. Since when is Sally Peterson quiet?"

"I didn't want to interrupt."

Lissa gave her friend a withering look that had no effect. "And I would have said yes to dinner, even if you hadn't kicked me under the table."

"I did no such thing."

"Well you might as well have."

"Hey. He's a nice man. Since he's been back he's dug right in and gotten involved in the community. He travels some, but when he's here he shows up once or twice a week to help at the food pantry. He's also been helping with the kids' summer rec program."

Sally abruptly turned her attention to her latte, as if to say, "So there." She didn't say anything more about Humpy, and neither did Lissa. The softness between the friends quickly fluffed up again like a favorite pillow.

"Sally?"

"Hmm?" Sally was mid-sip.

"I'm sorry I didn't call you the last couple times I was home."

"No problem. I understand. Really."

Lissa didn't doubt Sally's sincerity, but she wasn't sure Sally did understand. How could anyone understand until you've been through it. Losing a best friend at sixteen was bad enough, but to have your husband wrenched from you long before old age really was indescribable.

Maybe she could talk to Humpy. He would understand for sure. And with that, Lissa set thoughts of Humpy aside.

Sally leaned forward, "Hey, want to hear the latest in the Jessica Steuben Story?"

Lissa shifted uncomfortably in her seat. Hearing the latest gossip about Jessica was like watching a car race—you don't want anyone to get hurt, but at the same time, wrecks are compelling to watch.

"The buzz is that Jessica's on her fourth marriage. Some old guy in California. I heard she met him online."

"Well, you know, anyone about our age is old now."

"No, really. This guy's close to seventy." Sally reached up and patted the side of her hair, probably to make sure no errant tufts had escaped the exoskeleton of hair spray at the scandalous revelation.

FIFTY DAYS TO SUNRISE

"I just hope she's happy this time," said Lissa.

Sally fussing with her hair made Lissa run her fingers through her own hair, trying to tame it. Next to Sally, Lissa looked like an ad for herbal shampoo. Today she had taken no more time with her shoulder-length hair than a few swipes with a brush and a jab to fix a clip in place to keep her hair out of her eyes.

"You know her father died last year," Sally said. "I heard she didn't even come home for the funeral."

"That doesn't surprise me, I guess. Her dad always gave me the creeps. I remember them sitting in front of us in church once; he was rubbing the back of Jessica's neck and playing with her hair. Her mom was there, sitting on the other side of her dad. It was really weird. I've always wondered."

"Me too. Her mom divorced her dad, left town, and never came back. Right after the last kid left home." Sally shoved her bracelets down to her wrist.

Lissa couldn't stomach any more talk about the pits of life. "That's enough of the junk. Tell me more about your kids."

Sally immediately rummaged in her purse again and came up waving another photo. She snapped it down on the table in front of Lissa and waited.

 Sally didn't have to wait long for Lissa's reaction as Lissa clapped her hand over her mouth to stifle more giggles. A young man with a thatch of shoulder-length blond hair grinned impishly at the camera—Sally's youngest. His hair was streaked with red, blue, green, and purple.

The photo needed no explanation, but Sally offered one. "Sam's expressing his inner rainbow."

Chapter 25

Lissa walked home the long way: up to the northernmost bridge across the Dakota. She stopped in the middle of the bridge and looked upriver to Humpy's neighborhood. His house probably overlooked the river.

The houses were pretty, most of them well taken care of, several of them the Painted Lady colors of the Victorian era. These were the homes built by the monied founders of Gifford. The Angus Gifford House was now a museum, and a Gifford ancestor still lived on the street.

She would find out soon enough where Humpy lived.

Two blocks from home, Lissa's cell phone rang. "Hi, Dad. What's up?"

"Missy, I've got your mother at the ER." He quickly added, "Now, don't panic. She fell, and they just have her under observation."

Lissa heard the strain in her dad's voice.

"Is she all right? What happened?" Being told not to panic certainly wasn't going to keep her from panicking. The sour taste of fear rose in her throat.

"Well, nothing seems to be broken, but she bumped her head. She's got a nasty egg on her forehead and will probably have a shiner."

"I'm coming over to the hospital."

"Oh, good. They're going to keep her overnight. She has a mild concussion, and they want to watch her. I know she'd want to see you."

"I'm almost home. I'll be there as fast as I can."

"If we're not in the ER, just ask at the front desk."

Lissa caught her dad just before he hung up, "Dad? Where are the car keys?"

"Your mother's keys are on her dresser."

Lissa shot into a run, like she'd come off starting blocks. Fishing the key out of her pocket, she unlocked the front door and bounded up the stairs, two at a time, to Mom and Dad's bedroom. She grabbed the keys off Mom's dresser, ran back down the stairs, threw the front door bolt back to locked, and flew out the back door.

Mom's old white Toyota Camry hadn't been driven since Mom's stroke. The engine balked at first, but then it turned over, just before Lissa was about to stomp on the gas.

Pulling into St. Luke's parking lot, Lissa realized she hadn't been in this hospital since after Pip's accident. How could that be? Then she remembered she hadn't come home when Mom had her stroke.

Guilt jabbed her in the side, and she walked as briskly as she could without drawing attention to herself. Her mother was, after all, in the safest place she could be after an accident.

Besieging heaven with prayer, Lissa strode like a wooden soldier through the automatic doors.

Mom lay flat on a gurney in the ER behind a blue-and-white striped curtain. She tried to raise herself on one elbow

FIFTY DAYS TO SUNRISE

when Lissa came in, but Dad put a gentle hand on her saying, "Now, Eleanor, the doctor said you're to lie perfectly flat and still."

"Oh. Yes, dear."

After fifty-four years of marriage, Mom and Dad radiated a patient and tender love that was obviously rooted in a deep knowledge and trust of one another. The fire that once burned for each other could still be seen in a shared glance now and then, a lingering touch. Dad rested a hand on Mom's arm, without disturbing the monitor clipped to her finger. He stroked her hair with his other hand.

Lissa bent and gingerly kissed her mother's cheek—the cheek that wasn't bruised. She took hold of her mother's hand. The bruise on Mom's face was appalling. The lump on her forehead was fiery red and the size of a small hard-boiled egg sliced in half longwise. One eye was already turning a nasty purple, and the other eye was looking suspect for doing the same. The technicolor bruising made Mom's skin look all the more alarmingly pale. Her skin seemed fragile as eggshell. In the fluorescent lighting, the quilted lines on her face and neck appeared deeply scored. She looked like a very old woman.

Lissa was speechless for a moment. It was horrifying to see her mother looking so wounded, so frail. Tears dripped silently down Lissa's cheeks.

"Don't cry, honey. I'll be fine." Mom smiled a crooked smile that made her wince slightly.

"I know, Mom," Lissa said softly. Mom frowned almost imperceptibly. Lissa realized her mother didn't have her hearing aids in, and she repeated, "I know you will, Mom."

Mom looked tired; she closed her eyes.

Seeing her mother like this frightened Lissa, and she resolved to not let her mother out of her sight until she was sure Mom was fine. It was arranged for Lissa to spend the night at the hospital with her mother.

Lissa leaned against the frame of the studio's open door and admired her husband's broad shoulders and lean back. It was hot for June in Maine, and he'd taken off his T-shirt and thrown it over the tall stool he stood beside. She felt blessed beyond all sense.

"Hi, love." Lissa came up behind Sean and wrapped her arms around his waist, pressing her body against his back. It didn't matter if her clothes got covered in paint.

His head tilted back toward her; she could just see the corner of a smile. He threw a kiss back to his wife and returned to studying the canvas in front of him.

They stood pressed together, blissfully relaxed—Sean's brush poised, waiting for the next stroke of inspiration—or waiting for Lissa to let go of him. She peeked over his shoulder at the painting, a seascape at sunrise.

"You *are* good, you know."

The brush in Sean's hand became a long knife clenched in his fist. He slashed the painting, and the sun dripped blood.

Lissa woke with a searing inhalation of dry air. In her dream she was screaming, but the sound that woke her was a low gasp. She glanced over at Mom to see if she had disturbed her, but Mom looked peaceful in her medicated sleep. The monitors indicated she was fine.

Rubbing her face, Lissa reached for her glass of water. It was silly, but she didn't want to drink out of Mom's glass. Maybe it was against hospital rules to drink out of a patient's glass.

Lissa was so tired of these dreams. She let her head fall back and closed her eyes against the image of blood. Love destroyed. She was wiped out.

FIFTY DAYS TO SUNRISE

In recent months, she had discovered that alcohol dulled the dreams. Mom was right, that was no good. Lissa knew it, but had done it anyway, many times. She used to wake up crying several times a night. Lately she had just lain there—numb—until the respite of sleep came again—and with it the risk of more nightmares.

The air conditioning blew chilly. She quietly got up from the recliner and made sure Mom's blanket was doing its job. She gently tucked the blanket around Mom's shoulders.

Lissa wandered to the window, pulled back the edge of the curtain, and peered out at the night surrounding the hospital. There was no dark, only lights in the parking lot.

Exhausted, like she'd run a marathon at gunpoint, she settled back into the chair. It was only two a.m. There was a lot of night to endure yet.

She watched her mother sleep. From this side she couldn't see the terrible bruise on Mom's face.

Everybody had warned Mom about that rug, but she refused to take it up. Mom had several near misses where she'd caught a toe on the edge on her way to the sink. And here they were, in the hospital. Lissa was torn between annoyance at her mother's stubbornness and sympathy for her injury.

She had gotten the story from Dad while Mom was getting settled in her room. Mom was going through the kitchen cupboards, taking out things for the rummage sale. Apparently she'd put something on the table and was coming back to the cupboard by the sink when her foot caught the edge of the rag rug. She stumbled forward and hit her head on the rolled edge of the counter. Thankfully, they'd had to replace the old Formica with the metal edge nailed on, or she'd have needed stitches too.

That was the best guess for an explanation Dad could come up with; Mom didn't remember anything. Dad was in the dining room when it happened and was there in a flash. He said Mom was out like a light, but only for a minute. Mom refused to let Dad call an ambulance, and since she was talking and able to sit up, he reluctantly agreed.

Lissa thought of Dad, at home in his bed, and was glad she could do this for them. She didn't feel any less guilty for not coming home after Mom's stroke, but it helped.

Thoughts of Sean pressed on her, as they often did, but this time she let them come. She didn't have the energy to fight them off, nor the wine in which to drown them. And she had the good sense, barely, not to go for a run in the middle of the night, even in Gifford.

It seemed to Lissa she had coped better initially, when Sean's death was such a shock, than she had in the last few months. Then, there was so much to do, to take care of, to figure out. She wasn't as aware of the crushing loneliness she now felt, almost all the time.

She could hardly remember a time when Sean wasn't there. It wasn't true, but that's how it felt—that Sean had always been in her heart, making it swell to twice its size, filling her with love.

She drifted back to that warm September Saturday on the lawn at Columbia University when they met.

"Hi."

"Hi, yourself." She glanced up at the tall, rather forward guy looking down at her. Lissa waited for him to speak, not sure she liked being disturbed while reading.

"Mind if I sit down?"

"I guess not." She didn't want to seem very interested in him, although he was incredibly good-looking. His black hair reached just over his collar—all shiny waves, tucked behind his ears. His dark-brown eyes seemed to be trying to mesmerize her with a gaze as soft as chocolate. He looked good: a summer tan not yet faded, and very nice shoulders. Lissa rolled off her stomach and sat cross-legged with her book open in her lap. Her waist-length hair fell over her shoulders, and she flipped it out of the way.

"What are you reading?"

"*Return of the Native.*" Couldn't he come up with a better line?

"You have really pretty hair."

Now that was better. "Thanks. Actually, you do too." When he sat down in the sun, she noticed he had dark auburn glints in his hair. He smiled—a beautiful smile that made his eyes shimmer, like sunlight dancing on water—really dark, deep water.

"My name's Sean Maguire."

"I'm Lissa Makkinen."

"Makkinen? What kind of a name is that?"

They sat and talked until they realized the shadows were getting long, and they were getting hungry.

In one afternoon they gave each other almost their entire life stories. Like a card game, each playing a card in turn. They were both MFA students, but Sean was four years older than Lissa. He was studying painting, and she was studying creative writing. He had gone to college at the University of California, Los Angeles during the Vietnam war and missed the draft with a number in the 300s. She attended St. Lucia College in Gifford, Minnesota. He was the son of prominent parents in Washington, DC—his father was a Major in the Army and a surgeon at Walter Reed Army Hospital, and his mother was a painter of considerable talent. She was the daughter of musicians—Dad was a music professor at St. Lucia and Mom taught private cello lessons, but was mainly a housewife. He had a brother who served in Vietnam as a medic and made it back—she had a brother in seminary, and a sister who got straight A's and could do just about anything. Sean was from very East Coast Irish heritage—Lissa was from very Midwestern Finnish heritage, with Mom's English and German thrown in for emotional confusion. They should have been keeping score, there were so many cards thrown down.

Looking back, sometime after Jack was born, they laughed about how mismatched they might have been. But that first day they also discovered they both loved Jesus.

At UCLA, Sean had wandered into a Campus Crusade for Christ meeting, barefoot and stoned, and come out high on the presence of the Lord. The Jesus People Movement was catching fire in California, and it lit Sean up. His parents weren't pleased, but they came around when they saw what a difference it made in his life.

That day, the day they met, Sean and Lissa decided to become campus radicals at Columbia, and they resolved to attend the next Crusade meeting together. Radicals for Jesus.

That was the fall of 1972. They were joined at the heart since that first day.

The hospital room recliner was hardly a comfortable bed, and Lissa squirmed.

Lissa imagined herself spooned together with Sean, snug in their white, antique, wrought-iron bed that was their wedding present to each other—her grandmother's quilt bunched up around their ears. Life was good then.

The beeps of the machine at Mom's bedside jolted her awake. Panic balled up in her stomach.

The matronly nurse looked over at Lissa and smiled. The beeps didn't signal a problem. "Your mother seems to be doing well this morning." She unwrapped the blood pressure cuff from Mom's arm and wrote on the chart.

Mom turned her face toward Lissa and smiled around the thermometer. Lissa squeaked at the sight of the livid bruises and tried to cover the noise with clearing her throat.

"Good morning, George," the nurse warbled to Dad as he

came through the door.

"Morning, Margaret." Dad's attention was focused on his wife, and he immediately went to her bedside.

Nurse Margaret checked the thermometer and made another note on the chart, chattering as she wrote. "Doctor will be in shortly. Eleanor's as chipper as ever. She's got plenty of sugar in her. And you know, being so sweet helps the healing." With that, she patted Mom's hand, turned, and bustled out the door.

"Thanks, Margaret," Dad said. Nurse Margaret threw a backward wave and was gone.

An hour later, after the doctor had been in to check on Mom, Lissa left her mother and father together. She headed home for breakfast, strong coffee, and a run.

Chapter 26

Friday morning. Lissa checked the clock—again. She looked for things to do: pushed some already-packed boxes into corners, cleaned up after lunch.

Mom was upstairs, tucked into bed, resting. Dad read in the chaise beside the bed.

Fluttering around the house, Lissa noticed what was missing. Scissors in hand, she went out the back door to cut a bouquet of fresh flowers.

She decided the stargazer lilies and the roses were too strong-scented to put together. The pink shrub roses went on the dresser in Boots's room, and she set the lilies in the middle of the kitchen table. The crystal vases glittered.

Lissa leaned down to drink in the scent of a lily and heard a deep rumble from the street. An engine gave an abrupt growl, settled to a gentle purr, and was switched off. Boots had arrived.

Lissa tried to be nonchalant about seeing her little sister, but by the time she got to the front steps, she was tripping down the steps as fast as she could.

Boots was bent over the open trunk extracting an elegant, dark-red leather bag. She dropped it on the pavement behind the black Mustang, and the sisters threw their arms around each other.

"Boots!"

"Liss!"

They shrieked their greetings loudly enough that they could probably be heard up the hill at St. Lucy's.

Boots broke away from the bear hug and said, "Hey, I've got something for you." She unzipped the side pocket of the bag and produced a gold box tied with gold ribbon. "Chocolate, as promised. Not just any chocolate for my big sis. Pirkle's, the best."

"Oh, yummy. Thanks. I might let you have one." Lissa pecked her younger sister on the cheek.

Boots screwed up her face at Lissa and leaned back. "What have you got on your nose?" With a finger, she swiped at Lissa's nose. Lissa dodged and reached up to rub off whatever it was. "It's yellow. At least it was. You got it."

Boots slammed the trunk and shouldered her bag. "Hey, before we go in, tell me how Mom is."

"She'll be okay. But, wow, she really looks awful. I hope I warned you enough. You won't believe the bruises."

Boots had a grim set to her mouth. She cussed out the rug.

"No kidding. I put it away. She'll just have to like it or lump it. It hasn't gone in the rummage sale pile yet, but we have to convince her to let it go."

"How's Dad?"

"Oh, you know Dad. Nothing much gets him flapped. But he's sticking pretty close to Mom," Lissa said.

"Right, then. Ready, set, go."

Dad met Boots at the front door with his usual big towering-over-you hug. He kissed her on the forehead.

"Pretty good timing with your visit. Great to have you home, Bootsie."

FIFTY DAYS TO SUNRISE

Boots gave Dad a kiss on the cheek. "Missed you, Dad." Boots cast an inquiring glance toward Mom's chair in the living room.

"Mom's upstairs, waiting for you."

Boots set her bag on the bottom step and went to see Mom. Dad put his arm around Lissa's shoulder and steered her toward the kitchen. "Let's get something tall and cold, shall we?"

Some time later, Boots pushed open the back door and joined them on the patio.

"She's asleep." Boots looked ashen.

She sat down at the picnic table, pulled her ponytail loose, and ran her fingers through her dark, perfectly cut hair. The glossy weight of her hair fell into deep waves that spilled just past her shoulders. "It's unnerving to see her like this. The stroke was bad, but this *looks* worse."

"I know," Dad said, "but the doctor said she'll recover just fine. Apparently it was a mild concussion. It's that German hard head, you know."

"Sounds like the Finlander pot calling the German kettle black." Boots verbally elbowed Dad. Dad grinned, though not his usual grin that set his midnight-blue eyes sparkling.

"The doctor said she should just rest for at least a week. Good thing you girls are here. It'll make it easier for her."

"And for you," said Boots.

"Yes...yes it will." Dad looked tired as he stretched in his seat and ran both hands through his hair. Silver waves dislodged and poked out.

Lissa set her lawn chair bouncing lightly. She and Boots exchanged glances and nodded at each other in a sisterly pact.

"Hey, little sister, you want a pop?"

"Sure." Boots made a move to get up.

"Sit tight. I'll get it."

CRISTINE EASTIN

They set up TV trays in Mom and Dad's bedroom and ate together around Mom in her bed. Mom held court, like the Queen.

Looking around the room, Lissa's eyes fell on the three framed wedding photos on Mom's dresser. These were the candid photos. The formal portraits hung on the wall by the closet. She hadn't noticed the photos when she dashed in and grabbed the car keys off Mom's dresser. Mom and Dad had tried to be so considerate, taking down Sean's painting in the living room, but they no doubt didn't think about Lissa and Sean's wedding photos in their bedroom.

August 17, 1974. They looked so happy. They were. Lissa was twenty-four, Sean twenty-eight.

It was hot that day, and Sean had shed his tux jacket for the reception in the President's Garden at St. Lucy's. His sleeves were rolled up, his shirt bloused up over his baby blue cummerbund. They were both barefoot. The baby's breath and daisies in the circlet in Lissa's hair were a little wilted, but nothing mattered except how happy they were. Sean had pulled his bride tightly to him, one arm wrapped around her waist, and with the other hand, his fingers burrowed into her cascading hair behind her head. Lissa clung to her new husband as she reached up on tiptoe to meet his kiss. The photographer had caught them in this moment of promised passion; they thought they were out of view behind a big oak tree. This was Mom's favorite picture from the wedding.

Lissa nibbled at her meatloaf. Meatloaf was an odd smell in the bedroom.

Mom said, "I'm sorry, Lissa, I should have put that photo away. I didn't think of it."

"Oh," Lissa said, "it's okay." She must have been staring at the photo. It was hard to fight back tears—she could almost feel Sean's kiss.

FIFTY DAYS TO SUNRISE

Boots left only a moment of silence before she waved her fork at her sister. "Hey, Liss, where do you want to cruise in the 'Stang? I was thinking of Sjostrand Woods."

Lissa swallowed a mouthful of meatloaf. "Yeah, that sounds great. We could do a little cross-country run." She was trying to muster enthusiasm.

"I'll bet I can beat you at skipping rocks."

Lissa made an older-sister face at her, accepting the challenge.

"Dad, would it work if we do that tomorrow? It's supposed to rain Sunday," Lissa said.

"Sure. I don't see why not."

"Count me out." Mom smiled impishly. She still looked pistol-whipped: a yellowish tinge now added to the palette of purple and green around her eyes. But, apparently she was feeling a little better.

Chapter 27

Lissa handed Boots a glass of wine and sat down next to her on the porch swing. Soft notes of *Claire de Lune* on the Steinway floated out into the night. The swing chain creaked a duet.

"I suppose you've been told this before," Boots said. "You've lost weight."

Lissa closed her eyes and leaned her head on the back of the swing. She was really tired of this, but didn't want to snap at Boots. She tried to count to ten—didn't make it to three.

"I know, but my sins have been forgiven."

A muscle in Boots's jaw twitched, and she took a sip of her wine. Silence hung between them like a frayed rope. The odd rhythm of *Claire de Lune* grated.

"Sorry, I didn't mean to snap. It's just that this has all been so hard."

Boots nodded.

"You know, Boots, I'm just so ashamed after last Christmas, I don't even know what to do to try and make it right."

"Everyone understood, Liss. We're all just worried about you."

"Yeah, so what did I do? I went and did it again. I screamed the same thing at Mom again. And I…"

Lissa stopped, unable to expose her stupidity to her sister. Boots waited.

"And?"

"Quit it, lawyer. Let it go."

"No." Boots looked directly at Lissa.

Lissa looked away. "I got stinkin' drunk again. There. Are you satisfied?"

"What? You mean since you've been here?"

"Oh yeah. Just last Friday. You mean Mom didn't tell you?" Lissa flailed within herself. She wanted to fight, and she wanted to beg her family's forgiveness.

Boots was silent.

Lissa took her sister's silence for acknowledgment and launched an attack.

"You mean she *did* tell you?"

"Not about last Friday."

"I'm sick of everyone talking about me."

"Liss, there's no call to—"

"Yeah, right. Don't tell me—"

"Lissa!" Boots gently put her hand on Lissa's arm. Lissa closed her mouth and let her head fall back against the swing.

"What?" Lissa decided to accept the inevitable from her little sister. She had expected a verbal whipping, a cross-examination, anyway.

"I know this is hard for you. We all miss Sean." Lissa started to protest. Boots wasn't sticking to the no-talking-about-Sean rule.

"Let me finish. We can't tell you how to grieve, but you have *got* to stop being so self-destructive. I know you don't want that."

The fight gone out of her, Lissa drew a shuddering breath.

FIFTY DAYS TO SUNRISE

She thought a minute.

"No, you're right, I don't." She faced her sister. "I already decided after my last stunt, that I was done with this self-centered, self-destructive...I just can't stand it anymore. But, Boots,...I'm so scared. It hurts *so* much."

"I know."

"I've been trying. I've been thinking about Pip. Hoping that will help."

"Pip? How will that help?"

"I don't know, maybe remembering that I survived what I thought was impossible to survive." Tears welled up. "But missing Sean is *so* much worse. I just feel so...alone."

Lissa trembled, no longer able to contain her tears.

Boots took the glass from her sister and put both glasses down on the ledge by the screen. She gathered her big sister in her arms. Lissa pulled up her knees and melted into Boots's shoulder.

"I'm here. Liss, I'll always be here for you."

"I know," Lissa said through her tears.

Boots softly patted Lissa on the back and bent her head to rest her cheek against Lissa's hair.

Somewhere in a corner of her mind, Lissa heard the final *arpeggio* of *Claire de Lune* fade. Sweet again, as it had always been. She sat up, sniffed mightily, and did the best she could to mop her face with her hands. Quiet settled between the sisters —Boots reached over and brushed a finger down Lissa's cheek.

"All right?" Dad said as he stepped into the porch.

"That was beautiful, Dad. Too bad you're no good on those ivories."

"Oh, I know, Bootsie, but I keep practicing. Maybe I'll get to Carnegie Hall someday," Dad said with a grin. He'd gotten there thirty years ago.

He kissed his oldest daughter on the top of her head and stroked her hair. "I'll leave you girls to talk. Goodnight, sweethearts."

"G'night." Lissa was afraid she'd cry again.

"Good night, Dad. Kiss Mom for us." Boots kissed her fingers and pasted the kiss on Dad's cheek. Dad did the same and went up to bed.

Boots straightened. Taking Lissa gently by the shoulders, she looked her in the eyes and said, "Liss, you *will* be okay. You just have to talk about it. You can't keep it all inside."

"I know. I know."

By the light from the living room, Lissa could see a damp spot on the aqua silk of Boots's tank top where she'd had her face buried. "I'm sorry. I think I messed up your top."

"Doesn't matter, silly goose." Lissa's running nose was now an embarrassment, and she wiped it with the back of her hand. "You're disgusting. You know, for an older sister, you ain't got no class."

Lissa smiled ruefully and gave Boots a fond shove, but not hard enough to push her off the swing, something that had once gotten her in a lot of trouble.

"Boots?"

"Hmm?"

"Do you love Etienne?"

"That's an odd question. Why?"

"Because I need to know." Lissa twisted the wide, gold wedding band on her finger.

Boots retrieved their wine glasses. She rearranged the pillow in the corner of the swing and sat back. She gently pushed the swing back and forth with her feet on the porch floor. Lissa settled against the pillow in her corner, tucked her feet up, and waited for Boots's response.

"I think I did. Now I don't know. We work so well together. Honestly, Liss, Etienne's a brilliant lawyer. You should see him in the courtroom." Boots stopped the swing and faced Lissa. "But that's not enough, is it?" She turned away to look at the streetlight-lit boulevard trees flickering with the breeze. "I don't know, after we went through all that infertility nightmare. Etienne wouldn't even talk about adoption. I really wanted to adopt a child from India. I mean, I really wanted that. I think something in me just died for a time. And now—he says he loves me. I *think* I love him." She stopped.

"I'm sorry, Boots, I didn't mean to bring up something painful."

"It's okay. You've always said we work too much. It's true we don't spend enough time together."

The chain squeaked a soft and familiar rhythm as they swayed back and forth. A nighthawk's screech punctuated the cadence.

"It's just that I miss Sean so much. Sometimes I wonder if I loved him *too* much. I wonder if I can really live without him. I'm not even sure I know who I am without him." Having gotten that out, she took a deep breath, and found that her lungs still took in air, and her heart continued to beat.

"I always envied what you two had. No, not envied—I admired you. I wanted to love like you two. Liss, you can't imagine how difficult it was for me to watch you being a mother. Watching you and Sean grow in love as your family grew."

Lissa gulped reflexively, swallowing the bitter taste of her own self-absorbed grief—and the shame of not having fully understood her sister's pain. She paused before offering yet another apology. "I think I do now. Boots, I'm so sorry."

They reached for each other's hands. Boots's hands smooth and elegantly manicured, Lissa's rough from gardening, clasped together for a moment.

"Sometimes," Lissa lowered her voice, "when I watch Mom and Dad when they're not looking, I feel utter despair at missing Sean. They love each other so much. I'd catch Sean looking at me like Dad looks at Mom. I wish we could have gotten old together like Mom and Dad have. That's what we planned. I feel ashamed to say that it's hard to be around my own parents because they love each other so much."

Lissa cupped a hand on the side of her face and closed her eyes. Silent tears slid down her cheeks and between her fingers. "I miss him so much—it's like I can feel him touch me."

She opened her eyes and stared deep into her wine. "I didn't even get to say goodbye."

"Pardon? I didn't catch that."

"I said, I didn't get to say goodbye."

"I know." Boots reached over and brushed a tear off Lissa's cheek.

"How could God be so cruel?"

"That sounds like a question for Dad."

Lissa drained her glass. "Want another?" She reached for Boots's glass.

Boots hesitated. "Better not."

"You're right." Lissa sighed with once-again-renewed resignation. "No answers were ever written at the bottom of a glass."

Boots set their glasses back on the ledge.

The sisters sat quietly together until Lissa said, "Do you remember when Daisy stole Mom's apron, and Ray and I chased her all over the backyard?"

"Oh, yes. And Ray got it back from her."

"He did not! *I* got it!"

Boots gave Lissa an affectionate poke in the arm. "Gottcha."

Chapter 28

Boots tooted the Mustang's horn. Lissa gave Dad instructions on when to put the lasagna in the oven, and was up the kitchen stairs, down the front stairs, and out the front door. Boots put the car in neutral and gave the neighborhood a V8 blast of power.

Lissa slid into the passenger seat, the black leather warm on the backs of her thighs. Boots had her hair pulled into a ponytail stuck through the hole in the back of her baseball cap —her Cubs baseball cap. Lissa threw her sister a mostly mock disapproving look. Boots tugged on the bill in salute.

"Engage," Lissa said, pointing forward.

And Boots did. She slammed the gear shift into first and caught rubber—just a little. A squinty-eyed grin stretched her face, as she looked over at Lissa.

"I'm gonna get you a Twins hat," Lissa chided her sister.

"You know I won't wear it. Go Cubbies."

Lissa laughed. It was good to be with her sister.

The convertible rumbled down the street, passing under the noontime shadows of the boulevard trees. It was going to be a beautiful crystal-blue-sky day. Just a few puffy clouds to the west foretold rain, but for now the clouds glowed the color of pearls.

Gifford was in the rearview mirror in no time, and Boots settled the pony car to a loping canter, just a little above the speed limit. She took the long way to Sjostrand Woods, hugging the curves along the river.

Lissa let her hair fly free. She might pay for it later with wind-knots, but she didn't care. She reached her arms straight up and let the wind try to push them back.

Boots put in a CD she'd brought for the occasion—*Songs of the '60s & '70s*. "Jeremiah was a bullfrog!" They sang along, shouting into the wind.

"Joy to the world!..." Lissa turned to Boots, caught her eye, and mouthed, "Thank you."

"You're welcome, big sister."

The countryside slipped past. They drove through a pungent aroma: the first cutting of hay in a field. The farmer was baling the raked hay to get it in before the rain.

At the sign for Sjostrand Woods State Park, Boots turned in and downshifted the Mustang to a stately pace. The car snarled in protest. They paid their daily fee and parked at the end of the parking lot closest to the falls. Boots put the top up so they wouldn't get scalded on the hot seats later.

A quick stretch and Boots yelled, "Race you!" Lissa looked up to see her sister forty feet away, heels flying. She launched herself after Boots, but couldn't catch her. Boots stopped at the trailhead and leaned against the sign, pretending to file her nails.

Their shoes thumped a familiar beat on the packed earth. When Lissa was at St. Lucy's, she and Boots sometimes ran together. Boots had run cross-country in high school. The summer before Boots started law school she ran the first Grandma's Marathon in Duluth. To her credit, Boots had always been a healthy runner, avoiding the trap of addiction;

FIFTY DAYS TO SUNRISE

she continued to run because she loved it. Lissa ran because she had to, and sometimes, because she wanted to. Today she wanted to run. They easily hurdled a fallen tree.

Occasionally Boots called, "Excuse us," and hikers stepped to one side to let them pass. It was a mile and a half to the falls. Barely breathing hard, Boots stopped at the bank overlooking the pool below the falls. The waterfall was flowing only moderately, but the sound of the water hitting the pool twenty feet below was musical.

They picked their way down the bank over rocks and tree roots. Boots slowly cruised the edge of the pool, head bent, intently looking at the shore. Lissa knew she was looking for the perfect skipping rocks. Lissa did the same.

"Ready?" Boots straightened up with several rocks cupped in her hands.

"Ready."

They took turns skipping rocks, counting the skips at first, then firing rocks at will, laughing like loons, oblivious to the people around them.

"You win!" Lissa raised Boots's hand in victory.

"And you!" Boots grabbed Lissa's wrist and raised her hand too. They let their arms fall around each other and ended in an embrace of shared silliness, still laughing.

"That was fun. I can't remember when I laughed so hard." Boots splashed her hands in the pool to rinse off the sand.

"I know *I* haven't laughed that hard in a year and a half," Lissa said. Boots flushed and looked down. "It's okay." Lissa sighed. "You said I'd be okay. Maybe I will."

"Liss," Boots faced her. "Have you thought about writing about Sean? I mean, you're a writer. There's no way to beat around the bush to say this, but maybe you could write about your life together." Boots seemed to have this speech prepared. "It would probably be really healing."

It was Lissa's turn to feel her jaw tighten. "I know you mean well—"

"Really, Liss. I mean it. I just know it would be incredibly therapeutic for you. You've always journaled."

Journaling. That was a painful place she'd avoided. Lissa had thought about it many times, but had pushed it down with all the other shards of the past—as well as any thoughts about the future. But Boots was right. Doing it though...

"I guess I could try."

"Good." Boots squeezed Lissa's arm. "Let's go back through the woods and the meadow."

Lissa gave a thumbs up. "You lead."

Lissa watched her sister jog down the trail, shook her head before following Boots. She was feeling pushed around, just a little.

The jog through the woods was cool as the day heated up. Twigs snapped underneath their feet. A gray squirrel scrambled along a moss-covered fallen tree. He launched himself against the trunk of a shagbark hickory and shot up the tree. The squirrel disturbed a flock of crows in the canopy, and the crows lifted skyward, squawking indignantly.

After fifteen minutes in the woods, the trail rose uphill and opened onto a meadow on a plateau. The sisters fell into step side by side, jogging silently. They didn't look much alike, but running, they seemed as one. Lissa was a little taller, and Boots was finer-boned, but they ran together with a practiced rhythm and grace. The meadow dropped back down a slope, and they jogged through the campground.

The parking lot was in sight, and they slowed the pace. "Do you want to take the trail over to the river?" They were warmed up, and Lissa was up for another couple of miles on top of the four they had just run.

Boots didn't answer right away as Lissa expected her to. "I don't know, what do you think?" Boots said.

That was an odd response. A glaring lightbulb switched on—Boots knew. It wasn't just the drinking Mom had told her about. Lissa's eyeballs burned as she blinked hard to keep the tears down.

This time Lissa more effectively counted to avoid snapping at her sister and got all the way to five. "You're right. That's enough."

The drive back home was less euphoric, but still nice. It was hard to pout with the top down on a 2003 version of a muscle car and one's little sister singing as loud as she could, "I wanna hold your haaand."

"I lied," Lissa said. "I *did* laugh that hard one other time. Last week when Sally told me her twin granddaughters were named Violet and Verbena."

Boots's laughter peeled into the wind.

※

"Hey, Mom. You feel okay enough to be out of bed?" Lissa had seen Mom sitting on the patio and went out to her. Boots followed, looking equally concerned.

Dad straightened up from cutting out dead peony blossoms. "You girls have a good time?" He put a hand on his lower back and straightened some more.

"We sure did," Boots said as she sat on top of the picnic table. She took off her running shoes and wiggled her toes in the fresh air. "I beat Liss at skipping rocks."

Lissa almost blurted out, "Did not!" but caught herself and instead, smiled beneficently.

Mom reached for Lissa's hand. "How big was the falls?"

"About medium." Lissa was worried about her mother. She was a long way from her bed for being home from the hospital so recently. "Mom, are you feeling well enough to be out here?"

"Oh, I'm fine. Not to worry."

Boots folded her arms across her chest. "Well, from where I sit, it looks like somebody smeared grape jam, green bread mold, and mustard over half your face. So I wouldn't say you're fine. You either need to pick new friends, or that's the worst bruise I've ever seen."

"Your mother wanted to be outside." Dad lifted both hands in helpless surrender. "You know how she is."

Mom waved a hand at him and made a noise that sounded like *pshh*. They looked at each other and shared that knowing little smile.

"Right. I'm making tea. I'll bring it out here." Sometimes her parents could be exasperating and endearing, all at the same time. Lissa shook her head. A Finlander *and* a stubborn German for parents. She turned to the back door to hide her smile.

Dinner conversation revolved around what needed to be done yet to get Mom and Dad moved. It started a little rocky with Mom asking where her kitchen rag rug was.

Lissa informed her mother that the rug in question, the evil rug that had reached out and tripped her, was consigned to a place where she'd never find it. And further, what did she want done with it? *other* than put it back down on the floor anywhere in this house.

With pursed lips, Mom informed Lissa that she could do whatever she liked with the rug. Boots attempted to hide her smirk behind her napkin.

It was agreed that a rummage sale was too much work. And too dangerous. They would just continue to make donation runs to the various thrift shops and charitable groups in town.

After Mom went to bed, father and daughters sat in the living room and talked. With her hearing aids out, Mom wouldn't hear them.

More tears. Lissa snatched another Kleenex out of the box. It was painful to see Dad choked up. Stuck in desperate survival, Lissa hadn't realized how difficult Mom's stroke and her rehab had been for them. She had tried hard not to think about it at all.

Dad said he couldn't imagine how difficult it was for Lissa to see her parents aging—approaching a time when they might be separated by death—when she had already lost Sean. Lissa wanted to stop her dad, cut off his words, make them go away, but she didn't interrupt her father.

She hadn't been able to put her finger on the discomfort she felt around her parents, but there it was. It wasn't only their deep love for each other, it was seeing them headed for loneliness, when she was already there. Way too young. Dad said he and Mom had agreed they wouldn't live in fear that every moment might be their last together.

She couldn't stuff cotton in her ears. Couldn't make Dad stop. Couldn't deny it was true.

The sniffling and blowing subsided. They looked at each other, all clearly exhausted, not knowing what to say that hadn't been said.

After a few moments of no one speaking, Lissa looked at her father. "Dad?" She mashed a wad of tissues into a ball. "Would you please put Sean's painting back up over the mantel?"

"If you're sure." Lissa nodded. "Then I certainly will, Missy. First thing, right after breakfast." Dad got up from his recliner and patted her hand. "Good night, sweethearts. It's good to have you both home."

After Dad went to bed, Boots excused herself and went upstairs. "I'll be right back."

She returned carrying a flowered gift bag and handed it to Lissa. The bag was unexpectedly heavy. Lissa gave her sister a blank look. She had nothing to give in return.

"Go ahead. Open it."

Lissa dug through the lime-green tissue paper and pulled out a book. She drew an audible breath. A handmade journal bound in tooled Moroccan leather. In the lower right corner of the cover was her name in gold letters—*Melissa Makkinen Maguire*.

    She gently ran her hand over the geometric-patterned cover. The red goat hide was buttery soft. She untied the leather strip lashed twice around the sumptuous journal. The inside of the leather cover was rough. The cream-colored parchment pages were stitched in, at least 200 deckle-edged pages. Every surface was a delight to touch. Lissa flopped the journal closed, not taking her hands off it, and looked at Boots.

    "I didn't think you'd mind," Boots said with a tentative-looking smile.

    "Mind? Oh, no. It's absolutely gorgeous. I...I don't know what to say. Thank you so much."

    "That'll do just fine."

    "No, really. It's a work of art." She could feel her eyes start to fill up again. "Where did you get it?"

    "It's handmade by a guy who lives on Whidbey Island. I saw his work on display at a bookstore in Chicago, and I just knew it was for you."

    "Well, you shouldn't have. This cost too much."

    Boots gave her sister one of those you-dummy looks. "Doesn't matter. You're worth it."

    "You *are* a stinker. What if I just want to doodle in it?"

    "You won't."

    That was true. Lissa already knew the title page—*Sean*.

Chapter 29

The grumble of thunder in the distance brought Lissa to the surface of not quite awake, but not asleep. She lay in bed smelling the approaching rain. There was no hurry to close the window; she pulled the quilt up over her shoulders.

A clap of thunder startled her, and she thumped herself under the chin where her hands clutched the quilt. She must have dozed off. Lightning sizzled, and another boom smashed the air. The rising wind set the curtains flapping, and she jumped out of bed and closed the window.

She ran downstairs to check the windows in the rest of the house. Force of habit. Everything was battened down, and she went back to her room. Sleep would be impossible during this storm. She sat on the window seat and watched the wind whip the trees silhouetted in the streetlight. The rain lashed against the window, streaming down the panes in liquid sheets. Lissa wrapped up in the fluffy pink afghan Mom had made. It wasn't chilly, but it looked chilly outside.

Lissa liked storms. In a strange way a storm was comforting. There was nothing she could do but watch.

Nothing was required of her, and she relaxed against the pillows. She flinched at another thunderous burst. Thunder made her feel like a kid: brave in the face of danger, overcoming her fear.

She heard a light tap at her door. Boots quietly pushed the door open. "Liss, you awake?"

"How could I not be?"

Boots was wrapped in the green fuzzy afghan from her room. "Mind if I join you?"

"'Course not." Lissa moved her feet to make room.

Boots snuggled down into the pillows at the other end. "That was fun today, wasn't it?"

"Mm-hmm." Lissa was feeling that middle-of-the-night muzziness that instinctively resisted talking.

"Liss." Boots paused. "I'm going to India in February, and I want you to come with me."

Lissa looked at her, unable to come up with a response of any kind. Boots might as well have said she was flying to the moon and wanted Lissa to go with her. Why couldn't Boots beat around the bush once in a while?

"Hey, are you there?"

"Yes, but, no. I don't know *where* I am. And who are *you*? What did you do with my little sister?" Lissa caught herself and lowered her voice. "You know, the workaholic who never takes vacations."

"It's not a vacation. I'm going to work at an orphanage for two months."

"You're what?" She rubbed her face with her hands. Maybe she wasn't awake, or not hearing very well.

"Yeah, I'm taking your advice. You've always told me I work too much, so I'm taking some time off to do something I'm passionate about: helping orphans in India. I couldn't adopt all of them. Etienne wouldn't even let me adopt one. So I'm going over to do what I can, besides just send money."

Struggling to take in this latest pronouncement by Boots,

FIFTY DAYS TO SUNRISE

Lissa at least picked up on Etienne's name. "Is Etienne going with you?"

"I'm still trying to talk him into it. He might come for a week."

"You're serious?" Boots's expression confirmed it. "You're serious. What about your job?"

"I've got it all figured out. Being a partner helps....Well?"

"I couldn't possibly. The farm—"

"It'll be winter, nothing's growing. Get somebody to stay there like you did now. Anyway, you wouldn't have to be in India the whole time, just one month, just February."

"Boots, you've got to be kidding. I'm not made of money you know. And anyway, I don't know why I'm even talking about this, especially at two in the morning." Another shot of lightening split the night, followed by a drum roll of thunder, right on cue.

"Well, I'm planning on paying your way."

This was too much. Lissa gave her sister a dumbfounded look.

Boots shrugged her shoulders. "It doesn't matter, you know. I don't mean to sound like a pig, but you know I can afford it. It's that important, Liss, to have you with me." Boots drew her knees up and wrapped her arms around her legs. "To be honest," she drew in a long breath and slowly let it out, "I'm not sure I can face all those children by myself, especially the babies." She chewed her lower lip. "I need my big sis with me. Please."

Lissa crawled over to her sister and hugged her tight.

"I don't know what to say. Truly."

"Just think about it, okay? I'm not booking my flight till November."

Boots scooted over, and Lissa sat close to her in the pile of pillows. For a time they watched the rain pelt the window.

"You know, this has been one strange visit so far. Did I tell you I ran into Humpy Humphrey earlier this week? Sally tipped him off that we were at The Old Mill."

"No, you're kidding? Is he still mooning over you?"

"Don't be ridiculous. His wife died about three years ago. He moved here to help his mother."

"Oh, sorry, I didn't know."

"He wants to get together. I didn't really want to, but I said yes. How could I not."

"Wow. Strange is right. I'll bet it'll be good to talk to him. He was always your buddy."

"I know,...but it's all just too weird and too hard right now."

"I know."

Once again they fell silent. The rain slowed to a patter, and the thunder rolled away in the distance.

"Let's get some more sleep, if we can."

"Promise me you'll think about it. February in India. A dream come true."

"Promise. Now go away." Another sisterly hug, and Boots padded back to her bed and Lissa to hers.

Lissa lay awake until the gray of dawn.

Chapter 30

"Hey, are you getting up? Let's go to church."

Boots poked her head in the door and startled Lissa awake. Lissa threw a pillow at Boots, but she ducked back and jerked the door shut just in time.

Lissa could hear her sister laughing as she bounced down the stairs. Why did she have to wake up perky and talking?

With Boots by her side, Lissa could face church. This was a milestone for Lissa. By appearing in her old home church for the first time since Sean passed away, she was opening herself up to her wound being scratched and picked at by countless expressions of sympathy.

They arrived during the first hymn, so after the service was the only time she had to talk to people. She steeled herself for it. To her surprise, it wasn't so bad, or not so good. Only a few people said anything to her about Sean.

She realized many of the people she grew up with were

dead or gone, moved away. Some just nodded a polite "hello" in Boots's and her direction. She'd forgotten that people really don't know what to say after, "I'm sorry for your loss." The cards she got from the remaining church members who knew her had expressed their sentiments in someone else's words. Still, she had appreciated every card.

Boots never left her side.

Finally, Boots steered Lissa by the elbow toward the ladies room. "I really have to pee."

They each took a stall. It was like the old days at the cabin, using the two-holer outhouse together. Only this time Lissa didn't shine a flashlight up at the spiders, or down.

It was hard to believe Mom and Dad had already gotten rid of some things over the last few years. The basement still had plenty of unused Tupperware, empty coffee cans that might come in handy, a toaster that needed a new cord, and several boxes of ratty, fake evergreen garlands that hadn't seen daylight for many years. All but the Tupperware went in the pile destined for the dump.

Boots and Lissa each hauled a box of empty canning jars out to the garage to be added to the pile of no-longer-wanted stuff that had collected in out-of-sight spots. Next they planned on putting the remaining furniture from the basement rec room on the curb and propping a sign on the settee—*Free*. It would all be gone by evening.

Boots rubbed her nose and left a smudge of dirt under her nose and across her upper lip.

"You're a mess," said Lissa.

"Yeah? So are you. You've got cobwebs in your hair." Boots took a swipe at Lissa's hair.

Lissa dodged. "Time for tea."

They tiptoed down the back hall and into the kitchen,

FIFTY DAYS TO SUNRISE

hoping not to rouse the attention of the guests in the living room. Since Mom had stayed home from church and Dad with her, church had come to her. Two old friends and the pastor and his wife came for tea.

The door to the dining room was shut, but they could hear Mildred Nelson, Sally's mother, cackling at something the pastor said. The clink of china teacups on saucers let them know that Dad had gotten out the Crown Staffordshire for the occasion. After lunch Dad had told his girls to skedaddle, that he would take care of tea for the guests. Lissa and Boots decided to tackle the basement—and stay out of sight.

Lissa caught the teakettle at the first hint of a squeal. Not soon enough. In half a minute Mrs. Nelson swung the door open.

"I thought I heard you girls." She grabbed, first Boots, then Lissa, and smothered them with a hug. Her perfume seemed to have a hold on them even after she let go, something with a heavy dose of musk that didn't smell good. "Oh my, Leah, you've got a dirty face. And, Melissa, don't you look thin."

Lissa clenched her teeth, but managed to get out, "You look great, Mrs. Nelson." And she did, for her age. Mrs. Nelson was a billboard for the Mary Kay cosmetics she sold. The wrinkles in her face were well-troweled with foundation, which was fixed in place with powder.

"Leah, you must be doing very well. That's a nice car out front."

Boots smiled. "Oh, thanks, Mrs. Nelson. I do all right."

Lissa smirked, but Mrs. Nelson didn't notice. Back in the underground garage in Chicago, under their million-dollar condo overlooking Lake Michigan, Boots had a top of the line Land Rover parked next to Etienne's Jaguar XK8, both black.

Mrs. Nelson turned to Lissa. "Melissa, I do hope you're doing better."

"Sure. Sure I am." Lissa didn't know what to say, but that seemed to satisfy Mrs. Nelson, and she squeezed Lissa's hand.

Lissa wanted to stare and shake her head in disbelief at Sally's mother; Mrs. Nelson had the sensitivity of a stump. Clearly, Sally's mission in life was to overcompensate for her mother.

"It was so good to see you girls. Do have lots of the cake I brought," she said with a flourish of her hand in the direction of the dining table. And she was gone, back to the party, leaving the door open in her wake, along with a fetid cloud of perfume.

Now the sisters had a dilemma. They could see the towering layered chocolate cake through the door, but to get to it they would be seen by the pastor and his wife, as well as Georgina Hill. Helplessly, they looked at each other, shrugged, and got plates out of the cupboard.

"Ooooo, it's Lissa and Boots," shrilled Mrs. Hill. They were trapped: entangled in the net, fish caught by the gills.

The scene from the kitchen was repeated with Georgina Hill. Then they exchanged brief pleasantries with Pastor and his wife, telling him how much they appreciated his sermon this morning. They cut huge slices of cake and retreated to the kitchen where they grabbed their tea mugs and headed for the back patio. They collapsed on the lawn chairs, barely stifling their giggles.

Chapter 31

Too soon, Boots threw a goodbye wave back at her family as she pulled away from the curb. She said she wanted to go topless one more time before she had to turn in the convertible.

Lissa waved and sucked in her lower lip. She didn't want to watch her sister disappear down the road. What she wanted to do was stamp her foot in frustration. But she didn't.

They watched until the Mustang and Boots's flying ponytail turned onto College and out of sight. And with that—the air was let out of the tires, the champagne went flat, the fizz was gone from the Coke. Boots had that effect. The snap, crackle, and pop just drove off.

Lissa gave her Mom and Dad a wan smile. "I think I'll go for a run, okay?"

Before she could see her mother's reaction, she retreated to the house. She didn't need her mother's permission to go for a run, for heaven's sake. She couldn't believe she'd put it in the form of a question. Dad said something, but she didn't catch it as she bounded up the front steps.

Coming down the kitchen steps in her running togs, Lissa heard the phone ring. Mom called out from the living room. "Lissa, honey, it's Dwight Humphrey for you."

Rats. She picked up the kitchen extension.

"Got it, Mom." The phone clicked when Mom hung up. "Hi, Humpy." Lissa noticed she didn't have much enthusiasm in her voice.

"Hi. Did I call at a bad time?"

"No, I'm just headed out for a run."

"Oh...well, I'm calling about that dinner. What about Thursday?"

She remembered she had promised to go to dinner with Humpy. "Uh...sure. I guess that would work."

"What about the supper club?"

"Sure."

"Pick you up about six?"

Mild panic clutched at her stomach. "Um...how about I just meet you there." A split second of uncomfortable silence hung on the line.

"Sure. Six o'clock then. I'm looking forward to seeing you, Lissa."

"Yeah, me too. See you then."

Flustered, Lissa hung up. She hightailed it out the back door, not wanting to answer Mom's questions.

Thoughts pounded in her head as her feet pounded the sidewalk. She didn't consciously make any decisions about where to run. She ran because she had to, but she couldn't get her thoughts cleared out. She ran like a cat trailing a string of tin cans.

Boots. India. What a crazy scheme. But how could she let Boots down? She expected to hear a sharp *clang*: the jaws of a leghold trap snapping around her ankle. She pictured herself in India—imagined the smell of urine hanging over the country like a yellow-tinged cloud.

India? Why would she go to India? Well, just because

Boots asked her to. At least she said she'd think about it. Maybe even pray about it.

As she thought about praying about going to India, she cast a wary glance heavenward. Maybe if she kept her head down, God wouldn't notice her and He'd leave her alone, not ask anything of her. How could she give anything when she was running on fumes?

Humpy. Dwight. Whatever. Why wouldn't he leave her alone either?

She ran faster, harder. Sweat dripped in her eyes, and she swiped her forearm across her brow. It didn't help much.

Here she was, complaining bitterly about the miseries of her life, when over 3,000 people had been killed, turned to dust, in one act of terrorism. An act of madness—evil. And the country was at war. Was anything worse than war?

Nausea bubbled in her stomach. She slowed her pace and stopped—head down, hands on her knees, gasping for breath. Her breakfast left her in one convulsing heave. She wrenched herself upright to avoid falling.

This was ridiculous. She was sick of herself. She wiped the back of her hand across her mouth, but the sour taste was still there.

She glanced at the mess in the gutter and hoped it would rain soon to wash away the evidence of her weakness. She hoped no one had seen her, but didn't look around to find out.

She started running again, not quite so hard, but hard enough to stay near the edge of uncomfortable. She could only focus on her physical discomfort.

A hot flash engulfed her from the neck up. It felt scalding on top of already burning with exertion. She slowed to a fast jog, bewildered by the flames licking her neck. The more slowly she jogged, the more the burning sensation subsided, until, when she was down to a trot, it was gone. She continued at this pace another ten minutes or so, then dropped to a walk, hands on her hips, for the cool down before home.

Lissa shook her head. Not a healthy run. But she had done it anyway.

I love you, my child.

It wasn't an audible voice. More like a sentence that popped into her head. But it was there.

She stopped and hung her head in utter defeat—surrender.

"Okay, Lord," she whispered. "I give up." What else could she do. She faced a blank wall.

Time for a dose of Sally.

Sally stood, planted in front of her kitchen sink, fists pressed in where her waist used to be, resembling an indignant hen. Lissa had just finished confessing that she'd beautified Gifford with a pile of sick in the gutter. She cringed, waiting for Sally to take a flapping run at her.

"Well!" Sally stared intently at Lissa. "That does it. We're going on a retail therapy expedition."

Lissa opened her mouth to protest, but Sally raised a stop-sign hand. "Nope. Button it. My treat." Again the hand up.

Her generous friend had done this in the past, so Lissa knew there was no point trying to refuse.

Sally produced a large cinnamon-orange roll on a plate and clacked it down on the table in front of Lissa.

"Here, you keep your keister right in that chair and eat this while I change. I'm waiting till you take the first bite."

"Really, I'm all right."

"Eat."

Lissa obediently plowed her upper lip into the drift of buttercream frosting and bit into the roll. She nodded approvingly.

"Right. I won't be ten minutes. Then I'll drive you home so you can change."

"But..." Lissa spoke through a mouthful to an empty

FIFTY DAYS TO SUNRISE

kitchen. Sally was already on her way upstairs.

Chapter 32

Sean

Lissa leaned back on the chair and looked at the single word she had just written at the top of the first page, the pen leaden in her hand. She touched the pink enameled calla lily at her throat—the necklace Sally had bought for her—and stared past her reflection in the kitchen window out to the backyard darkness. Finally, resting her hand on the beautiful paper, pen poised, she began to write—the story of her life with Sean.

July 1, 2003

The beginning is the end. The end is the beginning. Both feel true.
Sean is gone. November 15, 2001, Sean died in Amsterdam.

The starkness of those words hung cold in the air, hovering over the page, waiting to shatter into a thousand icy crystals before landing on the page. Her lips fell stupidly agape. Sean's death was like a punch that had permanently knocked the wind out of her. She willed her hand to keep writing.

> Sean was in Amsterdam for the third annual showing and sale of his work at the prestigious Van Alst Gallery. We had been uncertain whether he should go or not after the terrorist attack on the twin towers. Mostly I was uncertain. In the end, he convinced me he should go. Sean reminded me that not a single person was going to go to heaven before the Lord's timing. Anyway, the paintings were already on their way to Amsterdam by container ship. He said we can't live in fear and let the terrorists win.
>
> The show was a wild success. All of the paintings sold, except one. Sean had called me the afternoon before, excited about the show. Art bigwigs from all over Europe had come to the champagne reception. He was bringing home a bank draft for $177,000. Two of his paintings would hang in museums. We kissed over the phone, said, "I love you," and hung up. He'd be home in two days.
>
> That night, while I slept, Sean was on his morning run along the Prince's Canal when he collapsed and died.

She wrote what she remembered of that night—the phone call. It seemed important. Later, if she couldn't remember, it would bother her. But it was hard to imagine not remembering something seared into flesh.

> My gut clenched as the ringing phone jolted me awake. But then I thought, it was probably Sean calling from Amsterdam—and I snapped on the light.
> "Honey?"
> A woman asked me questions. A woman I could barely understand, her accent was so thick. A woman I

did not want to be talking to.

"Mrs. Maguire, I regret to inform you that this morning your husband collapsed and died. The emergency medical team was unable to revive him."

My ears roared. As if trying to block out the woman's voice.

Hell must have visual hallucinations. Light from the bedside lamp seemed to flare. Splotches of brilliance ricochetted around the deep night shadows in the room.

The phone slipped from my grasp, and I vaguely heard it clunk to the floor.

I reached for the phone, desperate to hold on to the connection, wishing it wasn't true, and that the woman would take it all back. I kept falling and landed on my knees. I guess I fainted. Now I know I was falling headlong into a new and terrible life.

When I got to the phone I heard words that still run like ice in my blood: "The local authorities will contact you. They will help you repatriate Mr. Maguire's remains."

I hung up on her.

Choco wagged onto my lap, and I clung to her, deep moans rolling up from a place I'd never known. Choco backed away and whined, poor girl. Alone, I keened into the cold night.

My husband would not be coming home from Amsterdam.

I was told that a passerby administered CPR to Sean until the ambulance arrived. To no avail. I never knew who that man was. I wish I could have thanked him for trying to save my husband's life.

Idiopathic hypertrophic subaortic stenosis. The autopsy diagnosed the cause of death, but provided no reason that made any sense of his death. Sean was healthy, at least we thought so, and then he was dead.

Breathing short, shallow puffs, Lissa read over what she had written. Her hand cramped, and she shook it out. "Dead. Death." Words she could hardly say before, she now seemed compelled to put down on the page in front of her.

> *Death. There isn't any word more ugly. The period at the end of the sentence that was a life.*
> *I have felt like I've been dying with Sean—and I've been running for my life. But no matter how fast I run, Death keeps pace with me—a ravening wolf, running me down to the kill. I am exhausted.*
> *To die so young...*

Lissa was stuck. She put the pen down and wandered out to the backyard. She walked along the flower borders. The grass was springy and moist under her bare feet. The gentle night breeze smelled of damp earth and sweet flowers, the shrub roses.

She made a circuit of the yard and sat in a chair on the patio. Bouncing rhythmically for a time shook her thoughts loose. Resolved, she went back to writing her love story—the beginning.

> *We were lying on a blanket in the warm spring sun, May 4, 1974. We'd gotten out of New York City for the day. Away from noise and demands. Graduation was days away. Final projects were done. Sean wanted to go hiking and for a picnic.*
> *Sean poured us each a glass of wine, a Châteauneuf-du-Pape, and we toasted, "To us." We bent to kiss over our glasses, a soft, gentle kiss, and sipped our wine. We drank from the depths of each other's eyes.*
> *"I love you," Sean said.*
> *"I know you do." I was flippant and a little*

uncomfortable. The L-word hadn't passed between us that many times.

"Seriously, Lissa, I really love you." He put a lot of drama into the L-word and kissed me again.

"Seriously, Sean, I love you too." I caught the slight shift in his eyes and was afraid I'd hurt him. I hadn't meant to sound mocking.

"I really do love you." I kissed him a little kiss, then settled back on the blanket, holding my wine glass on my stomach.

I opened my eyes after a few moments of silence. Sean was lying on his side, raised up on one elbow, his head propped on his hand, intently studying my face. He reached over, took my glass from me, and set it on top of the picnic hamper next to his. I smiled at him.

Sean looked down at me. "Melissa Makkinen, will you marry me?"

The question I'd longed to hear hung between us like a gossamer thread. I searched his eyes and found what I wanted. "Yes," I said softly. "Yes, I will."

I felt unable to move, as if sitting up would break the spell.

Sean rolled toward me and wrapped his arm around my waist. His other hand gently twined in my hair behind my head as he drew me to him. Our lips melted together. Reluctant to end the moment, we drew breath from each other.

The kiss had to end, and it did.

Sean gave me another soft kiss. A kiss that sealed our engagement.

"Melissa Maguire," he said.

"That sounds nice." I had said it a hundred times to myself over the last few months.

At our wedding that summer, and for every anniversary for twenty-seven years, we drank

Châteauneuf-du-Pape and toasted—"To us."

Fighting tears, finally unsuccessfully, Lissa closed the journal. Tears dripped onto the soft leather. She didn't care. The tear stains were words unspoken, more eloquent than anything she could write. She clutched the journal to her heart and went up to bed.

Chapter 33

Lissa woke, feeling a spasm deep within her body. Such a familiar feeling. One she used to delight in. She shut her eyes tight, clinging to the fragile image of being with Sean.

Instinctively, she put her hands flat over her abdomen and gently pressed down. She didn't know if she was trying to hold the feeling there a little longer, or trying to comfort herself—or both.

And then it was gone.

Tears slipped down her temples. Her body had betrayed her—cruelly reminding her of what she could no longer share with Sean.

Lissa ached for Sean's touch. She wanted him to stroke her hair. To run his fingers over her cheeks, down her neck. To have him pull her to him.

Her hand reached out to the place in the bed where she wanted to find her husband.

It was torture to lie there, helplessly remembering. She got up and switched on the light in the window seat alcove. Writing would ease the pain. She sat cross-legged on the cushion and opened the beautiful journal on her lap.

> Sean was the best lover a wife could ever want.
> We loved each other with a love so pure and sweet that there were times we felt like we'd just bathed in honey.
> I trusted him completely.
> When we were together it was always good. No, that's not true. Sometimes it was unbelievably good. So good, we wanted to run outside naked and shout to the entire world how wonderful it had just been. But we didn't. No, that's not true either. Sometimes, at the dark of the moon, we'd run outside, jump in the lake, laughing, and embrace again, letting the water add its caresses.
> And our love got even better over the years. When we were young we couldn't have been convinced that it could get any better. But it did. There was nothing like the practiced, familiar, we've-been-here-before love that ended a busy day and sent us off to sleep in each other's arms.
> I miss his touch so much. The sweet way he'd lightly touch me as he passed. The deep, firm, longing way he'd touch me. So many ways and places we touched each other. I'm no longer sure of my body without Sean's touch. His touch traced the outline of me.
> I miss the scent of Sean.

Lissa stopped, pen suspended over her husband's name. She could go on, and on, and on about Sean—his touch, his body, his love. She was writing in ink, committed to the page. This journal wasn't meant for publication, but she realized she had to be conscious of her children possibly reading this someday, discovering it in a drawer after she was gone. Lissa didn't want Jack and Shannon to be embarrassed or revolted, just warmed again by their parents' love as they read her memories.

She didn't think she had crossed any boundaries her children would regret. But she decided to stop. She would have to silently live with living without.

Chapter 34

"Oh, goodness, honey," Mom dramatically put a hand to her chest. "I do wish you'd wear wooden shoes." Lissa had sat on the top step in the kitchen before Mom turned back to the sink and saw her.

Lissa grinned. "G'morning, Mom. I didn't mean to startle you. It would be a real tragedy if you dropped that coffee pot before we got our fix."

Mom filled the pot and finished the coffee-making ritual. The aroma of fresh-brewed coffee instantly permeated the kitchen as the water dripped through the grounds.

From her perch Lissa surveyed the familiar scene just below her and beyond to the garden. She rested her elbows on her knees, chin in her hands. The open kitchen windows let in the morning air, and let out the smell of coffee.

The house was more and more of a mess, with open boxes on the tables and boxes here and there on the floor. Stacks of newspapers for packing added to the mess. The corners of each room were starting to pile up with boxes already filled and taped shut. Each box labeled with its contents and destination room. It looked like a move was underway.

The garden looked the same as always. Except for the heap of trash next to the garage.

"So, you're going out with Dwight Humphrey."

Lissa was momentarily taken aback by Mom's comment. "I'm not going *out* with him. It's not like it's a date or anything." Lissa fought starting out the day annoyed at her mother. She knew Mom didn't mean to be insensitive.

"He's such a nice boy."

"Mom, he's older than I am. Has two grown daughters. And he's already retired from the Navy." She wanted to add, "And he's got a dead spouse too," but she didn't.

"I know, but I still remember the two of you doing chemistry homework at the kitchen table here."

Lissa closed her eyes and began counting.

"I hear his mother isn't doing very well. Getting very forgetful. She's in the assisted living at the Dakota Apartments."

Lissa was up to four, counting slowly.

"He was always so nice to you."

"I know, Mom. We're just having dinner. Two old friends. Just like Sally and me, okay?"

"Ready for coffee?" Mom apparently got the hint and changed the subject.

"Magic words."

Carefully holding her warm mug with both hands, Lissa meandered slowly around the backyard. The morning damp grass was cold, colder than last night. The flowered coffee mug seemed right for a stroll in the garden.

In the sunlight, the turmoil of last night, of the whole day, didn't seem quite so catastrophic. But her denial was fast coming unraveled, and she didn't have a grip on it yet.

Mom came out the back door. The sun on her face made the bruises shine yellow and green, but a lighter shade than they had been. "Phone for you, Lissa."

FIFTY DAYS TO SUNRISE

Oh, not Humpy again. She went inside to take the call and get it over with.

"Hi, Aunt Lissa, it's Ellie."

"Oh, hi, Ellie," Lissa was pleased and relieved to hear her niece's voice. When the twins called they were gurgling with enthusiasm about being at the farm and always had something fun to tell Lissa. Last week it was about the present of a live chipmunk Tigger brought them. Fortunately, they were able to save the little critter before he became a kitty dinner. Lissa hadn't told the girls about their grandma's fall. "How are things on the farm?"

"Oh, they're great. Couldn't be better. Rachel and I are just having an awesome time."

"What have you been up to this week?"

"Not much." Ellie paused. "Last week we went down to Camden with Jack and Meagan. We went for a couple hour sail. It was awesome. The wind was just great. We really screamed. Rachel and I got to help reef the sails."

"That sounds like such fun. Which ship did you go out on?"

"*The Dirty Whale*. What a riot of a name for a boat."

"I know the owners. They're nice people."

"Yeah." Again a pause. "Aunt Lissa?"

Lissa smelled a setup. "Yes, that's me."

"Um...Rachel found a kitten a couple days ago."

Lissa had to prompt her. "A kitten?"

"Yeah...a really little one. Someone must have dropped him off at the end of the driveway. He's way too little to have gotten there by himself. Rachel found him when she walked out to get the mail. He let out these tiny little mews when he saw her. He was hiding in the bushes."

Lissa knew where this was going. "That happens sometimes. People are so cruel to just abandon those poor little helpless things." She played it out, teasing Ellie.

"Aunt Lissa, he's so cute. He looks like a little bitty panda."

"How old do you think he is?"

"Well, the vet said—"

"The vet?"

"Um, yes....We took him in right away. We didn't think you'd mind. But we weren't sure what to feed such a little kitten."

Lissa heard the choked tears in Ellie's voice, so Lissa immediately let go of the teasing.

"Of course not. I would have suggested you take him in if you hadn't already. Well done."

"Thanks. The vet said he's only about four weeks old. It just makes me so mad at whoever dumped him off. He's way too young to be away from his mother."

"What did the vet tell you about feeding him?"

"We got some special milk formula he likes. And he eats wet kitten food. He's doing great. We take turns getting up in the night to make sure he's okay and to feed him.

"And Aunt Lissa, you wouldn't believe it. He's so little, at first he couldn't go to the bathroom by himself. The vet showed us how to help him, like the mother cat would. Only we used a wet cotton ball. He's fine now though. He uses the litter box like a champ."

"Wow, he must be young. Sounds like you and Rachel are being great moms."

Ellie was silent another moment. "Will you keep him?"

"Of course I will." Lissa smiled. It took Ellie long enough to get to the question. "There's always room for another cat on the farm."

"Oh, thanks, Aunt Lissa." Ellie bubbled over. "I told Rachel I was sure you would."

"Did you name him?"

"Galahad."

"My, that's a fancy name for such a little kitty."

"Galahad was King Arthur's noblest knight."

"Sounds like a good name for him. I like it."

"Well, gotta go now. I've got chores to do." Ellie sounded

FIFTY DAYS TO SUNRISE

like she couldn't be more pleased about the situation.

"Is Rachel there?" Lissa wanted to talk to her too.

"No, she went to town to grocery shop."

"Wow. I'm so impressed with you girls. I can't tell you how much I appreciate your help this summer."

"No problem. We love doing it. How about next summer?"

Lissa chuckled. "You never know. Love you. Tell Rachel I love her. And tell her thank you for rescuing Galahad. I can't wait to meet him."

"Gotcha. And back atcha. Bye."

"Bye-bye."

Mom came back into the kitchen for a coffee refill. "What are you grinning about?"

"I have a new kitten waiting for me at home. And the best nieces."

Chapter 35

As Lissa drove her mother's car out to Big Lake Supper Club, she thought about Humpy and how long they had known each other. His family moved to Gifford in the middle of the school year when Humpy was in eighth grade and Lissa was in seventh. He quickly gained notoriety as the class nerd, but it didn't seem to bother him. On a dare from Jessica, Lissa asked him to dance at a Sadie Hawkins dance. They danced a silly Mashed Potato, more like a grape stomp. After that, they just had fun. Humpy was by far the smartest person Lissa knew.

Life at home hadn't been easy for Humpy. His father drank too much, and his mother didn't drink enough. Maybe it would have mellowed her out. His mother was a hard woman: she probably had to be. A husband who didn't have a good job, when he had a job, and six children couldn't have been easy. But the worst was losing two children three months apart; one child died of pneumonia, and the other, the only girl, of crib death. Lissa couldn't imagine what that would do to a woman. It seemed to utterly break Humpy's mother, and she didn't have much to give to her surviving children after that.

Lissa wondered what Humpy's mother was like now. She dismissed the thought, assuming that it must be better, since Humpy had come home to help her.

Lissa pulled into the parking lot. She wasn't eager to jump out of the car. All this reminiscing since she'd been home was exhausting. She reminded herself this was most certainly not a date. It was no different than meeting Sally for coffee. She twisted the rearview mirror so she could see herself in it and applied lipstick. The fact that Humpy was a man had nothing to do with it, but she fervently wished Humpy was a girlfriend.

The hostess showed her to the table Humpy had reserved—out on the deck overlooking the lake. Humpy was already there, waiting for her. He got up when Lissa approached, and, on the inside, Lissa sank down.

"Sit. Please." She didn't want to be treated like a date. "Hi, fancy meeting you here." She tried to sound light-hearted.

"Howdy, ma'am. Mighty nice to see you." Humpy tipped his imaginary hat.

Lissa sat down, relieved. This was the Humpy she knew.

"Can I get you a drink, Lissa?"

"Sure. Red wine please."

He beckoned the waitress over and ordered Lissa's wine and a beer for himself.

They looked at each other over the table settings.

"Awk-waard," Lissa singsonged to him.

Humpy laughed. "Oh, don't feel awkward. This is just dinner with an old friend."

"I know, but we've never gone out to dinner together before."

"Prom doesn't count?"

Lissa laughed. "No, there was a bunch of us."

Humpy wore khaki trousers with knife-sharp creases, and a yellow polo shirt sporting a Pebble Beach Golf Links logo.

"I see you're a golfer. Have you played there?" She pointed at the logo.

FIFTY DAYS TO SUNRISE

"Yeah, many times. I was stationed in San Diego after Vietnam, so it was easy to get to. Not so easy to play, let me tell you. But what a great place. It's where I got my hole in one."

"Really?"

"No, but I wished for it a lot." He grinned mischievously. "I keep trying. Now I'm hoping for a hole in one here at the country club." Gifford didn't have a country club, but the municipal golf course was affectionately called that. "Do you play?"

"Good grief, no. Why would I do that? I have enough frustration in my life."

"You should try it."

"You're kidding? Stand like I have to pee and try and hit a little white ball with a stick, and then miss. Not a chance."

Humpy laughed. A familiar sound.

Lissa blushed. "Oh, sorry. I guess a simple no would have been enough."

Time passed as their conversation wound back and forth between the past and the present. They talked about their kids. They were all doing well. They talked about their siblings. Lissa's were great. Humpy's were distant or drunk. They talked about their jobs. His was good and very part-time. Hers was stuck. But they didn't talk about their spouses.

After dinner they shared a brandy alexander, two glasses, and watched the coots on the lake do their silly head bobs as twilight darkened. It was nice to not talk too.

Humpy wouldn't let Lissa pay for her dinner. Her mouth went dry, but she said, "Thanks."

They walked to the parking lot together. He opened the car door for her and she quickly ducked in. She wished she could have raced ahead and opened her own car door, but that was ridiculous.

Humpy held the door open. "Can I call you again?"

Lissa's stomach flipped over, and she gave him a pained look. "Humpy, don't ask. Just call. Like a friend."

"You're right. I will." He shut the door and stood back.

Lissa turned the key in the ignition. The engine chugged and died. She tried again. Same thing. Then she pumped the gas hard. It wouldn't start.

Now this was really ridiculous. She rolled down the window.

Before she could say anything, Humpy threw back his head and laughed. "This is like a Woody Allen movie," he said. "Pop the hood and I'll check it out. Although, I smell gas, so at the very least, it's flooded."

Humpy was under the hood only a minute. "There's the culprit. A loose spark plug wire. Did you have trouble starting it?"

"Sort of. It took a couple cranks, but then it started. It did seem to run a little rough though."

"Can you describe the sound?"

She looked at him and narrowed her eyes. "No." Silly woman makes fool of herself trying to imitate car noises—oh no, not falling for that. Humpy didn't try to hide his sly smile as he turned back to the engine.

He monkeyed under the hood for a couple more minutes. "Well, I think that should do it. You should take it in to the garage pretty quick and get the wires replaced. There's one that's a little frayed and the contact isn't good. New spark plugs wouldn't be a bad idea either."

He opened the door of the big silver truck she'd parked next to, reached behind the passenger seat, pulled out a rag, and wiped his hands. "Try it now."

The Toyota started up. "I'll follow you to make sure it's okay." Lissa nodded. "Hey, I enjoyed our dinner, Lissa."

"Yeah, me too. Thanks." She smiled, but felt mildly and irrationally annoyed. Humpy's truck roared to a start and off they went, a caravan of two, back the six miles to Gifford.

She resented having to rely on a man that wasn't Sean.

Chapter 36

She ignored the Fourth of July. Sean and Lissa used to enjoy going to fireworks, so she sat alone in her room with her journal. She wanted a glass of wine for company, but resisted. Lissa could have gone to the fireworks with Humpy; he asked. She just didn't want to.

Listening to the booms coming from the country club on the edge of town, Lissa opened her journal, her beautiful journal. The hours she'd spent on this window seat, writing—childish stories of smugglers and damsels in distress, poems drenched in teenage hormones and angst, stories of romance, hopes, and dreams. And now she was writing her own story, her own romance.

> *Sean was cleaning his brushes when I walked into the tiny bedroom upstairs that served as his studio when we first moved to the farm. He was working on a painting, a commission by the largest bank in Boston. It was of the Boston Harbor in the early 1770s: a tangle of ships, masts, rigging, and sails. It was magnificent, and it*

would bring in $7,000, a lot of money in 1975. The bank wanted to unveil it for the Bicentennial. The concept for the painting was that the Boston Tea Party had been done to death, so this painting was to portend the struggles to come. The mood of the painting was ominous with the Redcoats and the Colonists clearly divided and wary of each other.

Sean stepped back, at least as far as he could in the small room, to look at his work. "What does it need?"

I squeezed behind him against the wall and wrapped my arms around his waist. "It needs a dog."

He snapped his fingers and looked delighted at the suggestion. "You're right." He spun in my arms and kissed me solidly and quickly on the mouth. "You're a genius."

I let go, although to continue to try and hold on to him would have been like holding a wriggling puppy, and he reached for his sketch book on the table. He quickly sketched a dog, then two dogs playing tug of war with a rope on the wharf. "Got it. Perfect."

"Did I say the painting needs a dog? I meant, we need a dog."

"What?" The genius at work wasn't paying attention to me.

"I said, we need a dog, a big one."

Sean stopped, looked at me, and grinned. "You are so right."

"Well, that was easy. I thought now that we're married we're supposed to argue."

"Why? I want a dog too, a big one. Would you rather argue about it?"

"Of course not, Dopey."

"How about a Lab? Perfect for a couple that lives on a lake."

"Yeah? Sounds like muddy footprints all over the house all the time."

FIFTY DAYS TO SUNRISE

"In the house? I was thinking the barn."

"No dog of mine's going to live in the barn. If you can't have the dog with you, what's the point of having one?" I dug in on this.

"Oh-oh. This is starting to sound like an argument."

I folded my arms across my chest. "It won't be an argument if you agree with me."

Sean eyed me, a glint of mischief sparkling in his eyes, but then he folded his arms and said, "Yellow or black?"

"Doesn't matter to me, whichever you want. So long as it lives in the house."

"Let's go check the Sunday paper right now."

And that's how Black Bear came into our lives. He was the first in the litter to bound up to us. When I knelt down to him, he knocked me flat with his enormous paws and started licking my face. It was love at first lick. He grew and grew until he weighed in at a well-muscled ninety-six pounds. We had our big dog. Our first child.

And I had my house dog, which meant that everything tail height and lower had to be immovable. Bear once swept the coffee table clean with a single wag.

Sean loved Bear. Sean would run off the end of the dock, a blur of madras shorts, with Bear right behind. Double cannonballs, they hit the water. Sean splashed Bear, and Bear splashed Sean. Bear's huge paws slapped the water as he paddled in pursuit of Sean. Bear would have laughed if he could have, Sean certainly did. They played tag until Sean got tired, then Bear chased sticks in the water.

Life was good.

Lissa rubbed her eyes. The booms had stopped. She was tired of thinking, and tired of looking back at the past for tonight.

A short run couldn't hurt.

Chapter 37

Lissa was bored. On Sunday afternoon Humpy called and asked if she wanted to walk the course with him while he played golf on Monday. She agreed without thinking. Golf was a stupid game. She'd said so frequently.

She met Humpy at the country club. On the putting green, he waved her over. The ball clattered into the hole.

"Hi, Lissa."

"Hi back." She stopped in front of him, hands on her hips. "You know, I don't think I can keep calling you Humpy. It seems ridiculous to call you a nickname from when we were kids. What should I call you?"

He laughed. "Most people call me Dwight. It's my name."

"I know, but I don't think I've ever called you that. Feels kind of weird. It sounds so formal."

"My pa named me after Supreme Commander, Gen. Dwight D. Eisenhower. Pa was a swabbie in World War II."

"A what?"

"A swabbie, a sailor. He was in the Navy. Don't you know? That's why I joined the Navy."

"No, I guess I didn't." She realized there was a lot she didn't know about Dwight Humphrey. "Well, Dwight, are you going to show me how good you are at this game?"

"Yes, ma'am." Dwight shouldered the ridiculously heavy bag of clubs and headed toward the first tee.

"Are you going to carry those?" She knew enough about golf to know that golf carts had been invented and seemed to be a handy thing.

"It's good exercise. C'mon."

"If you're a masochist."

Lissa watched while Dwight balanced the stupid little white ball on the tee, stood there in that ridiculous stance, waggled the club around, and took a mighty whack at the ball. The ball sizzled through the air so fast she couldn't see where it went.

Dwight shaded his eyes against the mid-morning sun and pointed to where the ball had landed. She couldn't believe how far away it was.

"Wow. How'd you do that?"

"Oh, that's only about 250 yards. The longest ball I hit was 300 yards. Not as strong as I used to be. C'mon. Now we walk to where I hit the ball."

She fell into stride with Dwight. Though he wasn't more than a couple of inches taller than Lissa, he moved fast, even carrying a big bag of clubs.

"How do you know which club to use?" she asked as Dwight picked a club from the assortment.

"Practice." He grinned.

He said he parred the first hole. Apparently that was good. He marked his score card, and they moved on to the next hole.

The golf course was beautiful. Drifts of blue, pink, and white hydrangeas were interspersed among the trees bordering the course, and lavender clouds of Russian sage scented the air. A creek curved in and out through the holes, and artfully carved sand traps laid in wait here and there.

FIFTY DAYS TO SUNRISE

"Fore!" someone yelled. Dwight grabbed Lissa's arm and yanked her to the side as a ball arced over her head.

Her first instinct was to pull away. "Hey!" She rubbed her arm reflexively.

"Fore means 'look out'."

"Huh?"

"It's what you yell when you've hit a wild ball and someone might get hit. A golf ball can really hurt. Sorry, did I hurt your arm?"

"No, it's okay. You just startled me. I was busy looking at the scenery."

Somewhere, as they marched between spots where the ball landed, Lissa asked Dwight about his mother.

"She's not doing great. Dementia seems to be setting in."

"Is she still in the apartments?"

"For now, but she's gonna have to move to the assisted living section pretty quick now. She doesn't want to, but she's not gonna have a choice much longer."

"Oh, that's too bad. That'll be a big change for her."

"Not really so much. It just means going from small to smaller. She hasn't got much to move. It sure would be easier on me, knowing she's got meals taken care of and has medical people on call."

"Then why won't she do it?"

"Oh, you know Mother. She won't do what she doesn't want to do."

"Hmm, seems like I remember she was kind of strong willed."

"Strong willed. That's an understatement. Stubborn as a stake, is more like it. And nasty as a junkyard dog when she's crossed."

Dwight putted into the hole.

"Well, I'm sure she appreciates having you here to help her."

"Not so's you'd notice. But, yes, in her way, I'm sure she

does. I stop in every couple days."

"It must help having your brother in town."

Dwight snorted a laugh. "You're kidding. He's drunk most of the time. Lucky if he gets over to see Mother one Sunday afternoon a month." Dwight picked up speed walking to the next hole. He seemed agitated, but was trying to keep a lid on it.

"Dwight, I'm sorry."

"Yeah, me too." He looked straight ahead with a grim set to his mouth and clearly didn't want to say another word about his mother, or his brother.

He whacked the ball in silence through the next hole.

"One under par," he said with a grin, finally breaking the silence. "I got a birdie on that hole. It was a par four, and I holed it in three. That's good."

"Oh, well then, congratulations."

"You want to try hitting the drive on the next hole?"

"Me? You've got to be kidding. This is a stupid game, remember?" But Lissa admitted to herself that, up close, it was rather fascinating.

"You can do it. You'd have a great coach."

"Really? I don't see one anywhere around here. You don't mean that old guy up ahead?"

At the next tee he took out the driver and set up the ball. "Here, this is how you stand. And this is how you grip the club. Keep your head down, keep your eyes on the ball. Bring the club back and swing, keeping your eyes on the ball." And with that, he sailed the ball out of sight.

"Now you try it."

"Oh, all right." She was surprised how little coaxing it took to get her to step up and take hold of the driver. Dwight adjusted her hands on the club.

"Now, address the ball."

"Hello, ball, my name is Lissa. What's yours?"

He laughed. "No, hold the club face next to it, but don't

touch it, and sort of feel your body position. Make sure your grip feels good."

"My body position feels absolutely ridiculous, and my grip feels like a handshake that missed."

"Looks it too."

"Thanks, some coach you are."

Dwight stepped behind Lissa, reached around her, put his hands over hers, and started to draw the swing back.

Lissa jumped like she was stuck with a high-voltage cattle prod.

"Humpy!" They both dropped the club, the ball fell off the tee, and they split apart in a flap of arms and legs, trying to regain their balance.

"Geez, Lissa, I'm so sorry."

"What are you doing?" She didn't know whether to be hurt, angry, or just confused.

Dwight wiped a hand over his balding head and looked apologetically at her. "I'm really sorry. I just forgot myself there. Old wires touching I guess." He bent over and picked up the driver. His face was radish red.

"What?"

"Old wires in my old brain. I tried to teach Becky to play before she got sick."

"Oh."

"Yeah, I thought maybe we could find *something* we could do together that she would enjoy. But it didn't work. She hated it."

Lissa saw the anguish on Dwight's face and forgot her own jangling thoughts. She wiped her hands on her shorts and reached for the driver. "Here, give me that thing. It can't be that hard."

She replaced the ball on the tee and tried to do everything Dwight had showed her.

"Hello, ball. Now you be nice and go where I tell you to." She hauled off and walloped the ball as hard as she could, spinning herself around and off balance. To her astonishment, she actually hit the stupid little white ball. Lissa squealed like a girl who just got her first base hit at bat.

Dwight tracked the ball with his experienced eyes. He yelled, "Fore!" just before the ball splashed down in the creek—on the fairway next to them. The golfers standing near the splashdown point waved.

"Hey, that was great! You hit it! We're playing *this* hole, however, but it was a great start." Dwight gave her a light slap on the back, which she didn't mind one bit.

"Let's go get it. Can I keep it as a souvenir? The first golf ball I ever hit."

"You got it. I think we should get you on the driving range next time. You might be a golfer."

She grinned. Maybe.

They finished the ninth hole back at the clubhouse. During lunch under an umbrella on the patio, Lissa fired questions at Dwight about golf and all the unfamiliar terms she heard him use. He seemed happy to oblige her curiosity.

Sitting back after finishing her club sandwich, she dabbed her mouth with her napkin and looked at Dwight. There was no one sitting within earshot, so she asked the question that had been nagging her.

"How are you doing since Becky died?"

Dwight downed the last of his ice tea and looked thoughtful. "You know, Lissa, it was really terrible, Becky's death. Cancer's such a cruel way to die." He swirled the ice in his glass. "This may sound bad, but I grieved more about losing her during our marriage, than losing her to death. Hope for our marriage died with her. Now it just is what it was."

Lissa didn't know what to say. She knew Becky was a California rich girl, and seemed pretty snooty, but she didn't know Dwight wasn't happy in his marriage.

"She'd even wanted to separate. I don't know why, we lived pretty separate lives anyway. But then she got sick and decided

she'd stay."
"I'm sorry."
"Yep, me too." He threw his napkin down on his plate, smiled at Lissa, and said, "Now let's go show that little white ball who's boss."
"Correction—*stupid* little white ball. But I thought we were done."
"No. We've got nine holes to go—the back nine."
She groaned. But really, this was fun.

Chapter 38

Mom was out in the garden doing some after-dinner pruning, and Dad was in his chair reading the paper. Time to ask Dad one of those big questions.
"Dad?"
"Missy?" Dad was such a tease. He put his paper down and gave her his full attention. Lissa sat in Mom's chair.
"I feel ridiculous asking this, but I really need to ask something that you'd think I'd know the answer to, but I don't."
"What's that?"
"Remember when Pip died and I talked to you about how mad I was at God?"
"Hmm, I guess so. That was a long time ago. But go on."
"Well, sometimes...I don't know...you'd think, for as long as I've walked with the Lord, I'd understand His ways better, but I don't." She couldn't find the words, so she left it at that, hoping Dad would know what she meant.
Dad didn't respond for a minute. He stared at some spot straight ahead. "Missy, I think the older I get, the more of a

mystery it all is."

"Well, that's not very helpful. Come on, you're supposed to be the Bible Answer Guy."

"No really. But the older I get, I've also come to know beyond a shadow of a doubt that I don't have to figure it out. I just trust God completely. For everything. It's so complicated—it's really simple." Dad looked satisfied with his answer.

"But, Dad," Lissa whined like a sixteen-year-old again, "I need more."

"Why?"

She looked blankly at him, and he went on. "Missy, something terrible happened many years ago. I remember, I slammed my fists down on the arms of the chair, not understanding why God allowed it. Then I said, out loud, without even thinking, 'Though you slay me, yet will I trust you.' It really caught me up short because I hadn't consciously thought of saying that, it just came out."

"Hmm, sounds like Job."

"That's right. Did Job deserve what he got? His wife told him to curse God and die, but he didn't. He kept on trusting God. And God replaced all that he'd lost."

"But he didn't get his children back."

"No...I'm sure he mourned for them...the rest of his life." Dad shook his head. "Missy, honestly, I've given up trying to understand God. I just praise Him and thank Him for His love."

"I know. And I do. But..." She was feeling annoyed and trapped. Annoyed because she was starting to cry again. She was sick of tears. And trapped because, of course, what her father said was right. It just didn't *feel* right when she missed her husband. "Sean loved the Lord so much. I just don't understand why God let Sean die."

"I know." Dad's eyes reddened and misted over. "I don't either. And I've prayed hard about it, believe me." Dad patted her hand. "Just pray about it, honey." That pat and the admonition would have made her mad coming from anyone else.

Lissa nodded, smearing the tears off her face. "'Neither are your ways my ways,...' I know what God's Word says." She sighed wearily and slumped in her seat. "I know it, but I don't always like it, or understand it. But, you're right, there *is* no answer. Just God's love."

She absently rubbed her wedding ring. "You know, Dad, this has really felt like a test of my faith."

"Refining fire, honey. I don't know how people suffer without God's love. We keep praying for you and Jack and Shannon." Dad wiped a tear from the corner of his eye.

Lissa looked at her father and smiled a deeply sad smile. "Thanks, Dad."

She couldn't think of anything else to do, so she took her journal out to the front porch and sat on the swing. She couldn't open the journal, she just wanted to hold it.

Dad started playing the piano, warming up with a few slow *arpeggios,* undulating up and down the keyboard like small waves on the shore. He played an introduction and then began to play one of Lissa's favorite hymns, *Be Thou My Vision.* The music soothed her. She closed her eyes and rested. Dad played interludes and variations. He played the melody alone, so slowly she savored every thought it evoked.

"Heart of my own heart, whatever befall. Still be my Vision, O Ruler of all."

Whatever befall. She wanted to remember that.

Lissa opened her journal and released the words in her heart.

Sean was a man who had unshakeable faith in his Savior. As hard as this is for me now, I know where Sean is, and I know what he's doing: praising Jesus. So why would I take that away from him? Because I want him back here by my side, next to me in our bed. I need him.

It troubles me sometimes that Sean probably isn't even thinking of me anymore. Would heaven be heaven if, when we get there, we're still aware of what's going on back in our old lives? I know it's a comfort to think that our loved ones are looking down on us, but how can that be? It's heaven. Sean's with Jesus. And I'm alone.

Ah, the finality of writing in pen. When I write my books on the computer, I can erase the evidence of a thought or delete a bunny trail, and no one's the wiser that I was off-track. But here, my complaint to Jesus stands, accusing me. I feel panic grip my heart when I think of Jesus saying to me, "O ye of little faith." I feel so small. It feels like I'm trying to swallow a huge wad of guilt, and it won't go down.

But I didn't do anything wrong—did I? Intellectually, I know I'm not alone. I've walked too many miles with Jesus, and I know better. The disciples struggled in their faith, and they had Jesus in the flesh with them. David cried out in the psalms. Why should it be any easier for me? Or why should I do any better at it than they did? But I should try.

Lissa looked out at the street, her mind a dull blank. In a moment, in ten minutes—it could have been a half an hour—a scripture passage came to mind—the story of Jesus raising Lazarus from the dead. She knew the story, knew it well—but tonight she knew it deep in her heart—and she wrote.

Martha trusted Jesus. She knew if He had come earlier her brother would not have died, but even arriving four days after his death, she trusted Jesus to make things all better. Martha expected eternal life with Jesus for her brother though, not a bodily resurrection that day. Mary too cried in anguish and trusted Jesus would have healed her brother if He had been there before Lazarus died.

"Jesus wept."

Those are the two most beautiful words. My heart feels squeezed, not in fear, but with the grip of love that Jesus has on me. At this moment I know—I know—that Jesus has counted every tear I've shed since Sean died. He has known every raging thought I've had, every time I've snapped at my mother, or my daughter, even before I did it. And He still loves me, just as He loved Mary and Martha. Jesus's compassion is unfathomable. But it's there, whether I feel it or not.

I can grieve for Sean and still trust the Lord. At least I have to keep trying.

"And we know that in all things God works for the good of those who love him, who have been called according to his purpose" isn't a mockery, it's a promise.

Amen. So be it.

I'll remember that I wasn't alone the night I got the phone call at two in the morning. I'll remember that as I crumpled to the floor, the wreckage of my life exploded around me, Jesus was kneeling beside me, holding me together. And He wept with me.

She sighed. Lissa barely heard her sighs anymore; sighing merely seemed part of her breathing.

And that's my day.

She pressed the pen firmly on the period at the end of the sentence.

Chapter 39

Lissa was frustrated. What could take six weeks about a move? Even if they went through ever single item twice it wouldn't take that long. What was she thinking, agreeing to be here this long?

She called Humpy, Dwight, whatever his name was.

"Hi. It's Lissa."

"Hey. How's the golfer?"

"Honestly? I'm kind of itching to try it again. Tomorrow could we do that driving range thing you mentioned?"

"Oh, sorry, I forgot to tell you. I'm flying out to San Diego tonight. I'll be back late Saturday night."

"Yeah? What are you going there for?" She felt strangely crestfallen.

"Can't tell you."

"You're kidding."

"No, really. It's classified."

"Really? That's pretty exciting."

"Not at all. Most of the work I do is. Remember—I was a nuclear engineer for the Navy. Not a lot of open publicity about that sort of work."

"You know, I never thought much about what you did. I guess I pictured you down in the hold of a ship with a greasy rag in your back pocket."

Dwight laughed. "Me, a bilge rat? Sometimes, but not much. Actually, I'm a nuclear *design* engineer."

A lightbulb clicked on. "Oh, now I get it." She knew Dwight was brilliant, but now her respect for him shot up several notches. He was one of a very elite group in the world. "You *can't* tell me."

"Yep. I'd have to shoot you if I did."

"Funny."

"Hey, Lissa, want to grab a quick coffee at The Mill? I've got time. My ride doesn't get here till seven o'clock."

"Sure. I'll meet you there. Now?"

She heard a stifled chuckle. "Are you walking or driving?"

"Walking."

"Okay, see you in about fifteen minutes."

She was already sitting with her macchiato when Dwight arrived. He didn't notice Lissa right away; she was in the corner behind him. Lissa had a moment before he turned and saw her. He was wearing navy-blue slacks, perfectly creased, and a light blue Oxford cloth button-down, long-sleeved shirt, professionally laundered. Dark tan tassel loafers with just the right socks completed the ensemble. Dwight looked well-heeled. She tried to picture him with the hair he used to have. No, bald was better than slicked down.

He waved at her and went to the counter to order.

"So," he sat in the chair opposite Lissa, "you can't live without me, eh?"

She screwed up her face at him in half mock disgust. "You wish." An unwelcome blush heated up her cheeks.

"I suppose you don't want to hear that I like the hippie look on you either?"

She plucked self-consciously at the front of her hot-pink India cotton top to be sure no cleavage was showing and ignored the question.

Dwight launched into conversation. "What'd you think of golf yesterday?"

They chattered about golf for a surprisingly long time.

"Hey, you want to get a bite to eat?" Dwight looked at his watch.

"Do you have time?"

"I'm all packed and ready to go. Gotta eat."

"Oh, why not. I've got nothing else to do." She arched an eyebrow at him, hoping he'd at least wonder if she was serious.

"Gert's?"

"You betcha."

When Dwight led her to his truck for the three blocks to Gert's, Lissa didn't protest, though she wanted to.

Gert's Bar and Grill on Main Street was about as Midwestern small-town-bar as they come. The only significant remodeling since the 1960s was the addition of a shake shingled awning across the front. Most of the vinyl-covered tube metal chairs were in need of another reupholstery job. Pine booths, darkened with age and grime, lined the back and side walls.

Detritus from every Minnesota pastime covered the walls: beer signs galore, Vikings anything and everything, fishing gear, stuffed fish, an old Evinrude motor mounted on the wall, Twins this and that, bowling and softball trophies Gert's teams had won, and a green painted cedar strip canoe hanging upside down from the ceiling. All this viewed through a gray haze of cigarette smoke. But Gert's had the best hamburgers in a twenty-five mile radius, bar none.

Lissa sauntered up to Ginger, Gert's sixty-something-year-old daughter who had run the place for at least thirty years, and asked for the nonsmoking section.

"Ain't you a kidder, Lissa." Ginger smiled and set her cigarette down on a notch in a filthy glass ashtray.

Lissa had known Ginger since they moved to Gifford. Ginger leaned over, rested the number eighteen on the front of her Twins jersey on the bar, and handed them two single-sheet laminated menus printed on both sides. The menus were mostly wiped clean.

"Dinner?" Ginger pushed back a wisp of her frizzy bicolored hair: rusty gray from the roots out for four inches, then carrot red to the ends.

"You bet," Dwight said. "Lissa, you want a burger?"

"You betcha."

"Two burger baskets—the works." He looked at Lissa for confirmation. She nodded emphatically. "And a big slice of raw onion on both of 'em." Dwight winked at Lissa.

"How you want those?"

"Medium rare." Again Lissa nodded in response to Dwight's questioning look.

"Comin' up." Ginger strolled off to the kitchen and back. "Now, what can I getcha to drink?"

"Beer?" Dwight inquired of Lissa. She would rather have ordered for herself, but went along. Dwight was just being polite, but it grated. And what was all that winking about. Did he have something in his eye, or what?

Dwight carried their beers to a booth. Lissa wanted to jerk hers out of his hand; she'd do it herself, thank you very much.

"You are a dork." A grin broke through.

"What? I'm wounded."

"I'm not used to a Humpy…I mean, Dwight…with manners. Who are you?" That wasn't entirely true. He'd been a perfect gentleman when he'd taken her to prom after Pip died.

Just friends.

"But it's all right. Looks like the Navy taught you something."

"Yes, ma'am." They slid into the booth and faced each other. Just friends.

Again they fell into easy conversation. Lissa forgot the irritation she'd felt earlier.

Through a mouthful of French fry Lissa said, "Boots thinks I should talk to you about Sean."

"Do you want to?"

She gulped her fry. "I think I do. Do you mind? I mean, it's not like it could be easy to listen to someone grieving the loss of their spouse when you're in the same boat."

"I think I'd be okay with it. Our circumstances were pretty different. And I had a few months...well, I had a few months to get used to the idea, if you know what I mean."

"How about after you get back?"

"It's a date."

"No, it's not a *date*." She spat out the word "date" more harshly than she meant to.

"You know what I mean." He raised his glass. "To Pip and Sean."

Feeling a mist welling behind her eyes, Lissa added, "And Becky." They clinked glasses and drained their beer.

She almost protested, but she let Dwight drop her off at her parents'. As Lissa was getting out, she turned back and blurted out, "Do you want to come over for dinner after church on Sunday? Ray and Amy will be here."

Dwight's face lit up. "That would be great. I haven't seen Ray in years. Yeah, that would be great! What time?"

Lissa realized he didn't know when "after church" was since he didn't go to church. "Eleven thirtyish. Great. Have a good trip."

She shut the door with a heavy *clunk* and hoofed it into the house without a wave or a look back. The invitation had been impulsive, and she sort of regretted it.

But Dwight and Ray had been good friends in spite of their age difference. Lissa remembered Dwight had taught Ray how to build model airplanes. They periodically had aerial dog fights, punctuated with loud boy shooting noises, ending in piles of plastic airplane wreckage, necessitating starting the building process all over again.

Anyway, Dwight was coming over for dinner and that was that. Seeing how delighted Dwight was with the invitation, Lissa wished she had invited him over sooner. But that wink...

Chapter 40

Thursday. With Dwight gone and Sally busy, Lissa was a kid with no one to play with.

There was no point in cleaning the house for Ray and Amy's arrival beyond cleaning the bathroom. They wouldn't care anyway. Lissa was more concerned about cooking for everyone. Dwight for dinner on Sunday made six. Cooking would pass the time.

A lot of the kitchen things were already packed, boxes taped and stacked. She opened the cupboards one by one, made a mental inventory of what was left to work with, and planned the menus. Mom was happy to let Lissa take over the cooking for the weekend. Mom's bruises were fading to a mild yellow, but she tired easily and was often in bed by seven thirty.

Lissa grocery shopped at Piggly Wiggly and started on a tuna hotdish for Friday night after they arrived. Casserole for dinner would let Ray and Amy know they were back home, back in the Midwest.

She couldn't wait to see Ray. As kids they were sure to

exasperate each other. They scrapped to be the winner, but they also fiercely defended each other.

Lissa didn't know what she would have done without her little brother when Sean died. Ray immediately flew to be with her, and the day after his arrival they flew together to Amsterdam. She couldn't have made that trip without her brother by her side. The last time she saw him was last Christmas, the Christmas-from-hell. Could she call Christmas that? Well, it was. She was determined things would be different this visit.

She popped the casserole in the fridge for tomorrow and headed to the liquor cupboard in the dining room. Half empty bottle of wine in hand, she opened the upper door and reached for a wine glass—the cupboard was empty. She'd forgotten; all the good glasses were packed. A coffee cup would do. She started to pour a hefty shot, but caught herself. With a sigh, she poured only a small amount, put the bottle back in the cupboard, and went out on the porch.

A young couple walked by with their dog—their big dog—a Newfoundland. Neighbors at the farm had a Newfie. The web-footed giant was forever in the lake.

That would be a lot of hair in the house. She watched as the Newfie trotted down the sidewalk. She missed Choco.

"I thought I'd find you out here, Lissie." With one hand, Mom held on to the doorframe and stepped into the porch. "That was good soup you made for dinner." Lissa steadied the swing while her mother sat next to her.

"Thanks, Mom. You're up later than usual."

"Oh, I'm about to head to bed shortly. I came out to say goodnight."

They swayed gently. Mom glanced in Lissa's mug, but didn't say anything.

"Mom? Would you teach me to knit while I'm here?"

"Didn't you learn to knit in college? I thought I remember you knitting a scarf one year. Wasn't it for a boyfriend?"

FIFTY DAYS TO SUNRISE

Lissa grimaced. "Don't remind me. It was for Bill Gibbs. What a jerk. He unwrapped it and promptly stuck his fingers in all the holes that weren't supposed to be there. I quit knitting then and there. I also told him to take a hike."

"And a good thing too, the Bill Gibbs part."

"I think I'd like to knit now. Sally's always telling me how much fun it is and how it relaxes her."

"It's that all right, but it can be frustrating too. You just have to learn how to correct mistakes and consider them part of the knitting process. You know, I had a cello teacher who taught me to make mistakes and then to recover from them. I relaxed more about making mistakes, since I knew they weren't the end of the world, and then I made fewer mistakes."

"Sounds like knitting's some metaphor for life." Lissa had never been good at allowing herself to make mistakes. She smiled ruefully, thinking of all the rejection letters in a three-ring binder, to keep herself humble if she ever hit the *New York Time's* Best Sellers list.

Mom patted her daughter's hand.

"We'll start knitting tomorrow morning. We've got plenty of time. Ray and Amy shouldn't get here before teatime.

"Well, good night, honey." Mom kissed Lissa's forehead and patted her cheek.

"G'night, Mom. Love you." Lissa returned her mother's kiss.

Mom walked a little stiffly into the house. Lissa thought how grateful she was to be spending this time with her parents. She looked forward to tomorrow. Every bit of it.

Chapter 41

Lissa read Psalm 146 again. She closed the Bible and returned it to its place on the dresser. *"Sustains the fatherless and the widow,"* she repeated to herself as she had many times since reading it in the chapel.

In her journal she wrote a love poem to Sean.

Good night, my darling Sean.
I want my last thoughts of the day to be you.
Sweet thoughts, like our kisses were sweet.
Kisses in the rain.
Kisses in your studio.
Kisses under the pine trees in the snow. When I kissed you with such passion you lost your balance and bumped a branch, engulfing us in drifts of new snow.
Kisses when you smeared shaving cream from your face to mine.
Kisses skinny-dipping. Holding each other so close there was barely room for the wet of the water between us.

CRISTINE EASTIN

I thought we got in a lifetime of kisses in twenty-eight years. Now I know we were shorted at least a thousand kisses, maybe two thousand.
  I'm missing your kisses.

Chapter 42

Lissa settled onto the couch, her last cup of coffee for the morning on the side table. She glanced at Sean's painting: in its place over the mantel. It was hard to look at, but she also loved looking at it. Sean was an extraordinary artist. When painting his own children, he had put something special into the painting—Jack and Shannon's faces were so alive she could almost see their little brain wheels turning.

Mom reached in her knitting bag and took out two balls of yarn—one pink, one yellow—and two sets of knitting needles.

"I think it will work best if I just sit beside you and show you how to do it. You can knit along with me. I taught Ellie and Rachel to knit this way. One of them sitting on either side of me."

"I didn't know they knit."

"Yes, I taught them over a year ago. They were so cute. They were concentrating so hard, I was afraid they were going to stick a needle up their noses."

One more thing she had missed.

"Mom, who taught you to knit?" The question had never

occurred to Lissa before. As far as she knew, her mother came out of the womb knitting. Right now, it seemed an important thing to know.

"Why, it was our neighbor lady, Mrs. Fredrickson. I used to go over to her house after school and sometimes on Saturday mornings after I finished my chores. She was like a second mother to me. More like a grandmother, really. She taught me to bake Swedish cookies, and she taught me to knit."

"How old were you?"

"Oh, I was young. I must have been seven or eight." Mom had a wistful look on her face. "Mrs. Fredrickson had a Swedish accent that I just loved to listen to. She'd tell me stories about the old country when she was a girl in Sweden." Mom absently unwound some yellow yarn, letting it run between her fingers. "Hilda Fredrickson...She gave me that Swedish horse on my dresser."

"I didn't know that."

Suddenly, things Lissa had lived with all her life and taken for granted, or not noticed at all, became important. She realized if she hadn't asked her mother to teach her to knit, she might never have known about Mrs. Fredrickson and how important she was to her mother, or where that orange painted horse had come from.

"Here, honey, let me show you how to cast on."

Mom made each move slowly and carefully. She showed Lissa how to hold the needles and waited for her to catch up as Lissa fumbled with the awkward feel of the needles. Mom pulled more yarn from the ball, and Lissa did the same. Lissa's ball of pink yarn shot across the living room floor.

"Oops. I forgot to put your ball in a knitting bag."

Lissa recovered the errant ball. Mom plopped it in an extra cloth bag she had in her knitting bag. It was a lovely green and purple paisley bag with a flat bottom. "You can have this bag." Lissa could tell already that one reason to knit was all the pretty accessories that went along with it. The dark wooden needles felt smooth and warm in her hands.

"There. Now we have stitches cast on. Let's start to knit. Just follow what I do."

Lissa grinned, feeling inordinately satisfied, so far.

She looped the yarn around the fingers of her right hand just as Mom did and poised her needles, ready to knit. She watched Mom intently, then tried to mimic her movements. Lissa got the first stitch made.

As they worked their way across the row of twenty stitches, Lissa found herself propping the right needle on her leg while she maneuvered the yarn over the needles. It made her feel a little less clumsy.

At the end of the row she looked up and took a deep breath. She had been concentrating so hard, she wasn't breathing normally. She gave her shoulders a relaxing shrug.

"You did it! You knit a row. And it actually looks pretty good." Mom reached over and pulled Lissa's first stitch tighter.

"I think some of it's coming back from when I did it before. Only I tried to teach myself from a book. It didn't work very well. Obviously."

They slowly continued to knit along together until they had four rows completed. Lissa stopped to admire her work. It actually looked like knitting.

Lissa put her knitting down in her lap and looked at her mother. "Mom, I can't tell you how wonderful this feels, to be knitting with my mother."

Lissa's heart entwined with her mother in a new way. A book title sprang to mind, *Knit Together*. One day she would write a character who knits with her mother, and maybe with her sister, maybe with a whole group of women, two or three generations of women knitting together.

"What about purling?" Lissa wanted more.

"Let's just stick with the knit stitch today. Keep it simple."

Lissa knit three more rows by herself with Mom looking on. Lissa held up her knitting. It was starting to look like it could be something. Lissa's face sagged. Something for a baby, for a little baby granddaughter. She let the pink knitting drop to her lap, too dramatically, as she was prone to do.

"What's the matter, Lissa?" Mom looked concerned.

"I didn't know you could have such longings to be a grandma." At the same time she longed to hold a grandchild, there was the pain of no Grandpa. But she couldn't say that.

"Look what I'm knitting for Georgina Hill's great-grandson." Mom reached in her knitting bag and took out the start of a baby blanket in robin's egg blue. She held the needles apart, letting the footlong blanket hang on the length of plastic connecting the needles. The yarn in the complicated patchwork pattern looked luscious. Lissa patted the bunny-soft fabric.

"That's so sweet." Lissa turned back to her knitting, determined not to let the current lack of grandchildren in her life sour this experience. A mental pep talk kicked in. Jack and Meagan were busy with the restaurant, but they had talked about having children when Ship Ahoy was paying them a salary. And Shannon. Lissa smiled at the thought of her adventurous daughter. Right now Shannon was busy being young with money. Lissa just hoped she didn't marry the ski bum.

Lissa resolved to learn to knit. There would be a scarf or two for Christmas presents, only with no holes in them. She would be practiced and ready when the time came to make baby blankets for her own grandbabies.

"Mom, this is so much fun. Show me what you were talking about—correcting mistakes." So Mom showed her how to unknit a row. Then she showed Lissa how to make a mistake that makes a hole. Lissa unknit back to the mistake and fixed it. She got it.

"I think you can call yourself a knitter."

"I knit, therefore I am." They both laughed. And knit another row.

"Mom, I'm so glad I asked you to teach me to knit."

FIFTY DAYS TO SUNRISE

Lissa realized there was another question she needed to ask her mother. Another time. But soon.

Chapter 43

"They're here!" Lissa dropped her practice knitting on the couch and jumped to her feet. She was out the front door before Amy closed the car door.

"Lissa!" Amy threw her arms open wide, and Lissa dived into them. "So good to see you."

"Oh, yeah, I'm so glad you guys could come up."

"Hi ya, Mel." Ray ambled around the car and grabbed his big sister in a bear hug. Lissa felt happily smothered in her brother's bulk.

"Hey, little brother, give me air." They stepped apart and surveyed each other to check on the changes since they last saw each other. "You haven't changed a bit. When are you going to get fat like the rest of us middle-aged folks?"

"Fat? I'd hardly call you fat." Lissa could see it register in Ray's eyes that she was thinner than last Christmas, but he didn't say anything. Maybe it wasn't as bad as it was. She had gained a few pounds in the last three and a half weeks.

Mom and Dad emerged from the house all smiles. Mom waved her arms in welcome. More hugs and greetings.

"Come in, come in," Lissa urged. "You guys are in Boots's room. Dad and I already took your bunk beds apart."

"I could have done that," Ray said.

"Well, sure, but we needed something to do." Then Lissa remembered, of course Ray and Amy would sleep in the queen-sized bed in Boots's room when Boots and Etienne weren't there. She turned away to hide her blush.

Amy headed to the house toting a Styrofoam cooler, her blond Barbie pony-tail swinging. Ray and Lissa followed, each with a rolling duffle.

"I've got tea almost ready. I just have to put the kettle on." Mom bustled into the kitchen; Amy followed with the cooler.

"I brought some goodies," Amy said. "I thought we might like a gain-ten-pounds cake with tea. And I brought that apple caramel dessert Dad likes so much."

The scones Lissa had made after lunch would keep until breakfast.

The kitchen was delightfully crowded with the three women. Ray poked his head around the door to the living room.

Dad came in from getting something in the garage and said, "Hey, what's going on in here? Did the party start without me?"

"Out! Shoo! You men." Mom flapped her apron at the men.

The Crown Staffordshire tea set wasn't packed yet, not until after this special teatime. Mom set the platter of sliced pound cake on the table. The dining table looked like a flower garden. One crystal vase was left unpacked for this occasion. Mom had made a beautiful arrangement of snapdragons, bachelor's buttons, daisies, and roses. The Quaker lace tablecloth that was a wedding present from Mom's sister was the perfect backdrop for the tea set. The bluebells glowed on

FIFTY DAYS TO SUNRISE

the old white china.

Mom brought in the teapot and set it on the trivet. She stepped back for a moment, and Lissa noticed the mist in her eyes. Lissa put an arm around her mother. The scents of roses, tea, and butter and sugar hovered over the table. Mom was looking at the tea set.

"Well," Mom said, "have a seat and I'll be mother, since I'm the senior mother here." Mom poured the tea through the strainer set in each cup in turn. Lissa took the cups and passed them around as Mom poured. Mom was concentrating on keeping the teapot steady.

The family English teatime was bliss. But also sad. No one said it, but they all knew it was their last teatime in this house. It may not be their last at this table, but if not, the next would be in Toledo at Ray and Amy's house, since they were taking the table home with them.

Conversation was warm and the laughter sweet. Ray and Amy did almost a comedy routine telling about the twins at the farm. Apparently Rachel and Ellie had been calling their parents frequently, regaling them with stories of the fun they were having on the farm. Amy knew about Galahad as soon as Rachel found him.

Amy caught the family up on what Jason was doing: working on his Master's at Ohio State University. Next was a PhD and then finding the cure to cancer. Knowing Jason, he just might do it.

Teatime was over. Ray and Amy went upstairs for a rest; Dad, in his usual spot, read the paper. And Mom and Lissa were in the kitchen cleaning up. Lissa handed a cup to her mother to dry.

It was amazing how quickly they all settled back into the familiar, comfortable routine of being a family together.

"Lissie, I'd like you to have the tea set."

Lissa stopped mid-swish of the dishcloth on a plate. "Mom, you're not done with it yet."

"Yes...yes, I think I am. I would like you to have it. I think it means the most to you. You'd continue to enjoy it like I have. I'd like to give it to you."

"Oh, Mom." Lissa's nose prickled, like she was going to cry, again. She fought it. It didn't seem right, Mom giving away her tea set, yet she was thrilled. "Well, I can't take it on the plane anyway. I'll get it another time." Thinking the handoff was delayed, the tear urge subsided. "But thank you so much. I'll cherish it when the time comes." She leaned over, her hands still holding the plate in the dishwater, and gave her mother a peck on the cheek.

"Maybe you could take it home this time. We'll see," Mom said.

"Missy," Dad called, "can I talk to you when you finish up there?"

"Sure, Dad. Couple minutes." She wondered what this was all about.

Dishes done, Lissa sat on the couch. Mom eased into her chair. She looked tired.

Dad folded the newspaper and set it on the end table. "Your mother and I would like to give you her car—to give to Meagan and Jack. We thought it would be a good car for Meagan. She still doesn't have one, does she?"

Taken aback, it took Lissa a moment to respond. "Uh...no, she doesn't have a car. Jack told me just recently she could use one, but they aren't taking a salary from the restaurant yet, so they were going to wait till next spring."

"Well then, that would work perfectly. I just had it tuned up this week. I'm glad Dwight caught those frayed wires. New spark plugs, wires, battery—the works. So it should be good for lots of miles. It's only got a little over 60,000 miles on it. Just say the word, and I'll have new tires put on it too."

"Wow, that would be great, but I don't know how—"

"You could drive it home this summer when you leave. Change your ticket," Dad said.

FIFTY DAYS TO SUNRISE

"But...I've never driven that far alone." That was the first excuse that came to mind. She really wasn't sure about this.

"You can do it. You've always been a can-do sort of woman." Mom wasn't accepting excuses.

"I have?" Lissa had forgotten. "Let me think about it, okay?"

"One other thing, Missy. I've already measured, and Sean's painting," Dad waved toward the mantel, "would fit in the back seat."

"And you could take the tea set home with you," Mom added.

Lissa's mouth fell open, fish-like. She stared at them, then at the painting of her children. The prickle in her nose quickly turned to tears.

Mom moved to sit next to her daughter and patted her knee. "Does this mean yes, honey?"

"Yes." Lissa self-consciously wiped her nose with a finger and sniffed. "Thank you so much." She smiled at her parents through her tears. Mom took a clean hankie from her skirt pocket and offered it.

The confusion of emotions Lissa felt at her parents giving their treasured possessions away was overwhelming. But she was profoundly grateful and honored to have them entrusted to her.

Lissa already had a spot in mind for Sean's painting. In their bedroom, so she would see it first thing each morning.

Chapter 44

Rubbing sleep from her eyes, Lissa padded down to the kitchen through the living room. She could hear Ray and Dad talking.
"How do you think she's doing?"
Lissa slowed to listen to them talking about Mom.
"Well, she's finally crying instead of screaming at us, so that's a good sign."
"Poor kid."
"I'm sure she'll be fine. At least as fine as she can be under the circumstances. Missy's always been a fighter. I've got to tell you, Ray, we were worried about her."
Lissa stopped stone-statue still. They were talking about *her*.
"She really seems to have gotten her drinking turned around. Jack was really worried about that."
Heat crept up her neck like a grass fire out of control.
"Mom was worried about her running too much. She was really thin when she got here. But that's better too."
"I know. I talked to Mom about that a few weeks ago."

Lissa didn't know whether to tiptoe back upstairs, run out the front door and keep going, or charge into the kitchen, guns blazing.

"It's good you and Amy are here. Missy trusts you."

"Yeah. Man, I miss Sean too. I can't imagine what she's going through."

Lissa took a step backward, and a floorboard popped—loudly. Silence from the kitchen. They'd heard her. Slowly, she tried to gather what little wits she had and stomped into the kitchen. She didn't know what to say.

Lissa stared first at her father. He sat at the table, a mug of coffee in front of him. Then at Ray. Dressed in his running gear, Ray leaned against the counter, a half-empty glass of water in his hand. Ray obviously went on his run without her. That hurt. But what did she expect, given what they thought of her. Self-pity flooded in.

Ray broke the ear-splitting silence. "How much did you hear?" He looked stricken, so did Dad.

Lissa's mouth was dry—too dry to speak. Her hands felt unattached to her body. That was fortunate, since she wanted to take a swing at her brother. Emotions warred inside her, and she chose not to count.

"I'm sorry, Mel." Ray turned red, even redder than he was from running, and tears pooled in his eyes. "It's just that we all love you so much. It was breaking our hearts to see you in such pain."

"You mean...having me come home this summer was about *me*?"

"No, Missy," Dad's words tumbled out. "We also really needed your help with this move. Honestly, we've really needed you."

"But not for the whole...summer!" She almost swore at her father. "Well, that explains a whole lot." Lissa threw up her hands. Ready for a fight, her eyes flamed, and she glared at her father.

"Take it easy, Mel." Ray set his glass down and stood up straight. "Please. Don't be mad. Mom and Dad were trying to help. We all are."

She swung back and rounded on Ray. "Why weren't you honest with me?" Her voice cracked. Her mouth was so dry it almost hurt to talk.

"You wouldn't listen. You weren't *ready* to listen. Who would be with what you've been going through?" Ray took a step toward his sister. "I think you are now." He reached out for her.

Lissa jumped back as if dodging a body blow.

"Missy—" Dad stood up.

Panic rose in her, and she retreated further, bumping against the sink. To get out of the kitchen she would have had to push Ray aside.

"Both of you, leave me alone!"

Dad sat down again, looking defeated.

Ray yielded a couple steps and said, "Mel, what do you want? Seriously, what can we do to help you?"

"I want Sean!" She grabbed the edge of the sink behind her. The clunk of her wedding ring on the cast iron seemed much louder than it was.

"Missy, honey...please." Dad ran his hands through his hair and looked at his son.

"Mel, we miss Sean too."

"So now this is about *you*?" Ray didn't say anything, just looked steadily at his sister.

Her arms trembled, and she relaxed the death grip she had on the sink. Lissa swallowed the foul taste in her mouth and wished she could take back those words. She sucked in her lower lip and sighed, looking at the floor. "Sorry," she finally said. "I'm trying. I really am."

"We want to help." Dad tried again.

"I want to tell you all to leave me alone if you want to help, but obviously that isn't going to happen."

Ray folded his arms and slumped back against the counter. "I think we've all done a pretty good job of giving you space and at the same time being there for you. But when I see that you've lost about ten more pounds since Christmas, I've got to say something. Can you see that?"

She wanted to defend herself and point out that she'd gained a few pounds and not run so much since being home. Reluctantly, Lissa admitted to herself that her brother was right. But it was harder to let *them* know that.

"I suppose. But really, don't you trust me to come around on my own eventually?"

Ray's lips tightened, giving her his answer.

Lissa folded her arms. Brother and sister now appeared to be at a standoff that neither conceded. Dad looked from one to the other and waited.

"Well...if you must know..." Lissa wanted to stop, but got no encouragement to do so. She sighed and continued. "I've been working on a plan to deal with...my denial...and my short fuse." Still no response from Dad or Ray. "But, I've got to say... well, I think I'm going to keep that private."

"That's great, Missy. We love you so much, and just want to help you." Dad looked relieved, like he wanted the conversation to be over.

Ray didn't move. "You bit my head off when I suggested this last Christmas, but I'm going to say it again. I think you should see a therapist."

Lissa could feel her face redden, and she clenched her jaw. She didn't want to be angry at Ray. It was none of his business, but she knew it was said out of love. She decided to give the same that she wanted and be honest.

"I did."

"And?" Ray wouldn't let it go. Apparently, Boots had taught him how to cross-examine.

"I went a couple times."

"Was it helpful?"

"Geez, you're like a dog with a bone."
"Yep. Just call me Fido. Was it helpful?"
"I suppose. I liked her. But I just didn't want to talk. I told her I'd call her."
"When was that?"
Lissa realized she wasn't getting out of this. "Okay. It was months ago. But honestly, I've been thinking about calling her when I get back. Satisfied?"
"Yes." Ray cocked his head to the side and fixed a look on his sister. "If you *do* it." He uncrossed his arms and reached for his water glass.

Lissa hung her head and wished this world would go away.

Ray walked over and set his glass by the sink. He stopped directly in front of his sister and grasped her shoulders. Tears dripping onto the front of her robe, Lissa looked up at him. Tears sprang to Ray's eyes too, and he unashamedly held her gaze.

She couldn't be mad in the face of such love and devotion from her family. Lissa let her brother hug her. She half-heartedly thumped him on the chest once, then rested her fists on his chest.

"Ray," she spoke into his chest in a tear-strained voice, "I know I've told you this before, but thank you for going to Amsterdam with me. Thank you so much." She felt a quiet sob rise in his chest.

"I couldn't let you do it alone." Ray's voice was thick with his own grief.

"Thanks." Lissa moved away from Ray and started toward her father. She stood dumbly silent for a moment, too ashamed to speak.

"Dad, forgive me."

Now Dad was crying. He stood and wrapped his arms around his daughter. "Missy, there's nothing to forgive. Grief is a terrible thing. The whole family grieves. We just want to love you through it." Lissa pressed her face into her father's shoulder.

After a few moments she stepped back self-consciously and wiped her face with the sleeve of her robe. She didn't know what else to say. Neither Dad, nor Ray said anything either. The fight was drained out of her.

She broke the silence. "Coffee, the antidote for everything." Humor seemed out of place, but then, everything was. Why not? Fake it till you make it. That's what her therapist had said.

Lissa opened the cupboard next to Ray and took out the biggest mug. She wrinkled her nose at Ray. "You stink." Ray looked a little wounded. "No, I mean, you *stink,*" she said, pointing in the general direction of his upper arms. "You really do."

She fought the urge to run out the back door, bang the picket gate, run down the alley, and keep on running.

Chapter 45

Lissa bounced in a chair on the patio. She heard the screen door creak open and tried to resist the defensiveness she could feel lurking, ready to leap out and make a fool of her again.
"Good morning, Lissie. I thought I might find you out here."
"Morning, Mom." Lissa sipped her coffee, eyes fixed on the garage wall.
"Mind if I join you?"
"'Course not." Lissa set her mug on the table and turned to her mother. "I hope you didn't have your hearing aids in a while ago."
"Eh?" Mom cupped a hand to her ear and smiled.
"Did you?"
"Well, yes, I heard some of it."
"Hmm. Oh, well. One more time—Lissa yelling at her family." She swatted at a fly and almost hit it. "Honestly, Mom, I'm sorry. I keep saying that, but I mean it."
Mom reached over and firmly grasped Lissa's hand. "Honey, I appreciate your apology, I really do, but please

believe me when I say that nothing you say or do will make me love you less, or even think less of you."

Lissa put her other hand on top of Mom's and squeezed their hands together. "Thanks, Mom. I do know that, but it's good to hear." Lissa released her mother's hand. "But couldn't you and Dad have been more honest with me about this summer?"

"We were. We do need help with the move."

"Come on, Mom. The cat's out of the bag."

"Well, we just tacked a little time on for good measure."

"You didn't trust me."

"Should we have?"

Busted again.

"I was making a mess of it, wasn't I."

"Someday Lissie, you'll look back on this time, and you'll realize that it must just have been the way you had to deal with Sean's passing. There's no right way to grieve."

Mom hesitated, then took a deep breath. She too stared at the garage wall. "I remember when you and Sean—" Lissa loudly sucked in a breath, attempting without words to stop her mother from talking about Sean. Didn't they get it? She didn't want to talk about Sean. And she didn't want anyone else to talk about him.

Her mother proceeded. "Your dad and I were sitting right here. You and Sean were out there in the backyard with Jack and Shannon, playing Red Light Green Light. I was so proud of you—all grown up, and such a wonderful mother. I can still hear all of you laughing." Mom smiled. "Sean had such an infectious laugh." She paused. "Lissa, I want you to know how much I loved Sean."

Lissa responded to her mother's speech with silence. She chewed her lower lip, bit down on it. Mom said no more about Sean.

Finally, Lissa turned to her mother and said, "That means a lot to me."

FIFTY DAYS TO SUNRISE

Mother and daughter sat quietly for a time.
"Mom?"
"Yes, dear?"
"I remember that day too."

Chapter 46

Saturday was busy. Ray and Dad went to pick up the U-Haul; the women packed more of the kitchen. Mom told Amy and Lissa to go through the stacks of glass serving dishes and take what they wanted. How could one woman collect so many of those things?

Now that Lissa was driving Mom's car all the way back to Maine, she started a box of things to take home. When she had called Jack last night, he was thrilled about getting Mom's car. Lissa didn't tell her mother, but she was also taking the rag rug from the kitchen.

Mom put two heavy-duty boxes on the dining table and packed the Crown Staffordshire tea set. She said she wanted to pack it herself. She wrapped each piece in bubble wrap, setting each plate on end in a bed of bubbles. She made sure nothing would get jarred or put pressure on another piece. Setting the box flaps in place, she taped the boxes shut and wrote Lissa's name and *Tea Set* in marker on each side of the boxes. Then on the tops she wrote, *Fragile*.

"Lissa, why don't you carry these up to your room so they

don't get moved with the rest of the things."

Mom gave Lissa a look that gave away her mixed feelings about passing on the tea set. Silly to think of missing a tea service, but Mom had poured out a lot of memories along with the tea. And it was so lovely to look at.

"Use it well, honey, and pass it on to Shannon," Mom said, lightly resting her hand on the top of a box.

"Thanks, Mom. I will." It might as well have been a baton, or a mantle that Mom passed on. Lissa picked up a box and gave her mother a smile that didn't feel like much of a smile on the outside. She tried to make it better for her mother, but there wasn't anything she could do to prevent her mother from experiencing the unfair feelings that come with aging. All she could do was love her and try to make it a little easier for her.

Didn't she just hear someone say those words to her this morning? Does everything have to be so poignant?

When she returned to the kitchen after taking the second box upstairs, Mom was wiping off the kitchen table, which wasn't dirty. Lissa thought she saw her mother quickly brush her cheek with the back of her hand. Before her mother heard her, Lissa turned around to find Amy upstairs. Amy was on her cell phone talking to Jason, so Lissa slipped into her room and was about to pick up her practice knitting when she heard Mom coming up the stairs.

"Lissie, I just remembered, there's another box that I put aside for you. It's in the storage closet in our room."

Mom opened the door to the small closet under the attic stairs and pointed to a box. It too had Lissa's name on it. On all four sides, Lissa guessed.

"What is it?"

"Remember the day after Christmas last year when everyone was here; we divvied up most of the Christmas decorations?"

Lissa did remember, but she also remembered sneaking away to her room and not participating. That was not long after Melissa Makkinen Maguire's finest hour—drunk and screaming at her family.

"I put some Christmas things aside for you. I knew you'd want them."

"Mom, you are amazing. I'm so glad God made you my mom." Lissa kissed her mother's cheek and set the Christmas box next to the tea set boxes.

"Well girls, shall we take a knitting break?" Mom asked.

"Oh, yes." Amy clapped her hands. "Let me go get my knitting bag. I can't wait to show you the sweater I'm working on. It's my first sweater."

"You knit?" It seemed everyone Lissa knew was already knitting.

"Have been for about two years. I just love it." Amy wheeled around and went back to their bedroom.

For the next hour they knit together. Lissa advanced to the purl stitch. Sometimes Amy fell silent, counting stitches to make sure she had the correct number for the row. Her sweater was simple, but elegant, like Amy. The fluffy yarn looked like a watercolor painting of an early morning sky.

"I figured I'd better make my first sweater for myself, since I couldn't be sure if I made it for anyone else, that they'd actually wear it. I'll wear it no matter how it turns out." She held up the nearly-completed back.

Mom's wooden needles clicked softly as she worked on the baby blanket. She never looked at a pattern.

In the distance they could hear Dad and Ray in the garage. A lot of the gardening and lawn care things were going home with Ray and Amy. Now that they had an almost-empty nest, they wanted to get serious about growing their own vegetables. Ray talked about building a pond and a small waterfall.

"Oh, look at the time. We'd better feed those men." Mom set her knitting aside. She got up slowly and headed for the kitchen. It took her a couple of steps to work out the kinks.

"Be there in a sec, Mom." Amy and Lissa finished their

rows. Lissa stretched a big stretch, reaching her hands way up and arching her back. The sting wasn't gone from yesterday, but she was not going to hold a grudge against her family. What was the point? To make things worse? She was all too good at that.

Chapter 47

After church the kitchen bubbled with activity. The three women bustled around like chattering sparrows. Mom was supposed to be resting, but she refused to sit down.

The pot roast had simmered in the blue graniteware roaster all morning while they were at church. Roasted vegetables, potatoes and gravy, salad, relishes, crescent rolls, and the apple caramel dessert Amy made—enough food for the neighborhood. The dining table was dressed in its finest: the Quaker lace tablecloth, Mom and Dad's wedding present blue-flowered china, the sterling flatware, and the crystal vase of just-picked flowers.

"Dinner's served," Mom called out the back door, summoning the men to the table.

"Where would you like me to sit?" Dwight asked Mom.

She waved. "Oh, anywhere is fine."

Family members were so familiar with sitting down to eat together, it might as well have been assigned seating. Amy and Ray were already in their places. With Mom and Dad at each end, that left Lissa next to Dwight. She sat between Mom and

Dwight, to deflect Mom's comments to Dwight if necessary.

Ray and Amy were a handholding family when they prayed. Ray reached for Dad's hand and Amy for Mom's. The ripple effect went around the table. Lissa thought Dwight might break out in hives when Dad nonchalantly reached for his hand. Ray had gotten them all used to this, though it still wasn't Dad's way if Ray wasn't there. Lissa set her wrist on the table and turned her hand, palm up, toward Dwight. They exchanged awkward smiles and, as awkwardly, closed their fingers around each other's hands. She looked down, but didn't fully close her eyes. She noticed Dwight assumed the prayerful posture, but that it didn't seem to sit comfortably on him.

Dad asked a blessing on the meal and thanked the Lord—for all the family gatherings they'd had at this table, for the love the Lord had blessed them with through loving each other, and for the love they had through His Son Jesus. Dwight said "amen" with the rest of them. He gave Lissa's hand a quick squeeze and let go. With her thumb she absently reseated her wedding band at the base of her finger.

"Let's eat! Eleanor, it looks and smells wonderful, as usual. And I'm sure you girls had a hand in it, so thank you too." Dad rubbed his hands together and reached for the meat platter, passing it first to their guest. Dwight held the platter while Lissa speared a piece that was so tender it broke in half.

Dish after dish was passed. No one had ever gone hungry at the Makkinen house.

"So," Dad began the conversation, "what did you think of the sermon today?"

Lissa saw Dwight look up, fork poised between closed lips. Apparently, he didn't know this was standard dinner conversation fare on Sunday.

"Don't worry." She leaned toward Dwight. "We talk about religion all the time." He withdrew the fork from his mouth. "Then we move on to politics and the fun really begins." His eyes widened at Lissa in mock alarm. "Not really. Well,

FIFTY DAYS TO SUNRISE

sometimes, I guess."

Since Dwight had no idea what anyone was talking about from the sermon, Lissa excused herself and went to fetch Dad's Bible. She flashed the tiniest of sly smiles at Dwight. Come on, Lord. Make a believer of him.

"It was 1 Peter what?"

"Four, ten and eleven, I think," Ray said.

"Here's the passage we're talking about. 'Each of you should use whatever gift you have received to serve others, as faithful stewards of God's grace in its various forms. If anyone speaks, they should do so as one who speaks the very words of God. If anyone serves, they should do so with the strength God provides, so that in all things God may be praised through Jesus Christ.'" She set the Bible in its place and sat back down.

"It makes me hope I've been a good servant and wisely used what God gave me."

"Eleanor, I don't think you have to worry about that." Dad sent a warm smile to Mom at the other end of the table. "There aren't many people as good and kind as you. And could you ever make those cello strings sing." They shared a look.

"Well, you weren't so bad on the piano yourself, George." It was sweet to see Mom blush after all their years together.

"It's a tall order, that's for sure," said the pastor in the family. "In my position it's really hard to be a pastor and a miserable worm of a human being at the very same time. I feel the weight of it every time I say something that doesn't honor Jesus, or do something that shows Ray Makkinen, not Jesus Christ."

"Honey, your father and I pray for you every day, that God would provide people to hold up your arms just like He did for Moses."

"Thanks, Mom. That means so much." Ray reached over and squeezed Amy's hand under the table. Ray looked a little sheepish. "I really learned a lesson a while ago when Amy and I had a disagreement the night before, and we hadn't set it right between us by Sunday morning. I got up to preach my sermon, and it was an absolute flop. I sure wasn't speaking 'the very words of God.' So guess what I had to do the next Sunday? I had to confess my sin to the whole congregation." Amy smiled warmly at her man. Ray took a big bite of a roll.

"I don't know how you two do it." Lissa admired them both and, on occasion, felt really sorry for them.

"Missy, your writing is such a gift from God. I'm so proud of what you've done."

Lissa swallowed a mouthful of mashed potatoes, which seemed to have doubled in size. "It doesn't feel much like it right now."

Remembering her rages, it felt like she'd swallowed a wasp. Maybe that's why her novel was so stuck. The self-critical finger wagged at her. Since Sean died she hadn't written a word on *Pernicious Love,* nor had she done a good job of praising God—more like Peter—sinking beneath the waves. She swatted the thoughts away.

"Oh, honey, your *Lavender Stories* are so beautiful. I still read them over and over."

Lissa blushed crimson.

"Yeah, I agree. *I* even liked 'em." Dwight nodded in Lissa's direction.

"You've read *Lavender Stories*?"

"Sure. Sally loaned it to me a few months ago."

"Hey, what do you mean *even you* liked them?"

"Well, they're not exactly guy stories. Am I right, Ray?"

Ray lifted knife and fork in a leave-me-out-of-this gesture.

"No, you're right, they're not." Lissa settled her ruffled feathers since what Dwight said was true: men were not her intended audience. "Well then, I'm glad you liked them."

"I especially liked the story about the lavender cat."

"That was based on our naughty Boots." Mom told the story, as she had many times to her friends. "We had a cat named Scamper. Boots tried to share blueberries with Scamper

FIFTY DAYS TO SUNRISE

one day when I was busy in the kitchen. You can imagine the result. I couldn't wash the purple stains off that poor cat, or Boots. Boots's clothes were just a mess."

"How is Boots, the famous attorney?" said Ray.

Sarcasm tickled her tongue, but Lissa resisted. Ray probably knew how Boots was since they had all been talking—about her.

"She's great. It was more than great to have her here. Too bad you guys couldn't get your weekends here coordinated." Lissa almost let it slip that Boots had invited her, no, insisted, that she go to India with her, but Lissa didn't know if that was family knowledge yet. "She's still crazy. We bombed around in a hot convertible she rented."

"Sounds like fun," Amy said. "I wish we could have been here, but there was a ladies retreat that weekend. I'd have liked a little bombing around with you girls."

"Three would have been company. You know that." Amy was more like another sister. Lissa had always known Amy, but really got to know her after she and Ray married. The age gap between them quickly closed as they both found themselves married and mothers.

"Dwight, what have you been up to?" Dad turned to Dwight.

"If he tells you, he'll have to shoot you."

Mom looked concerned. Dwight shot Lissa a look that was apparently supposed to silence her, but didn't.

"Yeah, ask him about his work."

"Melissa," Dwight said with a slightly acerbic tone, "is referring to a trip I just got back from that I can't talk about." Lissa put her fork in her mouth, where her foot already was.

"Oh," Dad said, "top secret, eh?"

"Something like that. But I had a good time playing golf at Pebble Beach. Good place to do business. Do you golf, Ray?"

"I do, but badly, and I'm not afraid to admit it."

"We should play sometime."

"Depends on how much patience you have. I do a lot of whacking around in the bushes, looking for the ball."

Dwight cast a sidelong glance at Lissa. He smiled; Lissa rolled her eyes.

There was a lull in the conversation.

Mom cleared her throat. "Um...there's something I wanted to bring up." Mom's voice was a little thick. "Dad and I were wondering...actually..." Mom looked at Ray and Amy. "We would like to send this china and flatware home with you. To save for the twins."

Ray put his silverware on his plate and glanced at Amy. She shook her head almost imperceptibly. He considered a moment before responding. "I don't really know how we'd split it between them."

Mom looked disappointed. She thought for a minute. "Well, then, what about Jason. He'll get married someday."

"I wouldn't put your hopes on Jason. For him to get married would require dating a woman more than a few weeks, and that would require getting his nose out of the computer."

Mom nodded slowly. "Oh...perhaps you're right....I guess we can just keep it for now."

Dad tried to help. "I'm sure we'll have lots of people over at the new place. It'll be fine, Eleanor."

"I suppose so." Mom put on a fragile smile. "Who wants more pot roast?" She passed the platter down to the end where the men sat.

Lissa and Amy served coffee with dessert. Conversation became interspersed with yawns. And warm smiles.

As Dwight was leaving, he stopped to look at Sean's painting over the mantel. He turned to Lissa and put a hand on her elbow. "How about that talk tomorrow night. My place, six o'clock? I'll put something on the grill," he said, so as not to be overheard.

"Oh, okay." And just like that, she had agreed to see him again without giving it much thought. But, she realized, she

FIFTY DAYS TO SUNRISE

had asked to talk to him. "Where do you live?"

"The old Bergstrom house." She knew right where it was.

"Oh, and sorry about my foot-in-mouth episode."

"No problem. No government secrets got out." He winked at her and left.

The adult kids shooed the parents away while they cleaned up. Mom and Dad excused themselves to go upstairs for a short rest.

Lissa had to use the bathroom. At the top of the stairs she saw Mom and Dad through their partially open bedroom door. They were standing in an embrace; Dad stroked the back of Mom's hair.

Lissa's nose prickled and then the feeling subsided. She was glad she'd taken off her shoes. She didn't want to disturb her parents.

Funny, she must have avoided the creaky steps.

Chapter 48

Everyone had eaten way too much, but Sunday afternoon was busy with loading the U-Haul. Ray and Amy were leaving Monday morning. They tried to keep Dad from doing any lifting, but they couldn't stop him. Dad picked up an end of the dining table top, while Amy and Lissa nervously hovered. When Ray stopped to give Dad a rest before going out the front door, Amy just picked up Dad's end and motioned Ray to carry on. Dad didn't protest. He had a dining chair out to the curb before they knew it. Then he took a rest in his recliner while the rest of the chairs were taken out.

The dining room looked empty. The Persian rug glowed crimson and sapphire, the center medallion completely visible for the first time since the table was set on it so many years ago. It was a beautiful rug. The imprints of the table and chair legs were all that was left of the Makkinen family dining set. Lissa closed her eyes and imagined a symphony of voices from the numberless family dinners. The tinkling bell tones of children's voices, Dad's sonorous baritone, Mom the flute of the family orchestra.

The work done, a light supper consumed and cleaned up, they passed the evening on the front porch. Ray and Amy sat on the swing; he had his arm around her; she nestled into the hollow under his arm. Lissa felt a stab of pain, a knife in the ribs. It was heart-warming, seeing her fifty-year-old brother so happy with his wife at his side, but it was also excruciating. It would always be like this. She had to submit, or continue to be someone she hated. But what would she do, who would she be, without the pain? Maybe she could tolerate it in time.

Lissa excused herself to get a drink of water from the kitchen. She wandered out to the backyard. The full moon hung like an incandescent pearl, strung on a silver cloud-thread. Moonlight tipped the grass and made velvety shadows of the trees.

She sat in the chair and contemplated the moon. She cocked her head in surprise. The man in the moon was singing. It wasn't so many months ago he was howling in agony. It had been so unsettling, she couldn't look at the full moon, and had avoided it for months. But there it was, a cherub with round, open mouth, singing away. Lissa smiled, just a little smile. It seemed the Lord was restoring the beauty of the full moon to her. She had sat down to admire the moon without even thinking of avoiding it. She gave the chair a few bounces and went back to her family.

"Missy," Dad began, "there's something else your mother and I wanted to talk to you about." Gosh, now what? But at least they were talking to her face to face and not behind the closed kitchen door. "We've already talked to Ray and Boots about this, and they're in full agreement." Lissa aimed a glance at Ray. He nodded.

"We wondered if you'd like to move into the house. Move back to Gifford. Buy the house later, if you want."

Lissa stared at them. Had her family members just sprouted extra heads? She made her living with words, but just then she had no words available. Nothing came to mind. A

FIFTY DAYS TO SUNRISE

blank page.

Mom chimed in. "We weren't sure if maybe the farm would prove to be too much for you, one way and another. We thought you might want to come home."

"I don't know what to say." Lissa took a drink of water to ease her dry mouth. "But I thought you'd want to sell it."

"We don't need the money right now. And if it would help you out, that's what we'd like to do. That's what we'd *all* like to do," Dad said.

"No kidding, Mel. It's a no-brainer. That is, if it's what you want."

"Well, it's just an overwhelming offer." Buy the house. There was hardly any room in her brain for those three small words.

The glass halfway to her lips, she froze. "You mean, sell the farm?" The thought had never occurred to her. The weight of the glass drew it down to rest on her leg. She'd been too busy trying to survive to think that far ahead. She had no idea what she wanted. All she could think of for the last eighteen months was a frantic longing for peace.

"That would be up to you." Ray chuckled. "Rachel and Ellie would happily be caretakers for you and commute to school from there, but it's a long way between Seaton and Ohio State."

"Leave the farm? I just don't know."

"It's something to think about. We certainly don't need an answer now. Just wanted to let you know that the offer is on the table." Dad seemed so sure of this.

"But what about..." She didn't know how to delicately phrase this. "What about the legal ramifications? What about Ray and Boots?"

"You'd buy us out," Ray said, "and Boots and I would make that very affordable. The money doesn't matter. We've discussed that too."

"Oh." Lissa made a helpless gesture with hands that seemed loose on her wrists. She was again keenly aware that her family had been talking a lot *about* her, rather than *to* her. But, under the circumstances, she couldn't blame them. It was probably safer for them.

"We love you, honey, and just want to help, however we can." Mom reached over and patted her daughter's hand.

"Well, thanks. Thanks a lot." Lissa sighed. "I mean it. Thanks a *whole* lot. I'll think about it."

That night Lissa lay awake in bed, unable to switch off her brain. She thought of all that had gone on so far this summer. Three and a half weeks seemed like three and a half months. Scenes flashed through her mind. Conversations replayed over and over. She was restless. This weekend alone had been confusing enough. She felt as if she was playing crack the whip, like they did at the skating rink, only this was with her emotions, and she was at the end of the line getting whipped around from one emotion to another, barely hanging on.

Mom and Dad's offer of the house floored her. She never dreamed she'd have the option of moving home. She appreciated the offer beyond words, but yet, it didn't feel right. Her home was in Seaton, on the farm—Sean's and her farm. Their son and his wife lived two miles away. Jack and Meagan were putting down roots there and apparently had no intention of leaving. Shouldn't she stay close to at least one of her children? Shannon probably wouldn't want her too close anyway. Having options was unfamiliar. With Sean's death, the iron door to the future slammed shut on her nose. She was terrified to be hopeful.

Thoughts of Dwight wouldn't shut off either. They'd been such good friends in high school, it didn't seem right not to see him, talk to him like she used to. But they were adults now. It was different, yet no different at all. She remembered Sean had liked Dwight the couple of times they'd seen him at class

FIFTY DAYS TO SUNRISE

reunions, so that was all right. Dinner at Dwight's house tomorrow was no problem, she convinced herself. But then there was Boots and India. Crazy Boots. What was she going to do about that?

She'd call Sally in the morning. Talking with Sally always set Lissa back on the tracks.

Somewhere after three o'clock her brain gave up and surrendered to sleep. She dreamed of lavender cats.

Chapter 49

By the time Lissa hung up the phone after talking with Sally, Ray and Amy were probably nearly to Minneapolis, on their way home. Sally was good medicine.

Mom, on the other hand, had teared up when Ray and Amy drove off. It was always hard for her to say goodbye to any of her children or grandchildren. Lissa, at least, knew she'd see Ray when he came to the farm to pick up the twins.

Mom was packing the china on the kitchen table when Lissa got downstairs. She made sure to lightly stomp so her mother would hear her coming through the living room. Lissa tinkled the piano keys as she walked by.

The bruises on Mom's face were almost fully healed. The remaining yellow tinge was easily covered with a little makeup.

"Where's Dad?"

"He's out in the garage. Cleaning up after the mess he and Ray made yesterday."

"Is something wrong, Mom?" Mom had a look Lissa didn't know how to interpret.

"It's just that...well, I know your father's going to really miss his garage. That's all." She straightened up. "But it will be fine."

After seeing Mom and Dad comforting each other yesterday, during what they thought was a private moment, Lissa knew how hard this was on them. This was going to be a monumental lifestyle change for them.

"I know. I'm sorry, Mom, if I haven't been helpful enough."

"Oh, honey, not at all. We just love having you here. And you've done a lot. Really."

Lissa took her place beside her mother and joined in packing the china. There were a lot of pieces. When they finished, Lissa carefully lined the four boxes up along the dining room wall, each box labeled *China*, on all four sides, and *Fragile* on top.

"Lissie, the day of the move would you please take the china over in the car. I just don't want anything to happen to it. I'm so afraid the movers will pack something on top of the boxes."

"Sure. No problem."

Mom frowned. "I'm not sure what I'm going to do with it. I had wanted to send it home with Ray. I don't know if there will be room for it in the cupboards. We've always had the built-in buffet....I don't suppose you have room for it in the car to take back with you? Maybe Jack and Meagan would like it." She looked at Lissa hopefully, but Lissa shook her head.

"Not to worry. Something will work out." Lissa put her arm around her mother's shoulders and gently squeezed. The reality of their move was creeping closer. "How about a tea break?"

"But it's not teatime." Mom looked quizzically at Lissa.

"It's teatime somewhere."

"Oh, why not." She smiled like she'd just made a decision to be daring.

FIFTY DAYS TO SUNRISE

"Mom, can I ask you something?"

"Of course, dear."

Lissa set her mug down and faced her mother across the patio table. She didn't know how to ask the question, it had nagged at her so many years. But this time at home had made her realize she needed to ask her questions now.

"Sometimes you look so sad. Am I imagining that?"

Mom sighed and looked away to the flower beds.

"Mom?"

"No, honey, you're not imagining that."

Tense heat flashed in Lissa's belly.

"I hoped it didn't show. I'm sorry."

"No, I didn't mean to pry. I shouldn't have brought it up." Lissa hadn't expected to stumble into a thorn bush. "I'm sorry, Mom. It's none of my business."

"No, it's all right. I should probably tell you. It's just that your father and I have lived with this so long, it became too hard to tell."

Lissa stiffened.

Mom turned back to her oldest daughter. Tears traced Mom's cheeks.

"Lissie, you had another brother."

"Mom?" Lissa reached a hand toward her mother—grabbing for a lifeline. Mom grasped Lissa's hand and held on.

"Fourteen months after you were born, we had a little boy. But he was stillborn."

A sob stuck in Lissa's throat.

"A few days before my due date...well, he just stopped moving. My womb felt so empty."

"Oh, Mom." Lissa rushed to her mother and, on her knees, buried her head in her mother's lap, her arms desperate to comfort her mother. Mom stroked her daughter's hair.

"The umbilical cord was wrapped around his neck..." Lissa

felt her mother's stifled sobs.

"Why didn't you tell us?" Anguish twisted Lissa in double knots. "How could you and Dad bear it?"

"Honey, please don't tell your sister."

Wild-eyed, Lissa looked at her mother. "Please, Mom, please don't ask me to keep this secret."

"Well, I didn't want you girls to be frightened by childbirth. And then when Boots couldn't get pregnant...I just didn't want to burden either of you."

"You mean Ray knows?"

"Your father told him a couple of years ago. Dad thought that one of you children should know."

Lissa took this in and resisted getting upset. Ray had never said a thing.

"When was he born?"

"June nineteenth. It never stops hurting. Every year...His name is Nicholas."

"Nicholas? You named him Nicholas?" Her mother nodded and smiled the saddest smile.

"Mom, I'm so sorry." Lissa didn't know what words of comfort could help such an old hurt.

"I planted those poppies in remembrance of Nicholas." That bed of crimson poppies had been there for forever. They had bloomed year after year, with only Mom and Dad knowing why. To everyone else they were just pretty poppies.

Lissa sat, mesmerized, as her mother talked about her brother. Mom's voice flowed as a mother singing a lullaby to her child. Her mother told her what Nicholas looked like and where he was buried. Precious time. After so many years, Mom said all that needed to be said. Mother and daughter held each other's hands and shared their sorrow.

"And then God gave us Ray." Mom patted Lissa's hand and said no more about Nicholas.

Later, Lissa turned the shock of having a brother she never knew every direction in her mind. There was no good place to

FIFTY DAYS TO SUNRISE

get hold of it. This knowledge was a gift her mother had given her: a piece of her mother, a piece of herself. And it stung, like a handful of burrs.

She decided to just set it down. Not now. Nicholas would always be there. She looked forward to meeting him in heaven.

Chapter 50

Lissa was running late. Dwight's rented house, a red brick Victorian, was one of the smaller houses on the bluff overlooking the Dakota River. Carpenter Gothic trim in dark green lined the two dormer roof peaks. The porch across the front of the house was a well-done reproduction of the original, with turned posts and spindles, and fancy trim along the top.

Lissa shifted the hot dish she carried with potholders and tapped the front door with the side of her sandal-shod foot. This was the first time she'd been in Humpy's space. She never went to his house when they were kids. He always wanted to come to her house—who could blame him.

She worried she'd overdressed. She had on the nicest capris she'd brought: black, with lime-green embroidered flowers on the bottom edge. She wore her favorite black boat neck T-shirt with three-quarter-length sleeves. It was the most stylish look she could put together with what she'd brought.

Dwight opened the door. He wore khaki cargo-pocketed shorts, a salmon-pink Hawaiian shirt, no shoes, and a big smile. Lissa was overdressed.

"Hi. Sorry I'm late. The potatoes took longer than I expected." She held up the dish.

"Doesn't matter. The coals are almost ready. Come on in. Follow me to the kitchen."

She took off her sandals in the front entryway. Trying to balance the hot German potato salad, she fumbled with getting her purse off her shoulder. Dwight grabbed the dish from her.

"Wow, I didn't know you were an art collector."

Lissa surveyed the living room and dining room. Several paintings hung there—fine art paintings. Lissa recognized two of them. They were by Gilbert Brooks, an artist Sean knew from his California dreamin' days. Gil stayed and painted wild, evocative West Coast scenes. Sean moved and painted the East Coast.

"I know this artist. Gil's a character."

"So I hear." Dwight was on his way to the kitchen.

"This one's beautiful. The one of the rose." She admired a small, simple painting of a yellow rose, the petals tipped with a blush of pink. The shading was exquisite. Lissa was surprised by this one. It didn't seem to fit in the collection.

"My daughter Alexis did that. She's in London studying art."

"I'm impressed. Who'd she get her art talent from?"

"Her mother, of course." Dwight disappeared into the kitchen.

Lissa walked around the perimeter of both rooms taking in the paintings. It was an art gallery with a beautiful house for a backdrop. Nothing looked as fine as Sean's work, but she kept that observation to herself.

The house was lovely. Buttercream walls and golden oak all around cast a soft glow in the rooms. The original double pocket doors between the living room and dining room were stowed away. Another set leading to a room off the dining room were closed. The built-in buffet in the dining room sparkled with flashy quarter-sawn oak and leaded glass doors above. The oak mantel and blue tile surround of the fireplace set off an antique-looking gas fireplace insert. Lissa exhaled softly.

The living room furniture was nondescript, a little sparse, but high quality. A cognac-tan leather sectional, a large dark-blue leather recliner with a wrought iron floor lamp next to it, and a simple birch coffee table—that was it. The only thing on the coffee table was a large art book: *Twentieth Century American Painters: Volume 2, 1950-1999.* She could have turned to the pages featuring Sean; she had a copy of the book at home. The dining room was empty of furniture. There were no rugs on the wood floors.

Lissa counted nine paintings.

"What would you like to drink?" Dwight called from the kitchen.

"Doesn't matter. Whatever you're having." She followed Dwight's voice to the kitchen.

The kitchen was small, remodeled probably in the '80s. At the far end sat a bistro table and two chairs. Obviously, this was where Dwight ate his meals at home. The sheet linoleum flooring in a Delft tile pattern was jarring after two such high quality rooms. A tile backsplash covered the entire area between counter and upper cabinets: tiles in cobalt blue, marigold, and white. The cabinets were laminated and plain: blue on the bottom cabinets, white on the top ones. The overall effect was homey, if not chaotic. There was nothing left of the old house in the kitchen.

Dwight took out two big glasses and reached in the fridge. When he produced a pitcher of ice tea Lissa felt a twinge of disappointment. Dwight must have seen it.

"Would you prefer a glass of wine?"

"No, it's fine." She regretted those impulses. It shouldn't matter. She didn't want it to matter.

"Let's go out and check the coals."

He led the way out the back door to a brick patio. "Go

check out the view. It's great." He gestured toward the river.

She wandered toward the two Adirondack chairs overlooking the river. Downriver she could see The Old Mill and the apartment complex where Mom and Dad were moving. Straight across was Booth Park with acres of trees. Beyond, on the hill, was St. Lucy's. Beautiful.

The river, about thirty feet down a sloping bank, calmly made its way to the Mighty Mississippi. In the spring the Dakota was a torrent, and the whole town was glad for this bank.

"Looks like we're ready for the chicken. Back in a sec."

Lissa sat at the picnic table on the patio.

While the chicken cooked, they talked. The light turned amber as the sun dropped toward the horizon.

Dwight brought out a lettuce salad to go with the potato salad, and they ate outside. Conversation was easy. They still had a lot of past to catch up on: people to gossip about, a lot of questions to ask. Lissa put on her denial mask and talked about Sean and the kids. Dwight talked about Becky and his kids. But they didn't talk about the deaths of either of their spouses.

"Yow!" Lissa smacked a mosquito on her bare ankle.

"Time to go in," Dwight said as he finished the last mouthful of his seconds of potato salad. They gathered up the dishes and retreated into the house. "I'd sure like a screen porch."

He shooed her to sit at the kitchen table while he put food in the fridge and dishes in the dishwasher.

"Now," Dwight turned to her. "Dessert?" It amused Lissa that he was such a good host. Definitely a new dimension to the nerd he was in high school.

"You betcha."

Dessert was cookie dough ice cream and chocolate sauce. When Lissa finished, she clattered her spoon into the bowl and sat back. "Well, it's now or never."

"Let's go into the living room. Now you want that glass of

wine?"

"Sure." She wanted to say, "better not," but didn't.

Both barefoot, they padded out to the living room.

"Can I sit in the Papa Bear chair?" Lissa wanted her own space.

"Of course." Dwight sat on the end of the sectional. Several seconds passed. Lissa busied herself looking at the stained glass transom over the living room window. Her gaze moved to the nearest paintings and settled on Gil's painting of Big Sur.

"Have you been there?" Lissa asked, nodding at the painting.

"Yeah, many times. Brooks really captured the sea, don't you think?"

"Not bad. Good, really, but..."

"But not like Sean." Dwight smiled at her.

She was glad Dwight finished the sentence for her. It sounded unkind, but it was true. Gil's work wasn't in the book on the coffee table.

Lissa fell silent again.

"This is awkward, Lissa. You talked about Sean a lot this evening. Was there something more you wanted to talk about? ...about his death?"

She nodded, looking for words in the red depths of her wine. "I need to tell someone about it. I've avoided it, but I see it in my nightmares....I'm so tired of crying. Sometimes I wake up crying. Maybe saying it out loud will help." She paused, but Dwight said nothing. "I miss Sean so much, sometimes I think I'll go absolutely crazy if I think about it." She looked apologetically at her friend. "Oh, Humpy—I mean Dwight—do you mind? I don't want this to be tough on you either."

"Not at all. What are friends for? And I think we've done this before, remember?"

She did remember. She didn't know how she could have gotten through Pip's death without Dwight. Sometimes it had been too hard to be around Sally and Jessica: too hard when it was so obvious Pip was missing from them.

Dwight had tried really hard to make things better for Lissa. One of the corsages she found in the box in the attic was from Dwight when he took her to Homecoming. But she didn't tell him about the corsage.

She braced herself and told him everything about Sean. The phone call. Telling the kids. Flying to Amsterdam with Ray. Identifying Sean's body.

Oh, God, this was hard. Never. These details had never crossed her lips before. Not even to her therapist. Not to Sally. They were locked away in the back room of her heart.

The autopsy. Cremation. All the permits and details that Ray took care of. Flying back with Sean's ashes.

Repatriating remains, what a bloodless term. Her mouth ran dry. Empty. The police officer had just been doing her job, but Lissa had wanted to reach through the phone and shake her brains out. Jackie Kennedy must have felt that rage, accompanying her assassinated husband's body back to Washington. Shock and fury that can't be expressed, so you go blank, go somewhere else—anywhere else.

The memorial service. The months of sorting out the legal details. Standing in Sean's closet, weeping into the sleeves of his shirts, pressing her face into his collars. Then letting go of Sean's clothes, except for a few things she wore when she wanted to feel him close.

Lissa took a deep breath and sighed. Dwight had fetched a box of Kleenex from somewhere in the last hour and a half. She had several tissues wadded up in her lap.

"I still haven't done anything with Sean's ashes. First I had the urn in my closet, but I couldn't bear to look at it every time I opened my closet door. Then I moved it to Sean's studio. He's in the cupboard with his paints and canvases." She smiled a very sad smile at the thought of Sean at home in his studio.

"Really?" Dwight waited, but she said nothing. "Maybe that would be good to think about doing when you get back. Did you and Sean ever talk about what you wanted done with your ashes?"

"No, it never came up. I guess we figured we weren't old enough to need to have that conversation yet." She shook her head.

"What do you think he'd have wanted done with his ashes?"

She didn't have to think long. "He loved the sea. I think he'd want his ashes scattered at sea." She smiled. "Then he'd be close to home."

"You know, you can have a proper service and burial at sea, if you want."

Lissa was silent. She wanted to crawl back into the bottle of denial, firmly corked, bobbing on the Sea of Leave-Me-Alone. But she couldn't.

"No, I think just the kids and me." She avoided looking at Dwight and looked instead at Gil Brooks's wild seascape. "I'll talk to Jack about it when I get back."

It was strange, talking about Sean's ashes. She hadn't wanted to face it—so final, so real—tried not to think about seeing her husband in ashes. Lissa drew in a deep breath and let out an even deeper sigh.

Dwight offered the wine bottle in her direction. "No thanks. I should probably get home." Lissa gathered the soggy tissues into a wad in one hand. "Thanks for dinner." Holding her empty glass and the fistful of tissues, she looked at him. "And thanks for being such a good friend."

"No problem. I'm kind of used to it." He reached over, took the glass from her, and set it on the coffee table. Neither of them moved.

"Hey, you're here, what, another three weeks? You really want to learn to play golf?"

Dwight's question was a welcome tug back to the present. She'd never considered golf before last week, but it had been fun. She cocked her head and smiled. "I think I would."

"Well, then, I'm your teacher. I taught both my girls to play, and they're still speaking to me. I'll call you in a couple days."

Lissa got up to leave. Reluctantly, she slipped her comfortable bare feet back into her sandals, retrieved her purse, and jammed the Kleenexes into it.

"Oh, your dish." Dwight disappeared for a moment and was back with a clean dish. "Let me walk you out."

Dwight opened the door of the Camry, and she ducked in. He carefully closed the door. Lissa rolled down the window and put the key in the ignition. She hesitated and looked at him. She turned the key.

The little engine hummed its Japanese tune. "Whew. We have lift off." She put it in drive and eased on the gas. In the rearview mirror she saw Dwight standing in the street, waving. Lissa waved out the window and called, "Thanks again!"

Chapter 51

She let her cell phone ring three times before answering it. It might be Dwight setting up her first golf lesson.

"Hi, Mom."

"Jack. So good to hear your voice. It wasn't your ring."

"No, I'm calling from the restaurant. My battery's dead."

"How are you, honey?"

"Well, are you sitting down?" A knife stabbed Lissa in the heart. "Meagan and I just got back from the doctor." Lissa dropped down hard onto the window seat. "We're pregnant!"

She gasped, sucking in as much air as she could before letting it back out in a squeal of joy. Poor Jack probably had to hold the phone away from his ear. Relief hit her in the face like an icy bucket of water in the desert.

"Oh, honey, that's wonderful! I'm so thrilled."

"Yeah. We couldn't wait to tell you till you got back. I hope you don't mind hearing the news over the phone."

"Not at all. Oh, it's just so exciting." She was babbling. "When's Meagan due?"

"March 8."

"How's she feeling?"

"Oh, you know, what can you say, she's a pregnant lady. She throws up and she's a little grouchy now and then. Other than that, she's totally crazy fantastic."

"Well, this is such a surprise."

"Yeah, no kidding." Jack chuckled.

"Oh, really?"

"Yeah, but not something you discuss with your mother. We had about half a second of shock before..." Jack's voice sounded thick. "Mom, we're so happy."

She could only hug and squeeze her son with words. "Honey, I'm so happy for you."

Jack sighed. "I wish Dad...Sorry, Mom...I didn't mean to..." His words choked off.

"I know, honey. It's okay. Me too." Her nose prickled.

"I feel like I'm a little nuts right now. You'd think I was the one with the hormones. I mean, I'm going to be a father!"

"Well, you've got a few months to get used to the idea. The Lord knew what he was doing when he gave us nine months to think about it."

That was what Sean had said when they found out Lissa was pregnant with Jack. She pushed those memories to the side.

"Let me talk to the mom-to-be."

"Meagan's talking to her mother. Has been for the last half hour. I'm sure she'll call you when she's off the phone."

"Do you want to tell Grandma yourself?"

"You bet. Put her on."

Lissa fairly danced down the stairs to find Mom in the backyard. Mom took off her gardening gloves and took the phone. Her face lit up like a flare. She clapped her hand to her bosom and kept repeating, "Oh, that's wonderful."

After they hung up, Mom and Lissa hugged each other like fools. Lissa would have jumped up and down, clutching her mother, if she hadn't been afraid she'd break her. Lissa

FIFTY DAYS TO SUNRISE

knocked Mom's straw sun hat off the back of her head.
"I'm going to be a grandma!"
"I'm going to be a *great*-grandma!"
"Mom!" Lissa let go and gave her mother a serious look.
"What?" Mom's smile vanished.
"I need to start knitting a baby blanket. For my grandchild. Let's go get some yarn."
"Oh," relief washed over Mom's face. "Now?"
"Yes, now."
"Well, at least let me wash my hands." They couldn't stop smiling.

Lissa drove to Ewe Too, Mom's favorite yarn shop. The colors and textures of the yarns were intoxicating.

Mom suggested a simple, adorable pattern. After much patting and squeezing, Lissa picked out a dreamsicle-colored acrylic yarn, twisted with a pearly cream strand. She bought multi-colored wooden circular needles. Wouldn't Sally be surprised.

When they got home, Dad was back from the hardware store. Mom and Lissa again went through the joyful news of the first great-grandchild. Dad was thrilled, but in a much less exuberant way than Mom, but that was typical of them.

That evening there was a decided crackle to the air in the house—in a good way. They smiled at each other often. Mom's and Lissa's knitting needles ticked like clocks keeping syncopated time.

Chapter 52

Thoughts of her grandchild were Lissa's first thoughts of the day. She said a quick prayer for Baby Maguire and pushed away the irrational fears; today a doctor would catch a problem like what happened to Nicholas, she hoped. But what should she do about Boots and India? How could she leave when Amy was pregnant?

"Good morning, sunshine. You look chipper this morning." Dad set his coffee cup down and resumed eating his oatmeal.

"I *am* chipper. It's not every day you wake up knowing you have a grandchild on the way." Lissa poured herself some coffee and sat down across from her father. "Did it ever get old hat, having another grandchild?"

"Not at all. Although I have to say, there was something special when Jack was the first. Then Shannon the first granddaughter. Ray's Jason to carry on the family name. And then, it was something to have the twins." Dad looked contemplative. "But, no, now that I think of it, we were thrilled with each one. Your mom was flapping all over the place, telling all her friends, just like she is now. She's next door at

Gladys's."

Lissa put her feet up on the chair next to her. "Dad, about that offer of the house."

He waved his spoon in the air and chuckled. "I assume you'll be staying in Seaton now."

"Yeah, d'ya think?" A grin covered her face. "I can't tell you how much I appreciate the offer though."

The phone rang. Lissa jumped to answer it.

"Makkinen's."

"Hey, Lissa, it's Dwight. I just wondered if you're busy this afternoon. Want to start those golf lessons?"

"Isn't it supposed to rain?"

"Should hold off till this evening. I thought we'd start on the driving range."

"Then sure."

"Great. Wear your running shoes. I'll pick you up about two."

She hadn't spoken up quickly enough to say she'd meet him there. To do so now seemed rude. "Sounds good. See you then."

Lissa got off the phone, and Dad looked inquisitively at her.

"Dwight's going to teach me to play golf. He's coming over to get me at two. I didn't think we had anything for the move going on today. Do we?"

"No, I don't think so." Lissa caught the hint of a twinkle in Dad's eyes.

"What?" A slight flush crept up her neck.

"Nothing. Just glad to see you enjoying yourself."

"It's just Humpy." She gave Dad a look that included pursed lips and a mild scowl. Lissa whisked her coffee off the table, almost spilling it, and retreated to the patio.

She hadn't forgotten the conspiracy to get her here for the summer. She was resigned though, and mostly past the anger. She even admitted, to herself, that her parents were right.

FIFTY DAYS TO SUNRISE

Then her thoughts bounced back to Baby Maguire.

Assuming her newly acquired golfing stance, Lissa checked that her hands were in the right position. She waggled the club face behind the ball and looked at Dwight for confirmation. He nodded. It was an absolutely ridiculous position.

She whacked at the ball. And missed. Lissa whipped the club back down to try and regain her balance. The ball rolled off the tee with the force of the air currents created by her whiff.

Dwight broke out laughing. "That actually wasn't a bad swing. Remember to keep your head down."

"Grrrrr!"

"Animal noises won't help."

"Yes, they will. It makes me feel better."

"Here, let me show you again." Dwight took the five iron from her and demonstrated the swing again: twice in slow motion, then at full speed. "Now remember, close your eyes and picture what you just saw me do. Try to picture it and feel it in your body."

She did what he said. "Does this really help?"

"You bet. Visualizing and thinking something you're trying to learn helps get it into your movements. Now you try it."

Lissa stepped back up to the tee, put a new ball in place, and got into position.

"Now keep your head down and swing."

Concentrating, she sucked in her lower lip. She swung and heard the crack of metal on the ball.

"Owww!" She yelped in pain.

"Wow! That was great! You did it! A good sixty yards. Almost straight as an arrow."

"I didn't see it." Lissa missed seeing the ball arc out onto the driving range. Gingerly, she touched a fingertip to her lower lip. Her lip was bleeding, and it stung like fire.

"You okay?"

"Yeah. I'll do it again. This time without the lip biting."

She visualized, lined up on the ball again—and whacked. A gratifying *crack* sounded. This time she watched as her ball sailed wildly to the left.

"You hooked it. But you hit it."

Dwight coached her on a few more swings. Then they moved on to the putting green.

"We'll just have you get the feel for the putter today. We won't do much with it."

Putting was easy compared to swinging at the ball. However, getting the ball to roll into the cup wasn't easy. Several times Lissa came *so* close.

"Had enough for the first day?"

Lissa straightened up and put a hand to her sore back muscles, arching to stretch them out. She groaned in satisfaction. "Yeah. I think I have." The afternoon shadows stretched over the lawn.

"Seriously, Lissa, I think you're a natural. I can't get over how well you've done for your first day."

"Beginner's luck. But thanks." She really was pleased. "You're a pretty good teacher. Except when you laugh at me."

"But you were funny."

"Ha ha, but looks aren't everything, right?"

"Come on. I'll buy you a drink."

When they got their lemonades, Dwight proposed a toast, "To your new grandchild."

"Here, here," Lissa said, as they clinked glasses.

Chapter 53

The house was quiet and dark everywhere except the living room where Lissa sat knitting in Mom's chair. Her grandbaby's blanket was slowly taking shape. Through the open window behind her, she could hear the gentle thrum of rain.

She let her knitting rest in her lap and thought about the last few days. When she wasn't busy with something else, like trying to hit a golf ball, her mind immediately went to the baby. She smiled.

But an unpleasant feeling crept into her stomach: a feeling somewhere between nausea and unease. Her smile wilted. Fingers of guilt clawed at her insides, getting a grip on her heart and squeezing. She took a shuddering breath. Tears sprang to her eyes, and she trembled with the effort of trying to cry silently.

"Oh, Sean," she whispered to the dark, empty dining room, "I wish you were here."

Never in her wildest nightmares had she imagined she'd be a grandmother alone. It seemed wrong to feel joy in the midst of miserable grief. But she did. She couldn't push the joy away.

Yet the grief that was now part of her seemed to demand that she hold joy and grief together in some kind of balanced tension. Neither would fully give way to the other.

Her heart was a battleground. She realized that to love all the people so important to her, and now the promise of a new life to love, she had to fight for love. If she continued to turn inward, turn away from the love around her, she would lose—lose her family, lose herself, lose her grip on the Lord. It was bad enough she lost Sean; she couldn't lose those living, breathing, hugging people around her. Lissa couldn't let them down.

She got up to get her cell phone from her room. She needed to call her daughter. It was an hour earlier in Denver; Shannon would surely still be up.

"Hi, honey, it's Mom."

"Hey, hi! I was just thinking about calling you. Pretty exciting news, eh?"

"I know. I just can't wipe the smile off my face. You wouldn't believe—I've already started knitting a baby blanket."

"Oh, that's cool. I can't wait to be an aunt. This weekend I'm going to buy a stuffed animal for my niece. Or I guess it might be a nephew. Did they say if they'd find out if it was a boy or a girl?"

"Oh, I don't know. I didn't ask. It'll be a while before they can tell anyway."

"Well, it's all just so cool. I'll bet you can't wait to see them."

"No kidding. This has been a really long summer. I had no idea." She didn't say anything to Shannon about the ulterior motive behind her parents' request to have her come home. "I was already starting to miss being home. Now I'm *really* eager to get home. Two weeks and a bit. That's not so long now."

"Yeah. It'll go by quick."

"What have you been up to?"

"Not a whole lot. Matt and I have been biking quite a bit.

Gotta keep in shape for skiing, you know." Lissa stiffened at Matt's name and was thankful Shannon couldn't see it through the phone.

"Mom, I'm glad you called. There's something I've been thinking about asking you."

"Oh?" Her muscles got even tighter, and she could feel her breathing go shallow. Her relationship with Shannon was easily strained, and she needed to chose her words carefully.

"Yeah. I was wondering if you want to come out for Christmas. Everybody. We'd ski. In fact, I was thinking of renting a condo at Breck for the week. What would you think of that?"

"What?" The room tilted a little.

"I know we usually get together for Christmas, but I thought, hey, why not break tradition and make it out here. It would kind of be like at *my* place. *My* turn to have the family over." The excitement in Shannon's voice was endearing. "Everyone could come out if they want. Uncle Ray's family would love to ski. I know Aunt Boots would try anything. Etienne probably wouldn't come, but, oh well. I think Jack and Meagan might go to her parents'. And Grandma and Grandpa could come too."

"Well," Lissa bought herself some thinking time, drawing out the word. "What about Matt?"

"Matt?" Shannon sounded surprised. Apparently Lissa hadn't taken enough thinking time.

"I thought you two were—"

"Mom," Shannon sharply cut her mother off. "We're not living together or anything."

"Sorry, honey, I didn't know. I just thought—"

"Well don't think. *Ask.*" Shannon was clearly exasperated.

"I'm sorry. Really. Forgive me?"

"Of course." Shannon let out a huffing breath. "But only if you say yes."

Lissa chuckled inwardly. Shannon was her father's

daughter.

"Yes," Lissa said. Shannon squealed into the phone, and Lissa jerked the phone away from her ear. "It actually does sound great. But...now really, we have to think about this."

"I'll arrange everything. I'll be, like the tour guide. I'll call Uncle Ray and Aunt Boots. And I'll talk to Grandma and Grandpa after they get the move out of the way." Words tumbled out. "Then, depending on who all's coming, I'll book a place big enough for us. Maybe a whole chalet." She had clearly given this plot considerable thought.

"One thing, Shannon, Breckenridge is at a really high elevation. I'm not sure Grandpa and Grandma could do it."

"Oh, yeah, I forgot about that. Well, I'll ask them. There's portable oxygen, you know. Even an oxygen hookah bar." She giggled. "They could check with their doctor."

"Nobody besides me has to make an immediate decision, do they?"

"Oh, heck no, I'll just get the snowball rolling and see how many it picks up."

"It really does sound like fun. You had a great idea, honey."

"And if anyone wants ski lessons, Matt said he'd be happy to do it for free. There'll be a couple days during the holiday week when he's not scheduled with lessons."

"That's a nice offer." Lissa really was relieved to hear they weren't living together. "Tell him thanks. I know I'll take him up on it anyway." And it would be a good opportunity to get to know a little about this mystery guy in Shannon's life.

"Oh, Mom, this is so exciting. I can't wait for you to come out here."

"Me too, honey. This will be fun to plan." Time with her daughter and skiing? An easy decision.

"Give Grandma and Grandpa my love."

"I will. Love you."

"You too."

Lissa flipped the phone shut and grinned like she'd been

given an unexpected gift. Another thing to look forward to.

She thought again about hearing Sean's words from Shannon's lips. Sean used to say, "but only if..." in response to something Lissa and he were negotiating. It had made her laugh to hear Shannon say it, hadn't caused a stab of pain. It was comforting to hear Sean in his daughter. Lissa was likely to hear and see a lot of Sean in their children, and she made up her mind to find joy in it.

Chapter 54

Dad ran a hand through his thick white hair. "Maybe I should have sold the Steinway before we moved."
He and Lissa sat at the kitchen table going over Mom's list. Dad looked strained. He had just written a note to himself to confirm the piano moving date for the week after the main move.
"It'll be okay." Lissa didn't know what to say. Selling the piano seemed too much to contemplate. When Mom sold her cello it was difficult for her, but the arthritis in her hands was bad enough that she couldn't play at all. Dad playing the piano was like Dad hooked up to a respirator, life's breath.
"Yes, but your mother is fretting about the china set. We don't have a place to put it, and it certainly doesn't seem like a good idea to buy another piece of furniture. We won't have a dining table anyway, just this kitchen table. The piano is going to take up all of the dining area."
"Oh, well, I don't know, Dad." Not much can be done about a baby grand two weeks before moving day. Lissa tried not to show him how helpless she felt.

"Missy, do you think you could manage to take the china with you? I know it would be tight, but it would be a big help. We want Jack to have it anyway."

She could feel her shoulders sag and did a quick mental calculation of space in the Camry. A frustrated exhale almost escaped, but she covered it with clearing her throat.

"I'll just make it happen. Sure."

"Thanks, honey, that's a big relief." Dad reached over and squeezed his daughter's shoulder.

"Now, let's look at this list and tell me what you want me to do." Lissa sat up straighter.

For the rest of the day Lissa cleaned out closets under Mom's supervision and made two more runs to Goodwill. It was amazing how much stuff accumulated hidden out of view. Mom got more brutal as the day wore on, letting things go. She decided if she hadn't laid her hands on any particular item in a year, it was going.

It was hard for Lissa to watch her mother as so many bits and pieces of their life passed through her hands on the way to the donation boxes. Sometimes Mom held an item, and Lissa could tell her mother was looking back in time. Lissa felt like a voyeur as Mom's face told the tale of her memories and her struggle to let go. Mom said less about where she'd gotten something the longer they worked, until she worked in silence. With her mouth set, almost grim, she'd hand an item to Lissa and look away from it to the next item to be judged. Lissa had the thought, as she arranged things in the boxes, that she was the last family member to touch these things, things that were once worth keeping.

When Dad got back from running errands, he wandered in to see what Mom and Lissa were doing, but he didn't stay long. Lissa made a mental note to stop collecting so much stuff that didn't matter. She didn't want it to matter.

The accumulation of a lifetime. And this wasn't even all of it. Over the last few years, a lot of family heirlooms had already been distributed among kids and grandkids. Lissa thought of all the stuff she already had at her own home. What a confusion. She didn't know what she'd do without the comfort of the things that reminded her of Sean, things they shared, things that were his—a painful comfort. And she treasured the strength of family ties when she slept under her grandmother's quilt.

Her parents going through their past made her wonder about her future. She was sure Mom and Dad were doing the same.

She stuck close to Mom and Dad all day. She could feel their need of her, and, once again, she was glad she'd come home. Chinese takeout for dinner sounded good to everyone. They spent the evening watching TV—until the war news came on. Mom knit for a friend's great-grandchild; Lissa knit for her own grandbaby.

Chapter 55

Side by side Lissa and Dwight hit balls on the driving range. It was hot, but Lissa didn't care, she was determined to learn this game, and determined to keep busy.

Lissa had left Mom and Dad for the day, up to their elbows in dirt. They seemed to need a day of garden therapy. She called Dwight to see if he wanted to resume her golf lessons. He had work to do in the morning, but he was free for the afternoon. Lissa happily spent the morning with Sally and then met Dwight at the country club after lunch.

Time passed without noticing it was gone.

The ball sailed high and straight as Lissa chipped a shot.

"Whew, I thought you'd never finish that second bucket of balls. I'm hungry." Dwight slid his driver into the bag and topped it with the fuzzy black cover.

"What? Oh, yeah, hunger. I forgot about that. What do you want to do?"

It was once again easy to be with Dwight, and Lissa didn't give a second thought to continuing the day together. It was like old times, in a way.

"Let's go back to my place."

Without hesitation, Lissa bagged one of the tube chairs Dwight had brought and picked up her water bottle.

They sat in his backyard overlooking the river. The trees threw long shadows across the yard, and a warm breeze stirred the hot air. Lissa's muscles ached good.

"So, tell me, Humpy Humphrey, how did you get to be…well…you've changed. What happened?"

Dwight laughed. "Changed? How do you mean?" He put his empty ice tea glass on the arm of the Adirondack chair.

"Well, let's face it." She smiled impishly at him. "You've got to admit, you were a bit of a nerd. Wouldn't you say?"

"I'm crushed." He slapped his hand flat on his chest, producing a resonant *whump*, and let out an explosive breath.

"No you're not." She reached over and gave him a gentle shove. "Seriously, where'd you get the confidence you seem to have?"

"Me?"

"Seriously, I want to know."

"Seriously? I think I always had a fair amount of confidence, it maybe just didn't show when my pants were too short. I was determined to do well in school and get into Purdue. It's just that I had to study a lot. I needed that ROTC full-ride scholarship. Maybe that made me a nerd."

"No, I think it was the glasses with the tape on the bridge of your nose."

"Don't remind me." He smiled faintly and gazed out across the river. "You know, the truth is, I dressed the way I did because my pa never made enough money to take care of his family. And I studied as hard as I did because I was darned if I'd be like either of my parents."

Lissa sipped her coffee, too uncomfortable to intrude into

FIFTY DAYS TO SUNRISE

Dwight's thoughts.

"Sorry, I didn't mean to be a wet blanket. But it is what it was. My pa was a drunk, and my mother was pretty mean and bitter. Not that I blamed her. I just wanted to get out of Gifford." He said the last statement with a crooked half-smile. "And here I am again. But you know, it's okay. This time it's my choice. And I'll choose when I leave."

"I'm sorry."

He shrugged. "Confidence, eh? What makes you think I've got confidence?"

"Well." She was embarrassed she'd brought up the subject, but she'd gotten herself into it. "You have a confident way of walking. And you seem confident when you talk to people. Just very at ease."

He snorted a sort of laugh. "I'm sure the Navy had a lot to do with that. I did retire a Captain."

"That's good?"

He nodded and smiled. "That means I did just fine."

"Well, good."

She thought before asking the next question. "I don't mean to be overly nosey, but did Vietnam change you?"

He looked away again at something, or nothing, across the river.

Finally, he said, "Vietnam changed all of us."

Lissa stared at the past too—into the face of a Vietcong, hands tied behind his back, face contorted by the impact of a bullet fired point-blank at his head. A picture never forgotten.

"This war in Iraq..." Unable to finish the thought, she was sorry she'd brought up the subject of war.

Dwight clinked the ice cubes against the sides of his glass. "You know...we lost my brother Charlie in Vietnam."

"Oh," Lissa murmured—swallowed hard. She had forgotten. "I'm so sorry."

"The Easter Offensive. March '72." He stopped and ran a hand over his head. "It still gets me, after all these years. He was MIA. I searched the records for years. I would've gone over there and looked for him myself if I could've."

Lissa reached over and gently touched Dwight's shoulder. She didn't know what to say.

Still looking out over the river he said, "That just about did Mother in."

They sat in silence—a wounded silence.

Dwight softly patted Lissa's hand that was resting on the chair arm. "C'mon. I've got something to show you."

He picked up the plate that had been piled with cheese and crackers and led the way through the kitchen to the closed doors off the dining room.

"This is my office. I've got something to show you in here."

She threw him a quizzical look tinged with a frown. What was this all about?

He pushed back both sides of the pocket door and stepped into the room. A large desk took up most of the right half of the room. An oversized Mac computer screen dominated the desktop. Around it were neat stacks of papers and books.

She turned to look where Dwight was gesturing, toward the wall on the opposite side of the room.

Lissa gasped and clapped a hand to her mouth. In slow motion she staggered back, like getting punched in the stomach, and bumped up against the desk. A sound came out of her mouth, a quiet, pained groan.

"Lissa, I'm so sorry." Dwight put a steadying hand on her shoulder. "I didn't think. I should have warned you." His face was red, and Lissa could see the consternation in his eyes as she shot him a wild look. She didn't know whether to hug him or strangle him. There, side by side on the wall, were two of Sean's paintings.

"Can I get you a glass of water or something?"

She straightened up and shook her head, both arms wrapped around herself.

She couldn't remember the title of the larger painting;

Sean had painted it several years ago. The other was *Survivor*. She thought she'd never see *Survivor* again.

In their last conversation, Sean had told her all of the paintings at the Amsterdam show had sold except *Survivor*. She had been glad. It was one of her favorite paintings that Sean had ever done. Before she'd had the presence of mind to tell the gallery to send it back, it was sold. Gone. A separate check was sent to her for $7,500. She would much rather have had the painting.

"Why didn't you tell me?" She barely got the words out. Her eyes riveted to *Survivor*.

Dwight was clearly troubled by having caused his friend such a shock. He stood back from her. "I didn't know how. I kind of wanted to surprise you. I thought you'd be pleased."

"Oh, I am," Lissa said, breathless.

She slowly walked up to *Survivor* and touched the top of the weather-battered, lone pine tree on the rocky island. She ran her finger, barely touching the surface, down the tree and followed the trunk to the birch bark canoe pulled up on shore. In the canoe was something red. Sean had asked her what the painting needed—a muted red wool blanket. Her finger stopped on the unsettled, gray-green water. The paint was rough to her fingertip. She clenched her hand, realizing she shouldn't be touching the painting, especially someone else's painting.

"I never thought I'd see it again."

The painting drew Lissa in—she was part of the roiling steel-purple clouds. She knew this place. Not that she'd ever seen it. Sean had gone alone on a camping trip to the interior of Maine to sketch. But she *knew* this place.

"Lissa, it's yours."

She wheeled around. "What?"

"Really. I bought it thinking I'd give it back to you, if you wanted it."

She stared at him. "But...but...I couldn't."

"Why not? I want you to have it."

Lissa struggled for words. "Well...I'd give you the money back."

"No. I insist." He raised his hands for emphasis. "Absolutely no money back."

A flush edged up her neck. "I just couldn't. It's too much."

"That depends on how you look at it. If this painting means as much to you as it looks like it does, then I think you *need* it."

He was right. Lissa did need *Survivor*. "But don't you?"

"No. Sadly, I started surviving many years ago, and I pretty much just got used to it. I think that's part of the confidence, or whatever it is, you think you see in me."

She looked at the floor. Her face set hard.

Dwight must have guessed her thoughts.

"Free and clear, Lissa. You don't owe me a thing," he said softly.

She looked up at him. The hurt was unmistakable in his voice. How could she have thought he meant this gift in any way but friendship? Her nose prickled, and tears stung her eyes.

"I'm sorry." Lissa threw her arms around his neck. "Thank you so much," she said to the back of his head.

He relaxed and returned her embrace, his arms low around her waist. Lissa broke away—suddenly aware of her breasts pressing against his chest. Dwight immediately released her.

As she pulled back from him, they briefly made uneasy eye contact. Lissa was startled—Dwight's eyes were the same color as the water in *Survivor*.

She smiled at him from two steps away. "Thank you," she said again, wiping her hands across her hot, damp face.

"My pleasure." He smiled warmly. "I'll ship it to you. I still have the crate it came in."

She felt limp, all played out. "That would be great. I've really got a carful. Mom and Dad gave me boxes of china and Sean's painting of our kids to take home."

FIFTY DAYS TO SUNRISE

Dwight frowned. "Are you sure you should take the painting in the car? I mean, it'll take you at least two days to get home, won't it?"

"Yeah, but I've got no choice."

"I'll ship both paintings. No problem."

Lissa opened her mouth to protest, but Dwight put up a hand. "We've done this already. Just say thank you. I'll stop over and pick up the painting this week."

"Thank you." Her eyes resting on *Survivor*, she ran her hands through her hair. She smiled, a smile twisted by welling tears. "Really, thank you."

Chapter 56

Sean tipped his head to the side and smiled at me. I'd caught him looking at me. I thought he was reading, but he wasn't. He laid his book down on his lap and gave up the pretext, continuing to gaze at me.
　"Lissa, you're absolutely beautiful. Have I ever told you that?"
　"Oh, just a few hundred times." I waved him off.
　"Really. I'm the luckiest man ever, to have such a beautiful, brainy wife."
　We sat in our flea market chairs beside the fireplace. The leaping flames cast a red glow on Sean's dark hair. His Black Irish good looks shimmered. His dark eyes were lit with fire, and the blaze of the flames made them sparkle. We sat for several moments caressing each other without touching.
　I set my book aside and slid to the floor. I eased myself down onto the sheepskin rug in front of the hearth. Sean watched, his eyes melting to dark chocolate. I stretched catlike and beckoned him to me, gently tapping

a forefinger to my lips.

Later, we lay spooned together, watching the embers pulse and fade. Sean drew his plaid flannel robe over us. My long hair spilled over my shoulder, and Sean nuzzled the back of my neck. His chest felt warm and moist on my back.

"Melissa Louise Makkinen Maguire, I'll love you till I die," he whispered into my ear.

I pressed the back of his hand to my lips. "Sean Patrick Maguire, I will love you till I die."

He cradled my head on his arm. He tucked his other arm under mine, and we held each other tight.

This is a painful memory to write. Sean and I often reminisced about this evening: a night of making love, of making life. We were never again just the two of us, but a family. Jack joined us that night.

I want to remember everything about Sean: how he looked, how he loved, how he talked, how he walked. I still have his voice on our answering machine. I can't bear to hear it, but I can't bear to change it. I feel desperate to remember how his voice sounded. "We're not home right now." Sometimes I listen to his voice and think he'll be back soon, just stepped out. I cling to the "we" in irrational hope. But now, every day that goes by brings me reluctantly closer to reality.

Sometimes I think I've seen Sean. But it turns out to be a misinterpreted fleeting glimpse of a stranger who only vaguely resembles Sean. My husband isn't coming home.

I think of my life with Sean as that red plaid robe he threw over us to keep us warm. We were a shelter to each other—and the memory of the strength he gave me and that I gave to him—will comfort me. I still feel Sean's arms around me, pulling me tightly to him.

I had no idea grief could be like this. It felt like I was dying of cancer, something ravaging me from the inside *out. It felt terminal. That I had no right to live, no desire to live without Sean.*

I know I'll survive. But I will always walk with a shard of glass embedded in my foot.

She closed the journal and rested her hand on the warm leather. She pushed the candle further away on the porch table. The flame flickered lazily in the breeze, no more than a cat's breath.

Thoughts of her future were increasingly on Lissa's mind. Strange that there *was* a future out there after all. But she was getting more accustomed to the idea, even if she was still alternately resentful at having to face it alone, and hopeful.

Lissa looked at nothing in particular in the front yard and the street beyond. Her future was out there, somewhere. It was a shock Mom and Dad had offered her this house. *Where* she lived hadn't been a thought—some days it was enough just to still draw breath.

Survivor. What an overwhelming gift from Dwight. One she couldn't fully comprehend. When Sean was painting it she had been captivated by the evocative images, now the images were deeply personal. She *was* that tree, that canoe. She was battered, but embedded in rock—she would be adrift, but she was tethered. It seemed Sean had painted it for her.

Home to the farm. Lissa turned the thought over, let it tumble like a rock polishing.

But for what?

Lissa caught her breath at the memory of a conversation she and Sean had shortly before he left for Amsterdam.

It had been a dream of Sean's to have a summer art institute at the farm. He talked about it many times. Sean wanted to give back to the art community: share his talent and his blessings. The farm and his studio were perfect. It just

needed a dormitory cottage, he had said.
    Lissa's eyes widened—this idea was a precious gem.

Chapter 57

"I've been thinking about what I should do with the farm." Lissa and her parents sat in the living room after dinner. Mom and Lissa knit, and Dad read the paper—more news of the war in Iraq.

"Oh?" Mom said, "I thought you wanted to stay there."

"I do, but I've been wondering if I should do something more with it. Do something with Sean's studio."

"Maybe you could move your writing studio out there," Dad said.

Lissa frowned. "I don't think I could do that. Too many memories. Besides, I'm pretty stuck on doing my writing where I've done it for years. I don't think my muses would move."

"You could rent it out as studio space."

"I could. But, you know...I was thinking of something big. What would you think if I started an art camp?"

Mom stopped knitting. "An art camp? You mean, have a day school for children?"

"Actually, I was thinking of a summer residential program. Only serious art students—college age and graduate students.

More of a summer art institute."

"You mean have people stay there? In the house?" Mom looked a little skeptical. "That would be a big job."

"I think I can afford to have a small bunkhouse built. One side for women and one side for men."

"That sounds like trouble," Dad said.

"Maybe, but I'd try to have the students really well-screened. I'd invite a resident artist to give instruction. Heaven knows I know enough artists. I should be able to find someone interested, maybe even two or three different artists over the summer.

"Actually, it was Sean's idea. He talked about it for at least a year."

Lissa had been thinking about this idea of an art institute for a couple of days—really, a couple of nights, since the idea kept her awake. She hadn't had the nerve to say it out loud until tonight. She'd even thought about making the institute for artists and creative writers, but that seemed like eating too much of the pie at once.

She couldn't bear the thought of Sean's studio empty. Cleaning it out and getting rid of everything was unthinkable. It was equally inconceivable to leave it as some sort of shrine, untouched from the time he left it. Until now she hadn't even been ready to think about it.

"Sean's studio is so great, it seems a shame to let it sit unused. I could easily partition off part of it for a small apartment for the resident artist, or maybe make a loft area. When Sean designed the barn as a studio he had in mind to make the space flexible."

"Missy, I think you're really on to something. It would be a big undertaking though."

"I know, but I think I'm ready. I've even thought about how I'd feed people. I wish Jack and Meagan could help, but summer is their busy season at the restaurant, and now there's a baby in the picture." Lissa beamed at this. "I think I could do it if I hire a couple of high school kids to help me. Maybe the art students could help out weeding the garden. My kitchen is big enough. It could be fun: everyone eating together, pitching in."

"Wouldn't it tie you down for the summer?" Mom resumed her knitting, not looking at it.

"Maybe, but that doesn't matter. I do most of my writing during the winter anyway." She paused. "I know, I've thought about juggling everything. I'll want to spend lots of time with the baby. I'll have to talk to Jack and Meagan and see what they think." Lissa took a deep breath. "Gosh, there's a lot going on."

Dad nodded and smiled at her. "That's a good thing, isn't it?"

"Yes, it certainly is."

Mom looked down at her knitting and smiled.

"Oh, and I didn't tell you. Boots invited me to go to India with her in February."

"Yes, she told us she was going to do that." Mom didn't look up from her knitting.

Lissa shook her head. "She's such a stinker.

"Thank you so much for making me come home this summer. I don't know what I would have done without all of you."

"Not at all, Missy. We couldn't have done otherwise."

"It sounds silly, but it almost feels, not quite yet, but almost—like a new day."

"Joy cometh in the morning," Dad said.

"I know that passage. Where is it?"

"Psalm 30," Mom said.

"Joy. I'd forgotten what that was."

Dad handed her his Bible. She turned to the psalm and read silently.

"...weeping may stay for the night, but rejoicing comes in the morning....You turned my wailing into dancing..."

Those beautiful words wrapped around her heart like a cashmere shawl and made her nose prickle again. She closed Dad's Bible and sniffed the prickle away.

"I'm going to remember this one."

They sat quietly for several moments. "And I'm going to get a Newfoundland puppy in the spring. I think I'll name her *Sisu*. And call her Sissy, for irony."

Dad threw back his head and guffawed. "That's appropriate." He laughed some more. "Missy, I think of all my children, you probably got the most *sisu*."

"Yeah," Lissa smiled. "It takes a lot of guts to be the oldest Makkinen kid."

Mom rolled her eyes and kept on knitting. "You Finlanders."

Lissa put the purple tip guards on her needles and stuffed the baby blanket into her knitting bag. "Well, I think I'll quick run to the grocery store."

Chapter 58

Beef tenderloin tips, or the marinated chicken breasts? Lissa stood in front of the meat counter trying to decide.

"Lissa," she heard an oily voice from behind the counter, "I heard you were in town."

She jerked her head up, and her eyes ran smack into the last face she ever wanted to see—Leonard DeAngelo.

"Yep. Heard you were in town. I was hoping I'd see you." Her skin crawled at the sound of that voice. The creep.

Lissa couldn't respond. She nodded, brainless. The rabbit frozen before the hawk strikes.

"Hey, I heard your husband died. Real sorry about that."

With tight knuckles, she clutched her purse shoulder strap. She stared at him, eyeballs drying fast from her rising heat.

"I see you're still wearing your wedding ring."

A spark whooshed into flame, and Lissa blazed. "That's none of your business."

"Whoa, no need to get all defensive."

Yeah, right. She'd needed armor with him before.

"I didn't know you worked here." Or she would have gone

to the other grocery store. Really, she might have gone to the other side of the planet.

"Just started last week. Managing the meat."

"Oh." She was nailed to the spot.

"Yeah, I got sick of the exes with their hands in my pockets. Figured I'd move back here for a while."

"Yeah, I'll bet."

"Kids weren't much better." He put his hands on top of the meat counter and leaned toward her. "Hey, how's about you and me go get a drink after work?"

Her face stung. She turned, snatched a package of frozen chicken, and bolted. Memories flooded her. A lot of yesterdays ago, but it might as well have been only one.

Her senior year, Leonard DeAngelo had badgered her to go out with him for months. Finally, she gave in.

They'd gotten burgers at the drive-in, then he drove out to Carver Road, the make out spot. She'd never been there before. She begged him to take her home; he refused.

"Hey, you owe me for the burger," he'd said as he reached over and grabbed her arm.

He smashed his mouth on hers and thrust his tongue into her mouth. She fought his grip, but he wouldn't let go. He clamped his other hand on her breast and twisted.

She bit him, hard. Like a snake, he recoiled—and slapped her, slamming her head against the seat.

Lissa wrenched herself free, jumped out of the car, and ran for home. He let her go.

For weeks, every time he oozed by her in school, he made kissing noises. Graduation finally ended the torment, and Leonard enlisted in the Army.

"Nice talkin' to ya." She could hear his chuckle fade as she fled to the checkout counter.

Her stomach rolled.

Lissa threw the bag of chicken over to the passenger seat. She clenched her fists. It was all she could do to prevent herself

FIFTY DAYS TO SUNRISE

from having a first-rate temper tantrum. Instead, she got in the car. Not that anyone would have seen her anyway. It was late, and there weren't many people grocery shopping.

All those years ago. She didn't tell anyone but Sally. Especially not her parents. She wasn't "that kind of girl." It was like lying: sneaking into her parents' room to use Mom's makeup to touch up the bruise on her jaw, but she had to.

Now the bruises seemed to reappear.

She folded her arms over her chest and remembered how much she had hurt. The bruising on her face was nothing.

Back home she took the chicken out, looked at it, and slammed the package on the counter. She hadn't wanted wings! Didn't even like wings.

"Everything okay, Missy?" Dad called from the top of the stairs.

She took a deep breath before answering. "Fine, Dad. Sorry. I just dropped something."

Chapter 59

Driving to the country club, Lissa drummed her thumbs on the steering wheel, no tune in her head. Last night's encounter with Leonard DeAngelo had raked her and scratched open sores. She couldn't get out of here soon enough.
She pulled into the country club parking lot and parked next to Dwight's truck. They were meeting early today to avoid the heat. Dwight was on the practice putting green, intent on sinking a long one, his back to Lissa. The ball rattled into the cup.
She made an effort to sound bright. "Hey, Arnold Palmer. How ya doin'?"
He straightened up, grinning. "Hi, Lissa. Did you see that? Pretty good, eh?"
"Certainly was. You promise you'll teach me how to do that?"
"Absolutely. Here." He handed her the putter.
"Wait. First I have to tell you something....I've got to get it out, or it'll eat on me."
Dwight looked puzzled and concerned. "Sure. Shoot. Is it

something I said?"

"No, silly. Remember Leonard DeAngelo?"

"Yeah, tall, loudmouth punk? I remember DeAngelo."

"That's him. Well, I ran into him at the grocery store last night." She paused. "Did I ever tell you what he did to me my senior year?"

"No." Dwight drew out the word, a dark furrow between his eyebrows.

And she told him.

Dwight swore. "Lissa, I'm so sorry. That never would've happened if I'd been there. I didn't know." He was furious. His hands clenched, and the anchor tattoo on his forearm jumped as the muscle tightened.

"He asked me to go for a drink last night." Lissa took aim with the putter and lopped off Leonard's imagined head.

"Sheesh! I'll take care of this!" Dwight fumed.

"I'm leaving in a few days. Maybe you should let it go."

"No way! I'll have a *talk* with him."

She balled her fists. Leonard had done this to her before: put her in a terrible spot where there was no good way out. She refused to let Leonard DeAngelo think he got away with something again.

"Thanks. But I don't like being such a baby. It's not like I can't take care of myself." Her pulse thundered in her ears.

"Lissa,...guys who treat women like that..." He shook his head. "Here, give me that." He took the putter from her and, with a grunt, took a mighty swing that would have sliced DeAngelo in half.

"There," he said, handing the putter back to her. "Now, let's play golf. But I'm not kidding, he and I are gonna talk. Nobody's gonna treat you like that."

For the next half hour they practiced putting.

Lissa noticed Dwight shaking his head now and then, his lips pursed, but he said nothing more about Leonard DeAngelo.

FIFTY DAYS TO SUNRISE

That creep was not going to ruin this day too.

Dwight picked up the ball. "Now let's go take some practice swings with the driver. I've got a tee time for us in twenty minutes."

"A tee time! You mean to *play*?"

"Sure. You're ready. We'll just play the front nine to start."

"But I haven't got any clubs. Can I rent them?"

"Naw, it's okay. You and I are near enough the same height. You can use mine. Ideally, you'd want golf shoes with cleats, but your running shoes are fine. That is, until you decide if you really want to play the game."

Which she hadn't. It was one thing to play golf with Dwight this summer for something to do, but golf might not fit into her life at home—into her future—now that she could think further than the next day.

On the driving range her first shot was a clean whiff, so far from the ball it remained undisturbed on the tee.

"That's okay. Get it out of your system now. Leave it on the driving range." Dwight clapped his hands in encouragement. "Come on now. Smack it! Picture that—"

"Right! Oh, yeah."

She set herself and tried again. *Crack*! She sent Leonard DeAngelo's head out to land with all the other stupid little white balls.

"Attagirl!" Dwight shielded his eyes against the sun and tracked the ball. "You *are* amazing."

"Aw, thanks." She smiled so big it threatened to split her lips.

A few more swings, not all as successful, and they were off to the tee box. Dwight's name was called over the loudspeaker, and they were underway with her first golf game. Dwight led off. His drive was long and straight down the fairway.

"Now, we're not keeping score on this one. And if you hit a ball in the other fairway, we'll just go get it and drop it back in play on the hole we're playing. No need to make it more frustrating than necessary for you."

"Oh, definitely. I like less frustration. In fact, could we eliminate *all* the frustration from golf?"

He gave her a mock sardonic look and shook his head. "Oh, Lissa, you have *no* idea."

By the second hole she understood his meaning. At least she was getting a lot of exercise chasing the ball around the neighboring fairways. On the third hole they had to let another party play through so they didn't hold them up.

Yet, it was fun. Dwight chose the clubs for her and explained why he chose each one. She was slowly picking up the golf lingo.

On the fourth hole Lissa slammed the driver into the ball and sent it straight down the fairway. She jumped in the air and whooped. So did Dwight. Then the next shot she whiffed on three attempts, and finally sent the ball into the trees.

"I hate this game! Why are you making me play it?" she screamed for all to hear.

"To torture you, of course, why else?"

Lissa shoved Dwight in the arm, not coming close to knocking him off balance, and they marched off to find her ball.

"Remember to keep your head down. Don't move it," he coached.

"Yes, O Golf Master."

Dwight was really good at this game. Lissa learned what a birdie was, because he got two of them. And the bigger the bird, the better. An eagle was especially good.

By the end of the nine holes, she was dog-tired and exhilarated. She'd say she was hooked on the game, but she learned a hook is something you don't want in golf, unless you're trying to make the ball hook. She succeeded at hooking the ball a number of times, without trying.

Dwight clapped her on the shoulder. "Let's go celebrate. Lunch at Gert's?"

FIFTY DAYS TO SUNRISE

"Actually, would you mind if we went to your house? I'm not up for the smoke. I could pick up something on the way over."

"Oh, sure." Dwight looked surprised at first, but then quickly added, "I think I have plenty on hand that we can scratch up a decent lunch."

"Great. I'm right behind you." The other half of the truth was, Sean's paintings were there. And she wanted to tell Dwight about the art institute idea. Lissa wasn't ready to talk about it in public. Not that it was a secret, it was just very private yet.

The other painting, one of the wildest seascapes Sean had done, was *Cape Breton Island in November*. She read the title engraved on the small brass plaque tacked at the bottom of the frame. Sean's signature was hypnotizing.

A champagne cork popped, and Lissa turned away from Sean's paintings. Dwight appeared carrying two champagne flutes.

"Oh, this feels naughty for lunch." She took the glass Dwight offered.

"I was saving it for when you leave, but I thought it was pretty appropriate now, since you've got something to celebrate today. Here's to Lissa the Golfer." They clinked glasses.

Dwight put the shade umbrella over the picnic table and they ate lunch al fresco. In the time Lissa was in his office, Dwight had put together a plate of cold cuts, cheese, tomatoes, and lettuce. She built a sandwich that would have made Dagwood Bumstead envious. They replayed the golf game as they ate.

It was hot, and they retreated to the air conditioned living room. Lissa had been waiting for the right time to tell Dwight about her plans for the art institute. Now the ideas rolled out, and she told him everything she had told her parents. Dwight's eyes sparkled with excitement.

"Lissa, that's a fantastic idea."

"Glad you like it."

"Really? I can see it. I mean…Wow!" He had a big chimp-grin.

She laughed. "Really? Wow!" She teased him, and he laughed too.

"Seriously." He moved forward on the couch. "Can I help in any way?"

"Help?" She still chuckled.

"Yeah. Can I do anything to help with it?"

"Well, I don't need a nuclear power plant or anything."

"I'm serious, Lissa." He gestured toward the walls around them. "I am, after all, a patron of the arts of sorts, and I'd really like to be involved in something like this. I could consult with you, troubleshoot. Heck, I could even be a financial backer."

He put his hands up: surrendered.

"But I promise you, I'd never get in the way. It would be your baby, and I'd never forget that.

"I could see if Alexis would like to be one of your first students. Opening summer after next?" It seemed like a fire was lit in Dwight, and words tumbled out.

"You really are serious." She should have expected no less —this was Humpy, after all.

"Would you name the institute after Sean?"

"Do you think I should?"

"Yes, definitely."

"I've thought about it, but Sean Maguire Summer Art Institute doesn't have much snap to it."

"But it would have his name recognition. His reputation as an artist is incredible."

"I've wracked my brain, and I just can't think of a name."

"You'll think of something."

Dwight left a silence, but she could tell he was crackling with excitement.

Lissa peered into her champagne. "You know, I could probably use another brain to help me think through this." Dwight hooted and fist-pumped.

"But...now don't get too excited, I've got to think about this. It might be like letting a friend remodel your house. I'd hate to clash over it."

"Clash? It's *your* art institute."

She hesitated, then brought up her greatest concern. "Dwight, I don't mean to hurt you, but you know, you and I were friends a long time ago. Then we pretty much lost touch. It might be really weird that we'd be tied together by the art institute. That could be a long time."

"I know. But I'm willing to take that risk, if you are. Nothing binding."

She nodded. It sounded good. But, was it too good to be true?

"Lissa, there's something else. I was going to wait a few days to talk to you about this, but now seems the perfect timing." She frowned. "I'm going to be in DC in September. I was wondering if I could come up afterwards and visit you for a few days. Just friends." Again the surrender hands. "Of course, I'll stay in town, in Seaton."

Lissa sat, mute.

"In light of this art institute, I'd really like to see your place. Get a feel for what a summer school would be like there. What do you think?"

She sighed. "I think people talk. It's a small town."

He looked deflated. "Yeah, I suppose. I respect that." He sat back on the couch.

"But I think I don't care about that." His smile returned.

Expressionless, thoughts twisted inside her. "Dwight,...I've got to tell you, this has been kind of hard for me, spending time with you this summer." It was hard to get the words out. But it was that or choke. "I've enjoyed it, but...but it's hard. I haven't had a man near me...I mean, not even *near* me..." Tears welled.

"I just feel like I'm all twitched up sometimes. Other times it's okay." She swiped the tears off her face and sniffed. "Frankly,...I feel *guilty*."

Dwight flushed, but said nothing.

"It's ridiculous, but I feel unfaithful to Sean. I know it's irrational."

"Lissa, I don't want you to think—" She shook her head to stop him. Would have put a hand over his mouth if she could have reached.

She pressed her hands to her scorching cheeks. Finally, her confusion of emotions was out there. She had to draw a boundary here and now, or risk being dragged where she wasn't ready to go.

But this was silly. It wasn't like she was dating Dwight. Why couldn't she keep her mouth shut?

"Lissa, I'd never do anything—*anything*, to hurt you. You have my word on that. We're friends. Always have been, always will be. I promise." She saw Dwight's eyes redden as he handed her a Kleenex.

He looked so sincere. She had no reason to doubt Dwight. Suddenly, the Papa Bear chair was way too big, and Lissa's arms ached to be enfolded by Dwight's. His shoulders were just the right size to cry on. But she didn't move.

Instead, she looked at him through her tears. She had to know more about this man who was once again becoming a deeply trusted friend.

"It's none of my business, but...were you faithful to Becky?"

Dwight looked surprised, but he answered without hesitation. "Yes, I was."

Lissa caught something in his voice. "Was she faithful to you?"

"No." He looked very sad.

FIFTY DAYS TO SUNRISE

"Oh...I'm sorry...sorry I asked."
"It was a long time ago. Before we had the girls."
Lissa couldn't stop. "Have you...have you dated since...?"
"Have I dated since Becky died? Not really. I took a woman out to dinner about a year ago. A woman I met on the plane to London. She gave me her number at her hotel. We had dinner, I dropped her back at her hotel, said goodnight, and that was it." He laughed. "I shook her hand goodnight. She looked like— I don't know—like I was an alien. I remember thinking, how sad it was that she would invite a stranger to her room."
"Why haven't you dated?"
"I guess I haven't gotten over wishing Becky was someone she wasn't."
Lissa blew her nose and sniffed. "Thanks," she murmured. "Thanks for your patience."
"My pleasure. And I mean that."
She nodded, pursed her lips. Dwight let the silence be. "Right now I'm thinking we'd make pretty good partners on this art institute. Probably. Can you live with probably for now?"
"I can." He raised his glass to her. "Partners." He smiled. "Probably." He reached over and clinked the rim of his glass against hers. The crystal note rang sweet.

Chapter 60

Tension in the house ratcheted up. One week to moving day. They were ahead of schedule with the packing, which left them with too much time living in organized chaos. Mom and Dad weren't high-strung people, but it was clear this move was stretching them taut. A lot of unspoken coping was going on.

Mom was out in the garden; Dad played scales on the piano, and Lissa was in her room snuggled in the window seat with her journal, her door shut.

She wrote.

July 25, 2003.

I woke this morning from a dream, a wonderful dream. I was sitting on the floor with Sean's sketches scattered all around me. Dad's Bible was on the floor beside me. There were mountains of sketches. Preliminary sketches Sean had done prior to beginning a painting. Sketches of scenes he'd never painted.

I was picking up the sketches one by one and studying

them, then sorting them into piles. I smiled while I sorted. I think I woke up smiling.

I remember Sean painting out in his studio. He usually had music turned up loud. Often it was Christian music–2nd Chapter of Acts, Keith Green, Russ Taff. Occasionally I'd hear him singing along at the top of his lungs. Then I knew he was stepped back from his painting, deciding what it needed.

Early in the morning though, quiet covered the studio. Sean said he needed to hear the Lord speak to him about a painting through the sounds of the birds, or the rustle of the wind in the trees—and prayer. Sean said he had to get his battle plan fresh from the Lord every day.

Sean's art institute. Sean's dream will come true—I'm nearly certain of it. Excited butterflies collide in my stomach when I think of creating this living memorial to Sean.

Passion. If anyone had asked her three months ago, she would have said passion was gone, that she would never again feel passionate about anything. And, most days, she didn't care. But apparently, passion was just dormant, waiting for Baby Maguire to tickle it to life.

She mentally ran through her calendar over the next few months. Dwight's visit in September, skiing with Shannon over Christmas, India with Boots, Baby Maguire's arrival, the summer art institute and all the remodeling for it.

She took the small notebook out of her purse. After *India* she wrote—*Tell Boots I can only go for two weeks.* Next to *summer art institute* she wrote—*Call Columbia re resident artists.*

A kernel of panic tried to sprout in her stomach. She put a hand firmly over the spot and said out loud, so she'd hear herself say it, "Go away."

Chapter 61

Lissa was staying through the move and a couple of days afterward to help Mom and Dad unpack and get settled. Each day that kept her from her own home could have been a small agony, but she kept busy. She visited with Sally, went running, wrote in her journal, knit, started plotting the course of the art institute, and golfed.

Golfing meant time with Dwight.

They played three times in the week before the move. After each game, they unwound over ice tea at Dwight's house—a comfortable routine.

Lissa worked up to the full eighteen holes for the last game. At her insistence, Dwight kept score for her. It would have been a respectable bowling score.

And they worked on the art institute together—every day.

By the end of the week they had the basic structure of the institute laid out. On occasion they both blurted out the same idea at the same time. Partners, so far.

Lissa sketched a map of her property, and they drafted plans for the bunkhouse. Dwight suggested she keep the bunkhouse in sight from the house, a much better idea than down a path in the woods. He also suggested a strict no alcohol or drugs policy on the property. Like-minded partners.

    Every evening before turning out the lights, she wrote memories of Sean in her journal. Random memories in no particular order and of no particular importance. Just memories. Sweet memories. As her beautiful journal filled, her heart was no longer so empty.

Chapter 62

Moving Day. Dad pounded "Reveille" on the piano at six o'clock. And in case the entire household hadn't heard it the first time, he took it up a third and hammered it out again. The finely crafted plan they had for the day was set in motion.

By the time the movers arrived at seven thirty, Lissa and her parents sat at the kitchen table drinking coffee, waiting. Bedding had been stripped and stuffed into a box, toiletries packed, and the breakfast dishes were washed and boxed. Lissa's suitcases stood ready, and the boxes she was taking home were lined up in the dining room. Yellow paper taped to them with *DON'T MOVE* in big, black letters warned off the movers. Mom was concerned that the boxes weren't going directly in the car, but Lissa told her mother she just couldn't pack the car yet.

The first thing Dad directed the movers to do was to cover the Steinway with pads. There would be no risk of damaging the cherished piano.

The move was underway—a steady march of men shuttling boxes and furniture out to the black hole of the waiting truck.

Things disappeared fast.

Mom flapped around to the point that Dad finally suggested she go over and keep Gladys company for a while. Mom smiled at Dad and fluttered off. Lissa was sure Gladys was grateful too. With Mom and Dad's departure, Gladys was the last of the old-timers in the neighborhood. Mom probably still glanced out Gladys's side kitchen window from time to time.

The move to empty the Manitou house went almost flawlessly. Dad intercepted a mover heading for the front gate with an armload of garden tools from the garage. The garden tools Ray didn't take were staying. Mom and Dad planned to continue to tend the garden the remainder of this summer, and even into next summer, until the house sold.

Right on schedule, the house was empty, except for the Steinway. The piano, uncovered once again, looked odd by itself.

The movers got out their personal-sized coolers and sat on the front steps for lunch. Dad retrieved Mom from Gladys's, and they made sandwiches, using squares of paper towels for plates and napkins. The sun was hot at the picnic table, but they didn't linger.

There was no time or need for goodbyes to the house just now. After lunch they made a convoy to the apartment.

The unloading went equally smoothly. Lissa had taped a sign on each bedroom door with a number so that boxes with the corresponding number got properly delivered. The goal was to have as little uncertainty and decision-making involved as possible.

Once Mom was assured Dad and Lissa had the situation well in hand, as soon as her chair appeared, she sat down and knit.

The movers set up the beds, and by three o'clock the men were gone.

Dad and Lissa joined Mom and collapsed on the couch.

FIFTY DAYS TO SUNRISE

They all looked at each other and didn't know whether to laugh or cry, so they laughed till tears ran down their cheeks.

"I think I can find the tea," Lissa said. "Would you like some?"

Lissa worked all weekend getting things unpacked and put away. Her parents were exhausted. She tried to get them to pace themselves, which by Sunday, they were finally willing to do.

Slowly, the apartment started looking homey—somebody's home. The Persian rug was in the spot where the lacquered Steinway would sit. The rug would not only dampen the sound, but set off the piano like a jewel in a velvet box.

But so many things were missing or out of place. Where was her room? The dining table? Was there even room for her family here?

Fresh air on the balcony eased the little scream threatening. Mom and Dad had gone to bed before dark, and she bounced alone in a green chair. Some things hadn't changed.

Later, Lissa sat in the middle of the rumpled guest bed and wrote in her journal.

Sunday, August 3, 2003

My parents are moved. Mission accomplished.
All of their old things are now in a new surrounding. It's different, but yet, no different; they still have each other.
I'm going home to all my old things where they've always been, but everything is different. Nothing is the same without Sean. No kiss good night.
A broken heart never heals. Ever. The best that can be

hoped for is to contain the fragments in a silken bag, until, one by one, each piece finds its purpose and beats at its own pace.

She set her journal aside and pulled the pink flowered quilt to her chin. Gone was the wallpaper garden. Would nightmares find her tonight? Oh please, Lord, no.

She snapped off the light and said a prayer for Baby Maguire.

Chapter 63

From the balcony Lissa watched the sunrise inch its way pink and gold over the Dakota. Like a painting of a sunrise, Sean's painting, seen shimmering through Lissa's unshed tears.

God gave Sean such a gift for putting on canvas his vision of what he saw. He painted his world more beautiful, more vivid, than even the eye could see. Capturing and stilling the moment for time.

How blessed she was to have been Sean's wife. She would rewrite only the end of their love story if she could. Happy ever after should last a long, long time, shouldn't it?

She pulled the green afghan tighter around her shoulders against the morning damp. Boots's perfume scented the fuzzy yarn.

Resting a hand on the Bible, she whispered the verse she had just read.

"'He will quiet you with His love, He will rejoice over you with singing.'"

Her eyes drifted closed.

Robins' calls rattled from the lawn below, and sparrows chattered in the sun-tipped maples by the river bluff. God's song for her.

"Mmm," she breathed, as if to hum along. And in those moments she let beginnings and endings jumble together, their edges less sharp.

The softest, sweet moan passed her lips. And she bounced in the chair, oh so gently, rocked in love.

She felt blessed beyond all sense.

Chapter 64

Standing outside the apartment building, Lissa and her parents finally had to say goodbye.

"Missy," Dad said, his eyes reddening, "we can't tell you how much we appreciated your help this summer. You just can't imagine."

Mom stood by Dad's side, already sniffing and daubing her eyes with a hankie.

"It seemed to work pretty well, don't you think? We were a good team." Lissa kissed and hugged her parents. "I love you both so much. I'm glad you needed me." Lissa's eyes twinkled. Dad obviously caught the joke and smiled at her. It had worked *very* well.

"Oh, honey, you will drive carefully, won't you?"

"Of course, Mom. I'll stop whenever I'm tired. And I'll call you every night. I should get home late Wednesday."

"Give our love to Jack and Meagan and the twins."

"You bet."

Lissa turned and opened the car door. She looked back at her parents, then rushed to hug them again, almost knocking her mother off balance.

"I love you, my precious child," Mom said into her daughter's hair.

"Love you, Missy. God go with you."

"I love you," Lissa said again to her parents. She stroked her mother's cheek and whispered, "I'm so glad you told me about Nicholas." But Mom probably didn't hear her.

Lissa got in the car, started the engine, and pulled away from the curb. She waved back at her parents. They were standing together, side by side; Dad had his arm around Mom's shoulder, and Mom clutched Dad's waist.

Lissa turned the key in the back door. She had some time alone in the house before Dwight arrived to help her load the car. Time to say her private goodbyes to the house that had been her home for so many years. She might not be inside this house again. An army of cleaners and painters would descend on the house before it was sold, erasing the evidence of the life her family had here.

She entered the house and her stomach clenched, like a child forcing herself to walk in the dark.

She turned into the dining room, looking past all the boxes she had to take home. Where the Persian rug had been was glossy wood—around it the floor was scratched and dull.

Slowly, she made her way to the living room. Shadows of her family everywhere. The occasional pop of the wood floor was even louder in the empty space. She closed her eyes and stood in the middle of the living room, listening for the echoes of the years. Her stomach relaxed.

She imagined the thundering of little feet overhead—from the kitchen, Mom's voice, "That's enough running around!"—then Dad, at the piano, switching to the *William Tell Overture*, really the *Lone Ranger* theme—and everybody laughing.

FIFTY DAYS TO SUNRISE

Lissa sat at the old Steinway and played a slow rendition of "Chopsticks." The childish tune sounded strange: a slow waltz.
Upstairs she wandered through each room. She wasn't looking so much to see if anything was left, but to be reminded of what had been there.
Lissa found herself praying a blessing on the next family that would live here. She hoped it would be a family.
She went all the way to the attic, didn't switch on the light. Something caught her eye. On the floor, lit by narrow strips of light coming from the vent at the other end, was a small stuffed animal, a black-and-white cat. It must have fallen off the top of the last box Lissa carried down.
She stooped to pick it up. The old stuffed animal smelled musty and had dark smudges around it's embroidered pink nose, probably where it had been kissed repeatedly. Pokey whiskers stuck out at crazy bent angles. Its black floss mouth turned up, giving its green glass eyes a rascally sparkle. This cat could have been Ray's or Boots's, but it didn't matter, it was hers now.
Another stray cat in need of rescuing—in need of someone to love it—just like Galahad, the rescued kitten waiting for her at home. Her nose prickled, and she rubbed it.
"Hello, little kitty," Lissa murmured in greeting.
Hugging the stuffed cat to her chest, she went back downstairs. For the last time, Lissa stopped in her old room, burning the memories into the back of her eyes.
She turned down the stairs to the kitchen and sat on the top step. She could almost hear the clatter of dishes, the teakettle squealing, soft laughter—Mom.
Last on her route of remembrance through the house was the front porch. She sat on the swing and gently pushed off with one foot, the other foot tucked under her leg. She absently stroked the stuffed cat behind an ear.
No more tears. For now, she had cried all that needed to be cried. She closed her eyes and swung back and forth for several

minutes.

Dwight's knock at the back door carried through the house. "Anybody home?"

"Coming." The reverie was broken. Time to go.

"Hey, how ya doin'?" Dwight stood at the back door, hands in his pockets. His silver truck dwarfed the Camry in the graveled parking spot where the thicket used to be.

Lissa smiled as broadly as she could. "I'm good." She pushed the screen door open, and Dwight stepped in.

"Yeah? Really?" He stood in the back hall, hands still in his pockets.

She nodded.

"That's good." He didn't make a move.

Lissa smelled the clean scent of soap on him. She swallowed hard and led the way to the dining room.

"You won't believe how much we have to get in the car."

Dwight whistled when he saw the seven boxes.

"And nothing can go on top of any of the boxes." She pointed out the obvious *Fragile* written on the top of each box.

"Let me go take a look at the car. This could be a logistical situation."

They trooped out the back door to the Camry. Lissa already had her two suitcases laid across the back seat. In the front she had the atlas, a water bottle, snacks, a grocery bag with overnight necessities, her purse, and her knitting bag.

Dwight rubbed a hand over his balding head as he surveyed the back seat and the trunk space.

"It's gonna be really close. I think we can put four boxes in the trunk, two on top of your suitcases, and one up front. That should work. Okay to put stuff on top of your suitcases?"

"No problem."

"Then let's get 'er done."

They carried the boxes out to the car. Lissa left the heavier ones for Dwight. She set her newfound traveling buddy on top of the box in the passenger seat and laid the rag rug over the

FIFTY DAYS TO SUNRISE

boxes in the trunk.

She was packed, though she might barely be able to see out the rearview mirror.

"Oh!" she cried, and ran back to the house. The gate banged closed behind her.

"What?"

Lissa didn't stop to explain.

She reappeared carrying yet another box, not a large one. Dwight opened the gate for her.

"I nearly forgot my diaries," Lissa said breathlessly. "They were in my closet."

With the box of diaries and keepsakes stowed under the box of Christmas decorations in the front seat, Lissa stepped back to check the load.

"Whew!" She clapped a hand over her heart. "That was close."

Dwight smiled and shook his head.

"Hey. Are you making fun of me?" Lissa grinned too.

"No, but you *are* funny."

She gave him a light shove on her way to the house for the last time.

Dwight waited outside.

Lissa locked the front door. She stood in the living room and looked out at Manitou Street one last time. So strange. To think of never looking out this window again.

She gazed at the place over the mantel where Sean's painting of their children had hung for twenty years; she just let the ache be there.

Clutching the key so tightly it stung her palm, she left the house and locked the back door. She could feel Dwight's eyes on her as she walked down the sidewalk, but she didn't look up.

"Okay?" Dwight was at her side. His expression spoke what he didn't say.

"Yes...yes, I am." She made an effort to smile.

Lissa put a hand on the car door handle, but then turned back to Dwight.

"Thanks. Thanks for everything." She smiled warmly at him. "Humpy." Her nose did that prickly thing again, but she refused to cry.

Dwight reached out and, with a finger, pushed a lock of hair back from her face. "My pleasure." He gently held her arms, leaned in, and kissed her forehead. Reflexively, she cupped his elbows in her hands.

His kiss lasted a moment longer than she expected. When the pressure of his lips relaxed, she heard him breathe in before he drew back and released her. No, maybe she imagined that.

He took a step back. "It's been great, Lissa. Be safe."

She nodded. That brush fire crept up her neck again. "See you."

She got in and started the car.

Dwight winked at her and grinned. "See you in September," he said.

Lissa backed into the alley and put the car in drive. She took a deep breath and eased away.

In the rearview mirror, she saw Dwight standing in the middle of the alley, one hand in his pocket, the other raised in goodbye.

Lissa waved out the window.

September. She winked at Dwight's receding image in the mirror.

He was still standing there when she turned and headed home.

Epilogue

June 23, 2008

Four years and a thousand tears later, Dwight and I married. A year ago last week.
Dwight made it clear from his first visit in September that he hoped for marriage—had hoped for it since our first dance. Only this time, he asked me to dance. When he moved to Seaton, "to manage the art school," I wasn't fooled. We were good partners.
We danced and danced: around, back and forth, sometimes alone, but never with anyone else. Finally, I said yes. I even changed my name to his. Reluctantly, but I did.
We danced at our wedding—on the lawn overlooking the sea at Dwight's house, our house. Little Sean squeezed between us, giggling, his grandfather's chocolate eyes sparkling up at us.
Sean galloped away when Shannon beckoned him over. He grasped her pregnant belly like a beach ball and

pressed his ear against her, listening for his cousin. Matt swung Sean high, and crystalline squeals of delight tinkled down over the reception.

Dwight's daughters sat on the grass, rolling a ball to Keira, who clapped patty-cake in glee. My sweet little curly-haired, dark-eyed granddaughter.

A happy day for us.

After everyone left, Dwight took my hand and led me to the rocky promontory facing out to sea. We sat in the Adirondack chairs and watched the sunset cast strips of pink and purple and gold over our shoulders. Ribbons on God's wedding gift to us.

Dwight laced his fingers in mine. Tonight I wouldn't be going back to the farm.

"Lissa, do you really think you can be happy here—with me?"

"I do. You know I do.

"Hey, didn't I say that once already today?"

We squeezed hands.

The rhythm of the sea beat against the rocks. Usually the sea-music calmed or thrilled me; tonight, I shivered.

"Are you cold? You want to go inside?"

I shook my head.

He smiled at me, his I-know-what-you're-thinking smile. "There's no rush, Lissa. We've got the rest of our lives."

"We do." I smiled back.

He winked. "But..."

And we laughed. More than friends.

He leaned over and brushed a slow kiss on my lips, rested his forehead on mine. I cupped his cheek in my hand and kissed him.

"I do love you, Humpy Humphrey."

But I will always and forever be, a heart divided.

ABOUT THE AUTHOR

Cristine Eastin, PhD is a psychotherapist when at the office, but she's also a wife, stepmother, and grandma.

Cris has two grown stepchildren, a son-in-law, and two grandchildren; her husband, Dave, is a psychologist. The family includes two rescue cats and an Australian shepherd.

Raised in Minnesota, Cris is a grafted in Wisconsinite with a heart of woods and water.

She keeps busy collecting hobbies. For instance, in winter she's on the ski slopes, and in summer she might be kayaking. And in between she'd love to be visiting Scotland or England.

Cris works, lives, and writes by the motto "…because you can't pour from an empty pitcher."

Member of American Christian Fiction Writers.

Visit Cris at her website: www.CristineEastin.com.

ACKNOWLEDGMENTS

I'm thankful to have friends and family who were willing to help bring *Fifty Days to Sunrise* to completion. Not only did they make suggestions, they offered encouragement in abundance.

Thanks to readers Cathy Burns, Jane Kent, Peggy Konkol, Lisa Lynch, Gary Lynch, and Ce Turner.

Thanks to Dr. Bill Heifner for medical advice.

Thanks to Laura Jacobson for shooting my author photo.

Thanks to Jason Pape for the cover design, website, and rescuing me when I have computer questions.

And a special thanks to my husband, Dave. I couldn't have done it without him.

PLEASE TELL OTHERS ABOUT
FIFTY DAYS TO SUNRISE.

- Post it, pin it, tweet it—on Facebook, your blog, Pinterest, and Twitter.

- Write a review on amazon.com, bn.com, and goodreads.com.

- Tell friends in your book club, church small group, and workplace about *Fifty Days to Sunrise*.

- Give a gift of *Fifty Days to Sunrise* to someone who might be encouraged by the message.

- Visit my website and leave a comment regarding your thoughts about the book.

  www.CristineEastin.com

Thank you and blessings,

Cristine Eastin

Made in the USA
Middletown, DE
17 February 2015